BLACK OIL, RED BLOOD

by Diane Castle

A WISHLIST BOOK

http://www.wishlistpublishing.com
http://www.blackoilredblood.com

Copyright © 2012 by Diane Castle. All rights reserved.

DISCLAIMER

Please note: This is a work of fiction. Names, characters, places, and incidents either are the product of the author's imagination or are used fictitiously, and any resemblance to actual persons, living or dead, business establishments, industries, events, or locales is entirely coincidental or has been fictionalized. This book is not intended to be read as fact or truth. Read it for fun, and take it all in with a grain of salt.

For my dear husband David, the love of my life.
Without your love and support,
I would be utterly and completely lost.
Okay, I'll yetay now.

Acknowledgements

This book would not be complete without a giant thank you to my friend and mentor, Carole Nelson Douglas. Words cannot express how much I appreciate your help, encouragement, and friendship. To the readers—if you have not read Carole's Sherlock Holmes/Irene Adler books or her Midnight Louie mystery series, do so immediately. You're in for a real treat.

Secondly, I would like to thank my other beta readers: Angela Spring, Judy King, Julie VanDolen, and Jamie Spence. Angela, I can't thank you enough for reading every single revision and providing invaluable advice and support—your feedback on the ending was particularly helpful. Judy, thanks for going through the manuscript not once, but twice! And thank you for your ever-faithful friendship, which I will treasure always. Your kindness and generosity of spirit inspires me every day. Julie—thanks for your tremendous support during development and for listening to me rant about benzene, carcinogens, and the whole book submission process *ad nauseam*! Don't know what I'd do without ya. Jamie, this book would have definitely had a crummy opening without you! You're an amazing writer yourself, and I can't wait to see your book in print!

I'd also like to thank attorney Keith Patton for teaching me the basics of toxic tort litigation.

Thank you also to JoAnna Couch for teaching me how to write in the first place, and for never laughing at me for having the audacity to think I could actually write a book.

Many thanks and all my love goes to my husband David. Without your support, this project would not have been possible. Thank you also to Jana, brother David, Dad, Joanne, Gary, and Linda for your love and encouragement.

Another big thank you goes out to all my wonderful Gulf Coast activist Facebook friends. You inspire me every day with the work you're doing down there. Stay strong, and never give up fighting the good fight!

Finally, thank YOU—yes, YOU. . . the person reading this right now—for taking time out to read this book. That means more to me than I can ever express.

TABLE OF CONTENTS

Prologue 0
Chapter 1 19
Chapter 2 24
Chapter 3 24
Chapter 4 27
Chapter 5 36
Chapter 6 38
Chapter 7 43
Chapter 8 55
Chapter 9 62
Chapter 10 71
Chapter 11 76
Chapter 12 80
Chapter 13 92
Chapter 14 94
Chapter 15 104
Chapter 16 114
Chapter 17 121
Chapter 18 133
Chapter 19 136
Chapter 20 152
Chapter 21 162
Chapter 22 165
Chapter 23 172
Chapter 24 190

Chapter 25	194
Chapter 25	196
Chapter 27	202
Chapter 28	208
Chapter 29	226
Chapter 30	254
Chapter 31	257
Chapter 32	260
Chapter 33	266
Chapter 34	269
Chapter 35	274
Chapter 36	278
Chapter 37	292
Chapter 38	300
Chapter 39	325
Thank You, from the Author	337
Facebook, Twitter, and the Blue Bulb Project	337
About the Author	338

PROLOGUE

I didn't even know how to use a gun before yesterday, and I certainly hadn't become a crack shot overnight. That didn't bode well for my chances of survival at the moment —especially since I was currently staring down the wrong end of somebody else's barrel. What was I supposed to do? Duck? Shoot first? Run?

Maybe the decision would have been easier if I hadn't loved the guy pointing the gun at me. I watched his trigger finger tense as the smoky, toxic air around us seemed to grow even thicker. Walls shook and the floor rolled beneath me as an explosion thundered through the building. The PetroPlex flagship oil refinery was fast on its way to becoming nothing but a memory.

The doorframe buckled before my eyes—my only means of escape. Sharp orange tongues of flame lapped at me from above, sending down a rain of fiery particles as acoustic ceiling tiles disintegrated overhead.

That's when I knew that gun or no gun, I was going to die.

CHAPTER 1

The thing about cancer is it's hard to prove somebody gave it to you on purpose, but I can prove it. In fact, I make a living proving it. I sue oil refineries that would rather save a buck than comply with safety regulations designed to do important things like, you know, keep people alive. It's not unusual for my clients to pass away in the middle of a case, but I'd never had an expert witness turn up dead until today.

My favorite client, Gracie Miller, hurried toward me as I walked up the stairs to the courthouse. I had hoped to put off talking to her until after I'd spoken to the judge. Her untamed gray hair spiraled out of a would-be bun, curls going in a million different directions.

"Chloe!" she said. "Is it true? Say it ain't true!"

She didn't wait for me to answer.

"I didn't believe it at first," Gracie said, "because I heard it from crazy Mrs. Bagley, and everybody knows she ought to be in a home already. But then I called Mrs. Scott, and sure enough, her husband is out at the crime scene with all the other police, and oh! I've lived here for forty years and we ain't never had a murder!"

That seemed like a pretty big stretch to me, seeing as how we lived in Kettle, Texas, human population: four-thousand; gun population: thirty-four-thousand-three-hundred-fifty six. With all those guns around, there had to have been an incident at some point in the last forty years.

I took Gracie's arm. She was not going to like hearing that yes, Dr. Schaeffer—her expert witness and the key to winning her case—was indeed dead. He had been scheduled to present critical evidence at a make or break summary judgment hearing twenty-four hours from now. A loss tomorrow would mean the end of our case.

Gracie searched my face and saw the truth before I said a word.

"Oh Lord, a'mighty! What are we gonna do?" she said.

I had a plan, but it was kind of a desperate one—and Gracie didn't need to know about it, now or ever.

I smiled encouragingly as I carefully omitted the truth. "I'm about to ask Judge Delmont for a continuance. If he says yes, we'll have enough extra time to find a new witness."

"Sweet Jesus, Mary, and George W. Bush!" Gracie said. "You know perfectly well he ain't gonna agree to that! Ever since my husband died, it's been real lean times. I'm probably gonna lose my house. And I ain't got all his medical bills paid yet, neither." Her lip trembled and one big tear welled up and left a streak on her face before it fell to the ground.

Gracie's husband, Derrick Miller, had died only a month ago from a rare form of leukemia caused by exposure to a toxic chemical called benzene. Derrick had worked his whole adult life in the benzene unit of the PetroPlex oil refinery situated in the middle of town. PetroPlex had never provided Derrick with safety equipment and also had never warned Derrick that benzene would kill him. I was now representing the Millers in a wrongful death suit against the Big Oil industry giant, and tomorrow's hearing would have been a slam-dunk win if somebody hadn't offed our expert witness.

"You think it was just a coincidence?" Gracie asked. "Him turning up dead like that the day before our hearing?" Of course I didn't think it was a coincidence. The whole situation reeked. If your expert witness dies of a heart attack while surfing in Aruba, that's life. If he's murdered the day before he's set to testify at a hearing that can make or break a case, that's friggin' suspicious. But I didn't see any sense in getting Gracie more worked up than she already was.

"One thing at a time," I said. Let me go in there and get the judge to move the hearing date back, and we'll worry about the rest later."

Like it was going to be that easy.

Gracie nodded. "If anybody can do it, you can. I gotta get back to my cake. I left it in the oven, and the pastor's wife gets real snarky when I bake 'em too long. That woman hates a dry cake. It beats all I ever seen."

"Your cakes are always perfect," I said.

Gracie beamed. "I got another one mixing up just for you. Strawberry with cream cheese icing—your favorite. You come on by this afternoon and get you a slice, you hear?"

My mouth watered just thinking about it. "That sounds great," I said, omitting no truth there. I waved goodbye and hurried into the courthouse.

***

Judge Delmont was waiting for me in chambers. When I walked in, he had his arms folded across his chest and a look on his face he reserved for. . . well, me. He didn't like me too much. I was lucky he'd even agreed to an emergency *ex parte* conference.

Here went nothing. I mentally willed myself into super-lawyer mode.

We exchanged greetings, and I pulled a motion for continuance out of my briefcase and slid it across his desk.

He took a cursory look and laid it back down. "Look," he said. "I'd like to help you out, but it ain't my fault your expert's dead."

"Not dead," I said. "Murdered. There's a difference."

Delmont shrugged. "What do you expect me to do about it? I ain't Jesus. I can't resurrect him."

"I just need time to regroup," I said, pulling some more papers out of my briefcase and sliding them over to the judge. "I already drafted the order for you. All I need is your signature—no miracles required."

Delmont shifted uncomfortably in his chair. "If you had any evidence to support your claim—"

"I have it. I just need an expert witness to present it, but I can't find a replacement for Dr. Schaeffer by tomorrow morning."

"Well," Delmont said, "If you can get opposing counsel to agree to the extra time, I'll consider the motion."

Uh, right. "Buford Buchanan is conveniently out of town, and he is not answering his phone. Besides, you and I both know better than to expect that he would voluntarily agree to something so reasonable."

Delmont pulled a cigar out of the humidor on his desk and took a long whiff. "Smells good, don't it?"

He offered it to me. The gesture felt like an executioner handing a condemned prisoner his last cigarette before facing the firing squad.

I shook my head. "I trust your judgment."

"On the cigar. Just not the case."

This conversation wasn't going as well as I'd hoped, and that was saying something, considering I hadn't hoped for much at all. Everybody around here knew darn well the judge in this town had oil stains on his hands.

I sighed. "I'd like to hear your reasoning as to why you think a continuance wouldn't be appropriate in this situation."

Delmont leaned back in his chair and propped his custom-made snakeskin boots on his desk, which was decorated with a humidor, an ash tray (full), a cactus, and a jackalope head. No pictures of wife or family.

"The case has been on the docket for well over a year. Besides that, I got too many cases against PetroPlex floating around here already."

"And that ought to tell you something about the kind of business they're running around here," I said.

PetroPlex is notorious for flouting safety violations and dumping known carcinogens into the air and water. The EPA has been after them for years, but they don't care. It's cheaper to pay the fines than comply with regulations.

"It ain't their fault there's lawyers like you slinking around trying to sue 'em out of existence. They employ more than half the people who live here. If they leave, Kettle dies."

"If they don't clean up their act, Kettle dies anyway."

Delmont rolled his eyes.

Almost nothing makes me madder than an eye roll from a good ol' boy. I mentally pulled up my "big girl" panties, leaned over his desk and delivered my most intense "I-am-a-damn-good-lawyer-and-you-will-listen-to-me" glare.

"Look," I said. "Maybe you think cancer is something that happens to other people. Maybe you think you put on a pink ribbon once a year and you've done your part to fight the disease. But if you've seen cancer—really seen it—you know that all the pink ribbons in the world just aren't enough."

Delmont pulled out a match and lit the cigar he'd been holding. Clearly he wasn't concerned about cancer in the least. "You finished, Miss Taylor?"

I lapsed into a coughing fit as I waved the cigar smoke out of my face. "You *know* PetroPlex is dangerous," I said. "Even if you forget the cancer, how about the explosions? How about the toxic clouds?"

"You got an explosion in this case you wanna talk about?"

"Not in this one, but—"

"Stick to *this* case, why don't ya?"

I squared my shoulders and relaxed my glare—but only by a little bit. There was no way I was going to let this stuffed shirt redneck pawn intimidate me into backing down. There was too much riding on tomorrow's hearing to just roll over on it. Not only would Gracie wind up in a world of hurt if we didn't come out on top of this, but I would probably also lose my job. I'd had a pretty nasty string of *highly* questionable losses in this courtroom under this judge for more than a year now, which was fast destroying my reputation as a good lawyer. . . not to mention depleting my bank account. Wrongful death attorneys don't get paid if they don't win, and I'd been eating nothing but Ramen for weeks.

Meanwhile, I was pretty sure Judge Delmont was living fat and happy off the scraps PetroPlex passed him under the table, but I couldn't prove it.

"Okay," I said. "Let's cut to the chase, here. I'm gonna stop pretending like I expect you to be reasonable. So if you wanna stop pretending like anything I have to say matters to you, that'll be just fine with me."

Delmont shrugged.

"What are my chances of getting you to sign a continuance?"

"I'd say 'slim to none,' but I'd hate to give you any false hope."

I took a deep breath. What I was about to do was likely to land me in serious trouble if it didn't come off right. On the other hand, Delmont really didn't leave me any other choice.

I reached down to my briefcase and lifted out a manila envelope. Slid it slowly across his desk.

Delmont rested his cigar in his ash tray and pulled the envelope toward him. He cracked open the flap and pulled out a series of glossy eight by tens. As he looked at the photos, the lines in his face seemed to deepen.

"You really don't look good naked," I said. "And I wonder what your wife would think if she saw you with that blonde?" I leaned forward conspiratorially. "There's *no way* those boobs are real, right?"

Delmont shoved the pictures back in the envelope.

My heart felt like a jackhammer inside me. I prayed Delmont couldn't actually see it pumping. If I showed just one sign of weakness, this whole thing would backfire for sure.

Delmont put his hands on the desk and leaned over it, getting right in my face.

"You think this is a game, Chloe?" He spoke slowly, softly.

"I most certainly do not," I said. "The question is, *do you?*"

"I could have you disbarred for this. Throw you in jail."

"But you won't." I tried to put as much meaning behind those words as possible.

Delmont pulled back abruptly. "Where did you get those?"

I had gotten them from Miles, my fabulous paralegal. Where he'd gotten them I didn't know. Frankly, I had been kind of afraid to ask.

"It doesn't matter where they came from," I said. "What matters is the continuance. I expect to see the order signed and filed by eight a.m. tomorrow morning."

"Or what?" Delmont asked.

"I think you know what."

Delmont got up from his desk and paced back and forth across his bearskin rug, his fat rolls jiggling with each heavy step. When he turned his back on me, I could almost see his life-sized portrait of Robert E. Lee reflecting off the fresh perspiration on his bald head.

I waited. The courthouse was quiet today. It seemed as though the loudest sound in the room was the sound of my own heartbeat.

"Fine," he finally said.

Joy welled up inside me, but I didn't allow it to show.

"But you only get a week."

And just like that, the joy was gone. "A *week!* That is a joke! I need six months!"

"You get a week, or I will call your bluff and report you to the bar."

"What makes you think I'm bluffing?"

"What makes you think I give two pig farts about keeping my wife?"

My jaw dropped open against my will. Seeing as how this was my first attempt at blackmail, I was kind of at a loss. I had never considered the fact that he might not even want to keep his wife.

"Get out," Delmont said. "And pray to God the next time you stand in front of me you got a jury on your side."

I gathered my things together and stood.

"A *week*," Delmont said. "I don't care what else you've got up that sleeve of yours, that's all you get. That's the extent of my patience. Got it?"

I tapped the photographs on the desk with my index finger. "I'll just leave these here for you to think about. I've got my own set."

I didn't wait for Delmont to reply. I just walked out.

I was so distracted as I walked down the concrete stairs of the courthouse and into the town square that I stepped wrong and broke the heel off one of my Louboutin shoes. I tumbled down the steps, my briefcase popped open, and my papers scattered all over the town square.

I cursed at the shoe. The Louboutins were a relic of better times—the times when I'd actually had no trouble winning cases. The times when the deck wasn't completely stacked against me.

Even if I could find a replacement expert in a week (which was highly unlikely), all of Dr. Schaeffer's evidence and files were locked away in his house behind a whole lot of crime scene tape. We only had one set because my boss was too cheap to foot the Xerox bill.

If I couldn't convince the police to let me in and get those files, I'd just blackmailed the judge and put myself in jeopardy for nothing.

***

It was only three blocks back to my office.

I parked and limped indoors. Mountains of boxes lined the hallways—all of which contained my boss's files, not mine. Art hung on the wall, but you couldn't see it behind the stacks of cardboard.

I twisted and turned my way through the paper maze until I found my little cubicle, from which I daily fought Big Oil. My paralegal, Miles, was waiting for me.

He took one look at me and zeroed in on my broken heel. "Oh my gawd. Not the Louboutins! Please tell me you broke that heel wedging it between Delmont's butt cheeks."

Miles is the kind of guy who sets off even the most recalcitrant gaydars.

"Sadly, no," I said, tossing off the shoes and collapsing into my desk chair.

Miles crossed his arms and eyed me with concern. "Too bad. That would have been worth the loss. Did you get the continuance at least?"

I nodded, and Miles did the happy dance. "Woo-hoo! Atta girl!"

Our boss, Dick Richardson, heard the commotion and popped his head into my office. "Oh, good, you're back. Didja get it done, or are you fired?"

Miles glared at him, but I was unperturbed. Dick talked to me like that all the time. He's the kind of micromanaging, paranoid, jerk boss you want to avoid at all costs. His first name kind of sums him up. If I hadn't been out of other options when I moved to Kettle two years ago, I never would have agreed to work for him.

"I got the continuance," I said. "If you wanna fire me today, it's gotta be over something else."

"Hrmph. I'm shocked. 'Bout time you won one. How'd you manage it?"

"I used my superior persuasive skills, for which he was no match."

"You take your shirt off for him or something?"

Before I could figure out what to say to that, Miles chipped in. "She has other assets."

Dick made a noise that was something between a grunt and a laugh. "Not the kind that appeal to *you*, I bet."

Before Miles could launch into a tirade that might produce negative consequences, I said, "If you don't mind, we've got work to do."

"Yeah, get back to work," Dick said. "I gotta go into Houston to pick up my new car, anyway. Settle a case and generate some cash while I'm gone, will ya?"

Geez. Another new car. This guy was living high on the hog and I was at home eating Ramen. What was wrong with this picture?

I waited until Dick was well out of earshot before dropping my bomb on Miles. "Okay, so you've heard all the good news," I said. "Now for the bad news."

His face fell. "Oh no. There's *bad* news?"

"Yeah," I said. "Pretty bad. We only have a week to prep for the next hearing."

Miles looked like he was about to faint. I wouldn't have blamed him. I might have already fainted myself if the sheer urgency of the situation hadn't kept me moving forward.

Miles sat down hard. "We can't find and prep another expert in a *week*."

"I know that."

"Good Lord, Chloe! Why didn't you just come out and say so! You got my hopes up and called the boss in here and—"

"Um, I think he came in here on his own."

"Whatever. Details!"

"I don't want Dick to know about this until we have another expert in place."

"Chloe, you are *dreaming*. Dick and Delmont and the whole PetroPlex crew have a poker game scheduled for tonight, and all his poker buddies already know! How do you think you're going to keep it from him? This is not going to go well for you."

"You never know. Maybe they don't talk business at those games."

"And maybe a leprechaun will fly up your arse and leave a pot of gold!"

"It's the best I can hope for," I said. "I *might* get another case to settle before Dick figures it out. We have the rest of the afternoon. And besides, we *might* be able to find and prep a new witness before next week."

"But we haven't even got all of Dr. Schaeffer's research, and his place is a crime scene! You'll never be able to get your hands on it in just a week!"

"Extraordinary times call for extraordinary measures," I said.

"What are you going to do? Break in?"

"If I have to." Hey, I'd already committed blackmail today. One more moral breach wouldn't matter too much, right?

"Girl, you have *lost* your mind."

"Not yet," I said, "but I'll be there soon without your help. Have you found out who the detective on the case is yet?"

"Of course! It's Jensen Nash." Miles fanned his face with his hand and raised his gaze to the ceiling in a mock partial swoon.

Jensen Nash was one of the town's local detectives. I didn't know a lot about him except that he was an eligible bachelor and purportedly the sexiest male in a two-hundred mile radius. But this was according to the local girls, whose taste in men I seriously questioned. I was not really into the cowboy type, which comprised the majority of the male population in this town.

"Have you been able to get a hold of him yet?"

"Yes. I already asked him for an appointment on your behalf, and he refuses to see you today. I also told him there wasn't much time, and that you were dealing with matters of life and death," Miles said.

"And?"

"He wasn't impressed. He said he deals with matters of life and death every day, and that the living, especially living attorneys, can wait."

"He said that?"

"Yeah. But in a really sexy voice." Miles sighed. "You should call him."

I buried my face in my hands. Honestly. I just needed one thing—*one thing*—to go right, to be easy, just *one time* today. Was that really too much to ask?

"Go see him in person," Miles said. "Wear something low-cut."

"That is cheap and disgusting. . . and worth a shot." I rolled my chair back from my desk and inspected my broken shoe. "Are you up to finishing the draft of this motion?"

"Sure," Miles said. "Go get him, tiger. But take my advice and go home and freshen up first."

"That bad?" I asked.

"Girl, your hair looks like it went through a hay bailer. Change into something cuter. And do I even need to mention the shoes?

I sighed and limped out the door.

***

When I pulled into my driveway, the looming afternoon shadows of PetroPlex's largest refinery draped my sorry excuse for a rental house. The refinery was one of the largest in Texas and the town's supporting industry, employing over 1500 of Kettle's total population of 4000. The regional corporate headquarters were attached to this refinery and employed another 500 people. The complex was large and situated smack in the middle of town, right in everyone's backyard. Here, workers refined over 140 million gallons of crude oil into gasoline and other substances every day.

Residents whose property abutted the refinery, like mine did, were used to living under the refinery's continuous cloud of smoke and the frequent spurts of fire from the safety flares, which ignited every time the refinery needed to burn off excess vapors. Every now and then, something would go wrong, and the neighborhood would be filled with the smell of toxic chemicals. Sometimes alarms would even go off, warning nearby residents to stay indoors and seal the cracks in windows and doors with wet towels to keep the chemicals from getting in.

Worst of all were the explosions, and there had been a few. Most of them were minor, but several years ago a large one had killed ten people and shook the neighborhood's foundations.

I hobbled out of my car, grabbed the mail, and stumbled inside, kicking off the now defunct Louboutins. My long-haired Chihuahua/Sheltie mutt Lucy (so named for her red head—a characteristic she shared with me) raced towards me and jumped up and down, tongue lolling out, eyes wide. I put my stuff down and scooped her up to pet her hello. She licked my face and I kissed her on the head. "Are you hungry?" I asked.

She responded by leaping out of my arms and racing to the back bedroom where I kept her food bowl. I followed her, scooped some food into her bowl, and returned to the kitchen to look at the mail.

Bills, bills, and bills, all of which were 60-90 days late. Student loans in excess of six figures. Electricity. Phone and Internet. No cable, though—I had long since let that go. I swore out loud when I saw a demand letter from my landlord. I was sure to be evicted soon, at this rate. I really needed to settle a case and generate some cash.

There was also a notice from the City of Dallas threatening to repossess my dog if I didn't send them proof of vaccination within seven business days. I figured I could at least safely ignore that one, since I didn't live in Dallas anymore and I doubted they'd come all the way down here to get her. Still, I did need to find a way to pay for the vaccinations soon. Down here, you never knew what would jump out and bite you.

I threw open my pantry to see if maybe there was some hidden gem in there I had forgotten about. Sadly, there was only

Ramen. I was really much more in the mood for fajitas—and margaritas. Patron margaritas. The kind that were served in the big glasses the size of a human head with salt on the rim and a sangria floater.

Maybe if I played my cards right, I could get Detective Jensen Nash to buy me dinner. After all, he'd be more likely to spill his guts over drinks, right? Maybe I wouldn't even tell him I was a lawyer. Maybe I'd just go down there and turn on the charm and lure him out of the office and *wham!* Before he knew it, I'd know all about Dr. Schaeffer's murder and I'd have my files back.

This seemed like a pretty good plan, assuming I could get it to work. I have never considered myself beautiful. My bright red hair and pale porcelain skin are a bit out of place among all the tanned blondes down here in south Texas. Because I was hungry and really wanted those fajitas, I prayed Nash was into the red-headed type.

Trying to forget about my financial situation for a moment, I went to the bedroom, flinging off today's office wear as I went. I changed into a black lace number layered over a solid red cotton tank and very tiny, very fitted jean shorts, then I slipped on some red high heels. I felt pretty naked for what would essentially be a business meeting, but on the up side, I looked absolutely nothing like a lawyer, a breed of people Jensen Nash apparently hated.

I told myself this was totally going to work. Then I shut my eyes really tight while I tried to make myself believe it.

Okay, who was I kidding? I opened my eyes and took a moment to fantasize, not for the first time, about what my life would have been like if I had actually married my ex-fiancé, Dallas trial attorney Dorian Saks—a partner and colleague at my old law firm. He was more tall, more dark, and more handsome than the tallest, darkest, handsomest man you've ever seen. He owned a mansion in Highland Park, an area of supremely-concentrated wealth near downtown, and he was a movie star in the courtroom. When he looked at you, everyone else disappeared. I was absolutely certain that every time he stepped before a jury, each juror felt as though there was no one else in the room and that nothing mattered except producing a verdict in Dorian's favor.

If I had married him, I would have had a cook, a housekeeper, and a personal shopper to replace my broken Louboutins. I would have had a fireplace in the bedroom and a Jacuzzi in the bathroom. I would have had a diamond ring big enough to have its own zip code.

And I would have had an eternally broken heart. That was the fantasy killer.

Dorian was simply incapable of honesty and fidelity. This I discovered after we were engaged. Dorian's secretary knocked on my office door one day and told me Dorian had taken her out for a steak dinner. He told her he was going to marry me and asked her not to tell me she was sleeping with him.

Dorian's ego was such that he thought that would fly, but I'm no doormat. He lost both me and his secretary, but I was sure he'd had no trouble finding replacements for both of us.

The toxic torts circle in Dallas is a small one. I couldn't handle staying there and facing him every day, so I left town.

The only job in my practice area that was available anywhere in Texas happened to be here in Kettle.

Living in this crummy rent house buried under stacks of unpaid bills, I wondered for a fleeting moment if maybe I could have lived with the infidelity after all. He had loved me enough to propose. Couldn't that have been enough?

I thought about it for a moment, but in my heart I knew, even stuck down here in Kettle, Texas with a job that paid jack squat, I wouldn't trade places with whoever Dorian was with now.

I noticed a chip in my fingernail polish, and that brought me back to the present. I pulled out a bottle of top coat to smooth it over and tried not to let the situation get me down. Sure, I was feeling a little desperate, but I vowed to myself that Jensen Nash would never, ever know. I would be smooth. I would be charming. He wouldn't know what hit him.

I checked my mascara one last time, spritzed on some Michael Kors perfume, ruffled the fur on Lucy's head, and headed out the door and down to the police station. *Look out, Jensen Nash! Here I come!*

CHAPTER 2

The local police station consisted of one plain red brick building surrounded by a host of mobile trailers. Rather than buy or build a new building as the department expanded, the city just kept dropping in trailers and setting up offices in those. I found Jensen Nash in his office in one of the trailers. His name appeared in neat white block letters on a black sign attached to his door. I opened the door and walked in without knocking.

He barely bothered to glance up at me. It was hard to tell by the look on his face what he thought of me or my skimpy ensemble. That was not encouraging.

"You're off for the evening, I take it," he said.

"Um, yes, actually, but—"

"Chloe Taylor, right?" he asked without looking up.

"Yes, but—"

"I thought I told your paralegal I was busy."

Crap. So much for my "I'm not a lawyer" ruse. "You did, but—"

"You thought you'd come down here anyway and charm me with your feminine wiles."

Wow. I hadn't felt this out of control of a conversation since I was a zitty teenager trying to get up the courage to talk to my first crush. To make matters worse, Detective Nash was, in fact, the sexiest man I had seen in a 200 mile radius. He was even sexier than Dorian. He had Rob Lowe good looks. Even through his black suit jacket, I could see that he was incredibly fit. If he possessed even an ounce of personal charm, I might have fallen instantly in love. Instead, I found myself stammering and irritated.

"How do you know who I am?"

"I'm a detective," he said. "I know things."

"Would you care to share?"

"Nope," he said.

I bent over his desk, resting my weight on my elbows, chin in my hands, desperately trying to think of a way to get him to engage.

"Your victim was my expert witness," I said. "I knew him pretty well. We should talk."

Nash steadily refused to look at me. "I don't think so."

"I can help you," I said.

"I doubt it."

"Then maybe you can help me," I said.

"I doubt that, too."

Okay. Now he was starting to piss me off. "Well if you won't help yourself, and if you won't help me, how about helping Gracie Miller? Or are you just a heartless sonofabitch who doesn't care about old lady widows and their kittens?"

Nash looked up in surprise. "Kittens? What do old lady widows and kittens have to do with anything?"

I took advantage of the opening. "My client Gracie Miller used to be married to a guy named Derrick. He worked for PetroPlex in the benzene unit for forty years, starting right out of high school. When opposing counsel deposed him a year ago, his wife Gracie, who he married when he was nineteen, had to push him through the doors and into my office in a wheelchair. I had to wheel in his oxygen tank. He had no hair, not even eyebrows or eyelashes because of chemotherapy. He had radiation burns on his face and chest. He had to take off his oxygen mask and gasp for breath just to answer questions for the jackass PetroPlex attorney who spent the entire day trying to prove that even though Petroplex never warned Derrick that benzene causes cancer, that even though PetroPlex was too cheap to install the safety devices that would prevent benzene leaks, and even though PetroPlex never supplied respiratory masks or safety equipment, they were not to blame for my client's cancer and subsequent death."

I had finally succeeded in gaining Detective Nash's attention. I still couldn't quite read his face, though.

"Derrick," I said, "slaved away for years to save up for a down payment on a tiny farm. He took Gracie out to dinner at Olive Garden once a year for their anniversary because that was the best he could afford. And on my birthday last year, Gracie baked me a cake. From scratch. With homemade chocolate icing and *real butter*. And incidentally, my birthday was the day before Derrick's funeral, which was also the day after he died, at home, gasping for breath in his wheeled-in hospital bed. Gracie is thoughtful like that."

Nash's eye twitched almost imperceptibly. What did that mean? "And the kittens?"

"Gracie has a cat," I said. "The cat had kittens, but they all drank water from a toxic pond near the refinery and died."

He was silent for a few moments. I waited. Finally, he said, "All right. So your client's sob-story notwithstanding, I have to know. Are you a particular fan of Ramen noodles?"

"What?" My eyes went wide. "What kind of a random question is that?"

"Do you buy Ramen noodles because you like the way they taste?"

"I love them," I lied. I folded my arms and glared at him, nonverbally daring him to imply otherwise.

"I couldn't help but notice the redhead in the grocery store last Sunday wearing a thousand dollars' worth of designer clothes and buying fifteen or twenty packages of Ramen. Closer to twenty, I think, because you didn't check out in the express lane."

I'm not sure, but I think that if Nash had had a mirror on the wall in his office, I might have seen my face turn as red as my hair right about then.

"A woman like you buying food like that. I thought it was strange. Don't get the wrong idea. It's just that I'm a detective, and I'm trained to notice things that seem. . . off. So I was wondering whether or not you have a genuine love for all things Ramen."

"Well, I just, you know. . . the spice packets come in so many varieties." My fingers tingled. My head felt like it was floating up off my neck. I could feel my body shrinking. I thought I might die of embarrassment at any minute.

"I asked the checkout clerk if he knew your name. He did."

"I'm flattered," I said sourly.

Nash smiled. "So did you come down here dressed like that because you're looking for a dinner date?"

My jaw dropped open, but only for an instant. "You've got a lot of nerve accusing me of strolling around like a hooker in search of her next meal." Okay, of course I was cruising for dinner, but I'd been hoping not to be totally obvious about it. "I went to *law* school. I passed the *bar exam.* I am a *professional.*"

"So is that a no?"

I stopped short. "A no to what?"

"A no to my dinner invitation."

"You didn't extend a dinner invitation," I snapped. "And if you had, I wouldn't be inclined to say yes."

Nash laughed. "But you would go."

Well, yes. But no way was I about to fall all over myself rushing to admit it. "Let me tell *you* something," I said. "Every other girl in this town may be falling all over themselves trying to get a date with you, but I'm not that kind of girl. I don't just keel over in the face of good looks. I am a strong, confident, individual, highly accomplished professional, and you would be *lucky* to get a date with *me.*"

"I'm sure that's true," he said, glancing at me sideways. "So you think I'm good looking, then?"

"I didn't say that!" I said. "I was talking about other people. The ones who might think you're good looking. Not me."

Nash laughed again. I was really starting to feel like the village idiot, and that was saying a lot, considering that I lived in Kettle.

"Chloe Taylor," he said, "may I buy you dinner?"

I groaned. "Yes. But only because I need to ask you some questions about Dr. Schaeffer, and I feel like you'd be more talkative over margaritas. Pick me up in an hour."

I scrawled my address on a Post-It, flung it at him, and hurried out the door.

CHAPTER 3

Judge Delmont's cell phone buzzed. He picked it up. "Talk to me."

"The police chief said Nash is about to leave town with Chloe Taylor," said a gruff voice on the other end of the line.

"You got a tail on them?" Delmont asked.

"All my manpower is on the files. Schaeffer's laptop is encrypted, and there are ten boxes of stuff in print. That's just the stuff we got. There are thirty more boxes where that came from. We have to find out exactly how much he knew before we're certain we've plugged the leak."

"Thirty more boxes?"

"There wasn't enough time to get them all before Nash and his guys got there. We need to secure the rest before Taylor does."

"I see. You got any idea where Nash and Taylor are headed?"

"Some place for dinner. Nash is going to pick her up at her house at 6:30."

"A date?" Delmont rearranged the cigar ashes in the tray with the end of his pen.

"Not according to Chief Scott."

"How would he know?"

"He's got Nash's office bugged, as of yesterday. You know Nash and his goody-two-shoes reputation. If he happens to get wind of us, no telling what he might do."

"You think Taylor will find out anything we don't want her to know?"

"Unlikely. I don't think she's aware anything out of the ordinary is going on."

Delmont snorted. "Please. Her expert turns up dead the night before a summary judgment hearing, and you don't think she thinks anything out of the ordinary is going on? Get real. She's a big city lawyer. She ain't stupid. And you've got piss poor timing. You should have called me first."

"It wasn't your call to make."

"Maybe not, but just FYI, Taylor ain't playing by the rules anymore, either."

"What do you mean?" the voice on the other end of the phone asked.

"If I don't grant her motion for continuance tomorrow morning, I'm gonna lose my wife—that's what I mean."

The person on the other end of the line grunted. "Huh. Well, is that altogether a bad thing? Thought you were getting tired of her anyway."

"Yeah, but I'd just as soon the local tongues not go a waggin'."

"I'll cut you a deal."

"A deal! You've been hanging out with Dick Richardson too much lately. I'm sick of you guys and your deals."

"A deal," the voice said. "Here's how it is. You get somebody to man all the roads back into town, and I'll get somebody to go through her car and her house. There's gotta be something there you can use to get her to back off. Nobody's perfect. When you see Nash's vehicle, call me and warn me to get out. Things go my way, and you can deny that motion for continuance come tomorrow morning."

"Fine. I'll call you," Delmont said. "But I don't like it. Frankly, I think you and your guys are getting careless."

"I don't care what you think, and even if I did, you're not in a position to judge here. Just remember who put you where you are."

"I was elected fair and square."

"Sure, on my campaign money."

Delmont held his tongue. He'd always thought it was stupid that Texas elected their judges instead of appointing them. On the other hand, the system did offer certain advantages for people like him.

But now he was starting to feel a little out of control of the situation. "Listen here," he said. "I want you to keep me in the loop on all this. I don't want to get caught by surprise on this case, understand?"

"I understand."

"All right. Just so we're straight. Otherwise you may find you start disliking some of my more important rulings."

"That would be inconvenient," said the gruff voice.

"Darn straight." Delmont hung up the phone.

CHAPTER 4

Nash drove me to the nearby town of Rosethorn, which was slightly larger than Kettle and had a better variety of restaurants. We needed to leave town for dinner, seeing as how the exhaustive list of places to eat in Kettle included Dairy Queen, McDonald's, Grandma's Fried Chicken, and a place called Caliente, where the only flavor of food is jalapeno. I love jalapenos, but I haven't eaten at Caliente, mainly because I haven't been able to afford it lately. I've heard they serve jalapeno-flavored goat, and you can even get jalapeno-flavored rattlesnake there if you want to. (Apparently, some people actually like to eat rattlesnake—a fact I find hard to comprehend.)

When we got to the restaurant, Nash pulled out my chair and unfolded my napkin. I was just on the verge of thinking some nice things about him when he sat down and pulled a pen and small notebook out of his pocket.

An interrogation. Not a dinner date. Wow, how naïve was I? This guy was a real pro. He had gone out of his way to put me off balance so that *he* could ask *me* questions. Not the other way around.

Of course he would want to question me. I had been working with Dr. Schaeffer the day he was killed. As stupid as I had felt earlier, I felt infinitely more moronic now.

"Really?" I eyed his notepad pointedly. "You could have just taken my appointment request and asked me what you wanted to know down at the station."

"Frankly," he said, "I really didn't have time to see you today. I had just gotten back from the crime scene when your office called, and there were more important people to talk to."

"Like who?"

"Like people who actually had a motive to kill Dr. Schaeffer."

"Such as?"

"The details of the investigation are confidential."

"But here I am. So what changed?"

"Certain other people were unavailable. And you did show up in very skimpy clothes." If he were resisting the urge to leer or grin, he didn't show it. "And I'm hungry. A man has got to eat, and there's nothing wrong with multi-tasking."

I folded my arms across my chest defensively. "Are you always all work and no play?"

"Would you accept an invitation to find out?"

I rolled my eyes. "Stop it. We both know this is not a date. I want information, you want information, so let's have at it. Ladies first."

"By all means."

"What happened to Dr. Schaffer?" I knew he'd been murdered. I just didn't know how.

"The details have not been released to the public yet."

"I'm not the public."

"That's right. You're worse. You're the deceased's hiring attorney. My turn."

This guy was really a piece of work. "You don't get to insult me and then ask me questions."

Our waiter arrived, asking us what we'd like to drink.

"Two margaritas," Nash said, without hesitation.

"And you don't get to order for me either," I said through gritted teeth.

The waiter, sensing my agitation, hesitated for a moment before turning to me and asking me what I'd like to drink.

"Margarita," I said. "The big one in a glass that's the size of a human head. With Patron and a sangria swirl."

The waiter nodded and walked back toward the bar.

Nash looked at me with one raised eyebrow.

"And you don't get to look at me like that, either." In the looks department, he was adorable, which was seriously killing my game.

"When you are finished telling me everything I may not do, I'd like to know why you're so anxious to get inside Schaeffer's house."

I blinked, surprised. How could he possibly have known that? "Who says I want in his house?"

"Police Chief Scott. According to his buddy Judge Delmont, you haven't got a case unless you can get your hands on his laptop."

I frowned. "Not his laptop. His file boxes. Everything we had was in cardboard boxes at his house. I was supposed to pick up a lot of it the morning before the hearing. Then I got to his house and the whole place was a crime scene, and nobody would let me in."

"Imagine that."

"I need in," I said.

"And I need to figure out who killed him, preferably in less than a week, and I can't do that if you're tromping all over my crime scene."

I groaned. "Come on," I said. "Don't you get it? We can *help* each other."

"I doubt that our interests line up precisely." Nash fingered the frosty base of his margarita glass thoughtfully. "What would you say if I told you his laptop was missing?"

"I'd say there's nothing on it worth stealing. He was low tech."

"Everything was in the file boxes?"

I nodded.

"How many were there?"

A little shiver went up my spine. "Were?" I said. "As in *past tense?"*

"There weren't any file boxes in the house."

"There had to be," I said. "Unless you're telling me somebody committed a brutal murder and carted out forty boxes of documents without any of the neighbors noticing."

"*Forty?*"

"Yeah," I said.

Nash leaned back and scratched his neck. "I will admit that's unlikely."

"They're there," I said. "Maybe you just didn't know where to look." Schaeffer's house was full of hidden nooks and crannies. And I knew where at least one of them was—a little nugget of information Nash didn't seem to have. For the first time today, I felt like I was one step ahead of him.

"Maybe you can tell me what I missed," Nash said.

"Only if you let me in."

"Not gonna happen."

I sat abruptly back, exasperated. I *had* to get in. Some way, somehow. "Why not? I read detective novels! I watch *Castle*! I know I'm not supposed to touch anything! I will step where you step, touch only what you touch, *et cetera* and so forth. I swear."

"It would be a complete break of protocol."

"Sometimes you have to bend the rules," I said. "Sometimes it's just necessary."

Detective Nash narrowed his eyes. "It's never necessary," he said. "The rules are there for a reason."

"Give me a break," I said. "The people who have the money make the rules, which means the rules are not always in the interest of the greater good." This was a fact about which I had to thoroughly convince myself before deciding to go through with blackmailing Judge Delmont. Now that that deed was done, I refused to believe otherwise. And I would take anyone else I could get down that little mental path with me. Especially local law enforcement.

"Go on," Nash said.

"For example, did you know the oil refinery safety statutes which apply to refineries in the Houston area do not apply to the refinery in this town?"

"I did not know that."

"Well they don't, and here's why. There are only four-thousand people living in the shadow of our PetroPlex refinery, whereas in Houston and the surrounding areas, there are millions. The law dictates that more safety measures are required in places of higher population. In other words, the law says that the life of somebody who lives in Houston is more valuable than your life or mine. And all because some bigshot oil lobbyist funded some local representative's campaign in exchange for a vote to relax regulation in the area."

"You can't prove that."

"Maybe not, but it wouldn't shock me if Dr. Schaeffer could."

"So what you're saying is that it's okay to bend the rules in this case because PetroPlex bent them to start with?"

I took a deep breath. "It wouldn't be bending the rules. It would be returning to me what is mine. I'm saying I can help you in return. I'm saying we can help each other. Do you really feel like your life is worth less than that of someone who lives in Houston? Do you really believe your value is dictated by your geographic location? Help me show PetroPlex that your life matters, too."

Nash laughed—so not the reaction I was hoping for. "I can see how you'd be a threat in front of a jury. I'm not saying it's right. I'm saying that two wrongs don't make a right, so I can't break protocol and let you in. Meanwhile, if you have a problem with the current legislation, make sure you vote for someone who hasn't taken campaign contributions from Big Oil in the next election. That's how you right that wrong."

"Right," I said sarcastically. "Because it's that easy. Listen up, because I'm about to tell you how the system really works."

Nash raised his eyebrows.

"It's like this. Crude oil and gasoline contain dangerous hydrocarbons like benzene. The government has known that benzene causes cancer since about 1900, and the EPA has had it listed as a known human carcinogen for over thirty years. It is a Class A carcinogen, which is the most toxic designation the EPA hands out. It means we *know* benzene causes cancer. No ifs, ands, or buts about it."

"Okay," Nash said. "It's not like anybody thinks oil is actually healthy to be around. This is not news."

I ignored him and continued. "Benzene is so toxic that if you filled up one measuring cup and let it evaporate in a football stadium, ambient air levels would still be 3.3 times higher than the OSHA safe-air standard, and 6.6 times the NIOSH standard. Think about that for a minute. A single cup of benzene is enough to expose everyone in a football stadium to air that is six times more toxic than the legal limit. But a cup of benzene is *nothing*. Benzene is *everywhere*. This stuff is a natural part of crude oil and gasoline, and it's also found in all oil refinery waste products, which are rarely disposed of properly."

Our waiter arrived with the fajitas. I inhaled the scent of char-grilled bliss and stuffed my face with the meaty goodness.

"In fact," I said, not even caring that I was talking with my mouth full, "benzene makes up 1% of crude oil and accounts for up to 5% of gasoline vapors, which means you can also essentially poison everybody who is sitting in a football field with only six gallons of unsealed crude oil, or one and a half gallons of an uncorked bottle of gasoline. And yet, Corpus Christi, the U.S. City with more oil refineries than any other city except for Los Angeles, dumped seventy tons of benzene in 2007 alone. Seventy tons! That's *way* more than a single cup."

Nash's eyes went wide as he processed those numbers. Clearly this was news to him. "Seventy tons. . ." Nash's gaze went to the ceiling as he did some quick mental math. "That's. . . what? Almost 18,000 gallons, assuming a gallon of benzene is roughly equivalent to a gallon of water?"

"Or if you break that down even further into cups," I said, "enough to expose three-hundred-thousand football stadiums full of people to toxic air. Maybe my math is not perfect, but you get the idea. That's also the equivalent of benzene exposure you'd see in a twenty-nine million gallon oil spill, which would be almost three times the size of the Exxon Valdez. Data from the Texas Department of State Health Services reveals a birth defects rate in Corpus Christi that is 84% higher than the rest of the country. So if you're feeling romantic and want to settle down and have children, don't do it in Corpus Christi."

A strange look passed across Nash's face. I wondered briefly what his romantic ambitions might be, but I didn't dwell long on that thought. He was good looking, but what woman would ever be able to crack *his* shell?

"Meanwhile, our politicians allow this to happen. Both parties. They're both so beholden to Big Oil for campaign contributions they don't care who gets hurt. Everybody who lives in this town—and countless other towns just like this one—is exposed. A lot of people have died—including Gracie's husband. I work my butt off every day trying to hold these polluters accountable, and I get virtually no help. I'm asking you for help. Help me get justice for Gracie. Let me in to Schaeffer's house, and I'll help you get justice for Schaeffer."

Nash stared down at the table for a long moment, drumming his fingers on the polished wood surface. When he raised his eyes, he almost looked sad. "I'm sorry," he said. "I just can't. But if you really want to help me get justice for Schaeffer, you can tell me where you think he stashed all those files."

The fajitas I'd just inhaled felt like they had turned to rocks in my stomach. I snatched the napkin off my lap, wiped my hands on it, and tossed it on the table as I stood up. "I'm sorry," I said, putting all the ice I could muster into my voice. "I just can't. Dinner's over. Take me home."

Nash paid the bill, and we drove back to Kettle in silence.

CHAPTER 5

The phone in Delmont's chambers rang.

It was about time. Delmont was sick of waiting around. Sick of waiting for a call that he shouldn't have had to wait for in the first place. Taylor and Nash must have really been talking it up. He was gonna be late for the poker game, at this rate. His wife had been nagging him to host one of their bi-weekly poker sessions at his house for years, and he'd never given in until tonight. If he showed up late, he'd never hear the end of it.

These losers had really screwed up. They couldn't have offed the guy at a worse time. Not only did it look bad in light of the docket schedule, they had to go and do it right when Nash was sure to be assigned to the case. Delmont knew Nash's history, and he knew Nash couldn't be bought off. If these screw-ups had consulted him first, as they had discussed, they wouldn't be in the pickle they were in now. Delmont would love to get his hands on the guy with the happy trigger finger.

He picked up the phone. "Talk to me."

"They're en route. Maybe five minutes."

Delmont slammed the phone down, not bothering to say "thanks" or "goodbye."

Immediately, he picked it back up and dialed another number.

The call connected. "Chief Scott," barked the voice on the other end.

Delmont said, "Five minutes. What's your status?"

Chief Scott hesitated. "I'm sorry. Best I can tell, she was squeaky clean before today."

Delmont swore. "Clear out. We're late for the game, anyway. My wife is gonna have my hide."

"You shouldn't have let her talk you into hosting in the first place."

"I know, but a man can only take so much nagging before he gives in."

"She's not gonna *play*, is she?"

"Course not. But I gotta warn you, she's been buying all kinds of ridiculous paraphernalia for weeks. Just put it on and humor her, all right?"

"All right, then."

The line went dead.

CHAPTER 6

Anna Delmont looked at the clock for maybe the hundredth time that evening. Where the heck was her husband? Joe Bob always acted like he could hardly wait to get out the door and get to the poker games at Dick's house. He was *never* late to Dick's house. How come he'd be late to his *own* party? And why in tarnation wasn't he answering his phone?

She kept calling up to the courthouse, but all the staff had gone home by now. Maybe she ought to go up there and drag him out of his chambers with her own two hands. But what if the other guests arrived while she was gone and there was no one here to greet them when they finally got here?

Anna paced back and forth across the living room, wringing her hands. She took a detour to the window, hoping to see someone approaching the house, but there was no one there. She sighed. Had she gone to all this trouble for nothing?

She'd spent weeks picking out all the decorations. Joe Bob had never, ever let her come within a mile of one of his "guy's night outs" before, and she was dying of curiosity to see what happened during all these poker games. She wanted everything to be perfect. She wanted all the boys to want to come back.

She'd set out the green felt-top table and bought everyone buttons to pin to their shirt. They were battery-operated gadgets with red flashing lights that said stuff like "High Roller" and "Pit Boss." She'd also put up seventies-style beaded curtains all around the room, except they were made of strings of various sizes of red dice instead of beads. She'd also bought everyone their very own pair of green suspenders covered in diamonds, hearts, clubs, and spades, and matching green transparent visors to match. Mylar balloons decorated with cards and dice were tied to the back of every player's chair, and she'd set up a real fancy slot machine centerpiece on the green felt table to spruce it up. Everything was looking mighty fine. Joe Bob was sure to be proud of her handiwork.

Her doorbell rang, playing the melody to *Stars and Stripes Forever.* Her interchangeable custom chimes were the envy of all the women in the neighborhood.

She plastered on a big, welcoming smile and threw the door wide. A little man with a big cigar in his mouth stood at her entryway, puffing foul smoke into the house. It was Dick Richardson, who she knew through Joe Bob, of course—but even if she hadn't, she couldn't have failed to recognize him from his obnoxious television commercials. Anna didn't want to let him in with the cigar, but she didn't want to be rude either, especially since this was her very first poker party. Her dismay must have shown on her face.

"What? No smoking in the house?" Dick asked.

"Well. . ." Anna said.

Dick took a long drag from the cigar, dropped it on her custom welcome mat, and ground it out with his foot. "Don't worry about it," Dick said. "Long as you got Jack and Coke in the house, everything'll be fine."

Anna eyed the ruined mat. Well, it wasn't like she couldn't get another one. Joe Bob always gave her plenty of spending money. And who could expect men to really pay attention to niceties like welcome mats, anyway? Men would be men.

Dick strode past her into the room and eyed the set-up. He let out a low whistle. "Wow," he said. "You sure got the place done up."

Anna beamed with pride. "You like it?"

"It's. . . something else," Dick said.

Anna couldn't help but notice the look of astonishment on his face as he took in the balloons, pins, dice curtains, and centerpiece. That wow-factor had been exactly what she'd been going for. She felt herself warming up to Dick in spite of the whole cigar incident.

"Don't tell me I'm the first one here," Dick said.

"You are. For the life of me, I can't account for everyone else. Sit down. Let me get you a drink."

She bustled into the kitchen to pour him a Jack and Coke. She had tried to bake a spade-shaped cake, but the darn thing had burned, so there were no refreshments other than the booze.

She returned to present Dick with his drink when her doorbell chimed again.

This time it was old Judge Hooper, the town's criminal court judge. Judge Hooper was a nice, elderly man with a kind grin who walked with a cane. *He* didn't show up on her doorstep with a cigar. No siree. She ushered him in and he patted her on the back kindly.

"How you doing, little lady?" he asked, and looked around. "My goodness. Ain't you just gone all out!"

"Nothing but the best for you," Anna said, smiling. Really, she ought to host poker games more often. She couldn't understand why Joe Bob had always seemed so against it.

Right then, she heard Joe Bob slam through the back door. He stomped into the living room and stopped short.

"I'll be darned. It's worse than I thought," he said.

Anna's face fell.

"What the. . ." Joe Bob muttered as he strode toward the felt-top table. "Why you got a *slot machine* in the middle of our playing area? What's the matter with you, woman?"

She'd just wanted to break up all that empty green space. And after all, every good party table had a centerpiece.

"As long as real money comes out of it, I like it," Dick said.

"Yeah, I've never seen *you* turn down a buck." Joe Bob picked up the slot machine and dropped it unceremoniously on the sofa, then turned to Anna. "Where's the snacks?"

Anna's heart started beating rapidly, her lower lip threatened to start trembling, and her eyelids started to sting. She didn't want to admit she'd burned the cake in front of all of Joe Bob's friends. "I was expecting you to be more thirsty than hungry at this hour," she said. "I restocked the whole bar. Can I get you a drink?"

"Don't tell me you burned the cake?" Joe Bob said.

Anna flushed.

"Never mind," Judge Hooper said. "I already had dinner."

"Me too," Dick chimed in.

"Well I ain't," Joe Bob said. "Anna, you run on out and get us a pizza, all right?"

"All right," she said.

She left just as Police Chief Scott, Mayor Fillion, and a couple of other men were arriving.

Once inside the safety and relative privacy of her car and surrounded by the open road, she let a few tears fall from her eyes. Just a few. It wouldn't be a good idea to indulge in unseemly emotions out in public.

Of course Joe Bob wasn't the perfect husband. But he had always given her so much—he always made sure she had the best dresses and the best house in the neighborhood, and he was always sending her into Houston for overnight spa vacations and shopping trips. All the other neighborhood ladies were so jealous. So if she didn't often receive the affection from him she felt like she needed, she couldn't really complain. After all, he was a man, and she couldn't blame him for bottling up his feminine side.

Really, she figured she had done pretty well snagging Joe Bob. It was too much to expect to find an absolutely perfect man. They just didn't exist. She and Joe Bob had been married and faithful to each other for over 30 years, ever since she was crowned the Kettle beauty queen her senior year in high school. Sure, maybe she sometimes longed for a man with a softer side, but she and Joe Bob had such a solid history, and she would never throw that away or betray his trust. Even if he sometimes hurt her feelings, her eye had never really strayed. She loved Joe Bob, and Joe Bob only, and she was sure he felt the same way about her.

All that notwithstanding, she'd have some strong words for him after all the guests left tonight. He'd been late to an event he knew she'd been planning and looking forward to for ages, and then he'd embarrassed her in front of his friends. That would never do.

CHAPTER 7

Nash walked me to my front door. I was unclear on the protocol. I knew it hadn't been a date, but he was hovering awfully close. I thought maybe he might even lean in for a hug, if not a kiss, but given the fact that I knew I was about to break the law for the second time that day, I stepped back.

"Well," he said. "Thank you for a lovely evening."

"No, thank *you*," I said. "For nothing." Nash had frustrated me to no end. It was hard on my already bruised ego. It made me feel like being rude. Not the best way to be, I'll admit, but I hated feeling like an ineffective, pansy pushover.

"Nothing?" Nash ran his hands through his hair in a way that might have seemed self-conscious, if it were possible for Nash to feel such an emotion. "How about for dinner? If it weren't for me, you'd be eating Ramen."

"A temporary inconvenience," I said.

"I have no doubt."

He lingered. I could hear Lucy scratching at the door, impatient for me to come inside.

"Have a good night," I said, shifting my weight back and forth on my feet uncomfortably.

"You too."

We shook hands, and he left.

When I went inside, Lucy seemed unusually perturbed. She was always excited for me to come home, but tonight, she seemed more hyper than usual. She danced around, eyes bulging, tongue lolling out. She was shaking, kind of like she does when a big thunderstorm rolls through town, or when a stranger invades her territory.

Alarmed, I looked around, but nothing seemed to be out of place.

I scooped her up to soothe her. "Whatsamatter?" I asked. "Did the big, bad detective scare you? It's okay, baby. He's a nice detective. But between you and me, he's a little anal."

Lucy wagged her tail slightly, but continued to shake.

"Honeypie!" I said. "It's okay! What's wrong?"

If only dogs could talk. No matter how much I stroked and soothed her, she wouldn't calm down. I couldn't leave her like this, and I knew I had to leave immediately. Or at least once Nash was good and gone.

"Ride in the car?" I asked. She perked up. Those were the magic words. "Yeah! Momma will take you for a ride in the car!"

Lucy *loved* to ride in the car. One time I had taken her on a car trip to Florida—a thirteen hour drive. When we got there, I was exhausted, and so was she. As a joke, after I unpacked, I asked her if she wanted to ride in the car again. She hopped back in, ready to go. I had to forcibly pull her out and bring her inside.

She leapt out of my arms and pranced in circles in front of the door.

"Ride in the car?" I cooed again. She bucked like an impatient horse.

I fished around in my purse for my car keys.

I debated about whether or not to call Miles. The bottom line was, I needed Schaeffer's files. While I knew Miles would love to get his hands on them, his livelihood wasn't on the line like mine was. Right now, Miles just flat out had more options in life than I did. And if I was about to break into a crime scene illegally and disturb the evidence, why should I involve him? If I called and asked, I knew he would come even if he didn't want to. But if I didn't call him and I got caught, Miles would have complete deniability.

I decided that Lucy would be a perfectly good lookout.

I glanced out the window to make sure Nash was long gone. I didn't see any trace of him. Just to be on the safe side, I waited another five minutes before loading Lucy into the car and heading to Schaeffer's place. I used the time to do a quick and dirty Internet search on how to pick locks with credit cards. Schaeffer, who had been extremely paranoid in life, had about five on every door. It was going to be interesting trying to get in. For good measure, I also dropped a small hammer in my purse, in case I had to break a window—but that would be my last resort.

After sending the lock-picking information to my iPhone and double-checking my credit card count, I hit the road. If I ruined a couple cards in the process, no biggie. They had no credit left on them that I could use, after all. I was completely maxed out.

Schaeffer's house was an old 1950s ranch-style house with beige brick, a low-pitch roof, and small windows. It was his second house, which he'd had custom built to keep him comfortable while he was doing research here in town. Seeing as how he charged seven hundred dollars an hour, he could afford it.

The exterior was pitch black. The crime scene tape glinted yellow only in the gleam of my headlights. Everything else was dark. I drove past the house a few times to make sure everything was quiet. If any of the neighbors happened to be window-gazing tonight, I would surely appear suspicious. But somehow, "casing the joint" made me feel a little better about what I was about to do.

But what did I know?

Only what I'd seen on TV, that's what. And of course, what I'd just learned on the Internet. Ahh, the Internet. How did anyone ever live without it?

I shut off my lights, pulled the car around back, and parked in the shadow of a fence. I cracked the windows for Lucy and got out of the car. Ordinarily, I would never leave my dog in the car on a summer day, but the evening was cooling off significantly. I estimated the temperature was now back down into the eighties, and there was a nice breeze blowing. I knew Lucy could handle that.

"Good dog," I said, leaning in to pet her. "Stay right here and guard the house, okay?"

She wagged her tail. Her eyes widened in slight confusion, but she didn't make a sound as I crept away.

I felt certain that if anyone came around, she would bark and warn me.

After pulling on a pair of latex gloves, I crept slowly toward the back door and listened.

Nothing. No sounds. No light. No nothing. Good.

I slid one of the credit cards into the crack in the door and ran it down. Only one of the five locks was locked! I had totally lucked out. Obviously the local police weren't nearly as paranoid as Schaeffer. I wasn't surprised. It was such a small town that most of the residents never even used their locks at all. Some of them even left their keys in the car. There wasn't a lot of property crime in this town, and there usually wasn't much violent crime either, although there had been a slight uptick in stats lately, which had resulted in the hiring of some new police—Nash among them.

Best of all for me, the lock the police had chosen to fasten wasn't a deadbolt. It was a plain-old key in the doorknob contraption—the kind that was so easy to break into you might as well not even have installed it on the door in the first place.

I held my tiny, high-intensity flashlight in my teeth, glancing around furtively, working the credit card until the door was open.

I carried my light low, trying to make sure the beam stayed well below the window sill line and closed blinds as I came to them, shutting my tiny light off from the outside world.

A thrill of excitement vibrated through my core. I had never, ever done anything like this before. I felt high, lifted into the air on wings of pure adrenaline. Part of me wanted to never feel this way again. The other part of me wanted to feel this way every day of my life, from today henceforth to ever after.

I stepped slowly, one foot in front of the other, careful not to disturb anything on the floor.

The body had long since been removed to the Rosethorn morgue. But flicking my flashlight around, I happened upon a small pool of blood in the living room. I shivered, one part nauseated, one part . . . I don't know what.

Out of the corner of my eye, I saw light.

Headlights blazed in severe, horizontal lines through the blinds.

A car drove past the house slowly. More slowly than necessary, it seemed.

I might have been imagining things, but I felt tailed. Watched. Like I didn't have a lot of time. But no one could possibly know I was here. Could they?

I made my way through the house, looking for document boxes, but not expecting to find them right away. They wouldn't be anywhere obvious, or Nash would have found them already.

I crept into Schaeffer's office, which really looked more like an old European-style study. You'd never guess the interior of the house looked this way judging from the outside. After pulling all the blinds tight, I clicked on the light. I bypassed a grandfather clock, an entire wall of bookshelves, a shiny black grand piano, some parlor chairs, and a sofa, heading straight toward his middle desk drawer. Schaeffer had mentioned once that it had a false bottom, which was a little tidbit of information I'd decided to keep from Detective Nash. If he were thorough, he may have already found it. But if not. . .

The drawer was full of the usual desk knick-knacks. Paperclips, pens, pencils, rubber bands. A stray business card or two. I pulled the whole thing completely off its rails and dumped it upside-down on the rug.

Everything fell out—including the false bottom.

And an envelope.

With my name on it.

The false bottom was only a few millimeters deep, which is probably why Nash hadn't noticed it.

Feeling as though my illegal expedition had somehow just been validated, I snagged a letter opener from the pile of stuff on the floor and slit the missive open.

Inside was a single sheet of paper.

Another car drove past the house on the street outside. Faster than the first one, perhaps?

I froze and watched the lights fade away.

Once they were gone, I examined the sheet of paper. A literal letter from the grave.

In handwritten block print, Dr. Schaeffer had written: "The end of time."

That was all.

What on earth? I had risked my livelihood and broken the law for this? For *this?* A cryptic message that meant nothing?

Time. Time. I racked my brains, trying to think of any discussions we'd ever had about time.

We weren't rocket scientists or quantum theorists, for crying out loud. When had we ever discussed time?

We did know filing this case meant we were in it for the long haul. We knew we weren't up for a quick win. So the end of time meant. . . what?

The literal end of time? Surely not.

I flicked my flashlight around the room, stopping at the grandfather clock. I rushed over to it, opening its cabinet and poking around.

I found nothing.

What else?

I went back to the desk and went through the drawers. I found a pocket watch and opened it up. Nothing. I grabbed a pair of scissors and pried open the case. The thing fell apart. Still nothing, except a freshly ruined watch.

Frantic, I rushed to the bedroom, examining his watch case, his bedside clock, anything related to time.

Nothing.

Frustrated, I went back to the office and stared at the note once more, silently willing it to tell me its secrets. There was nothing else on it except for the bare block print. I even shined the flashlight on it, looking for watermarks or smudges or *anything* else except the uninformative words neatly printed in black ink.

I sat in Schaeffer's desk chair, debating about whether or not to turn on the light. Maybe if I could see properly, something else would come to mind.

I decided against it, but flicked the flashlight around the room, hoping something would stand out.

A gleam of red caught my eye.

Yes! Not time, but TIME with a capital T! As in, the magazine! An entire row of Time magazines filled the second bookshelf down on the south wall. It was not an external wall. This wall backed up to the bedroom, if I was not mistaken.

I stepped out into the hall and peered into the bedroom, trying to gauge the distance between the door and the wall that divided the bedroom from the office.

It was dark. But either it was my imagination, or there was a slight discrepancy in the distance to the end of the room and the distance down the hallway to the office.

Could the boxes be in a chamber be behind the shelves somehow? But if so, where was the switch? These shelves felt like they were miles long. They covered the entire length of the wall, which was not insubstantial. The house itself, being ranch style, was unusually long to start with. The trigger could be anywhere, assuming there was a trigger at all. It would take me all night to empty the shelves. There had to be a better way. *Think!* I told myself. Brains over brawn. The only way a girl could survive.

In the distance, I heard a dog bark. But it wasn't Lucy, so I figured I was still okay.

I checked the windows again, and seeing no car lights, I crept back to the office and went back to the magazines. They were organized by date, the earlier ones to the left and the most recent ones to the right. I pulled out the last chunk of magazines—the ones to the far right. The "end of Time." When I stuck my hand into the bookshelf, I felt nothing out of the ordinary.

I pressed the back wall.

Nothing.

I pressed in various other places.

Still nothing.

Plopping onto the floor, I propped up my light and paged through each of the magazines, hoping to find a dog-eared page, a piece of paper. Something. Just something.

Finding nothing, I started to work my way backwards through all of the magazines, pressing in various places on the shelf, paging through each copy. I worked my way all the way through the very first issue of the magazine on the shelf—the January 1991 copy—before I finally admitted to myself that I had reached a dead end.

Now what?

I scrupulously replaced all of the magazines in the correct order.

As I bent down to pick up the last magazine, I noticed an old copy of a family Bible crammed into the corner of the bottom shelf. Unlike all the other books around it, it wasn't covered in dust.

Surely not. But there it was. *Revelation*, I wondered? A book about the literal end of time?

I pulled out the old Bible and flipped to the last page of *Revelation*. Tucked inside was a small scrap of paper that read: "A Scandal in Bohemia."

Was he kidding? Sending me on a goose chase like this just for the files that were *already mine?*

It was a good thing I happened to be familiar with the reference. I took the clue and ran my flashlight over the bookshelves until I found a volume of Sir Arthur Conan Doyle. I flipped it open and found the short story titled "A Scandal in Bohemia," which featured Irene Adler, the only woman to outwit Sherlock Holmes. I riffled through it. Nothing. I crossed my fingers, replaced the book on the shelf, and pressed it firmly in.

A clicking noise shattered my blanket of suburban silence, and I jumped.

Realizing that I, myself, had caused the sound, I blew out a sigh and relaxed. Feeling along the wall, I found the uneven space where the bookshelf had popped away from the wall.

Pulling it back, I shined my flashlight into the newly revealed space.

One, two three. . . thirty boxes of files.

Ten boxes were missing.

Someone had been here.

And yet, the envelope with my name on it in the desk had been sealed. How could anyone else have known?

Visions of men in black going all Jack Bauer on Dr. Schaeffer flashed through my mind. Had he been tortured? Had he died a slow death?

I thought about that for a second, and then wished I hadn't.

A high-pitched bark ripped my attention away from horrifying past and future possibilities into the even more horrifying present.

It was Lucy. Her bark was not one of idle boredom, or a mere shout-out to the neighborhood dogs barking in the distance. Its pitch was the one she reserved for neighbors trespassing on her sidewalk, or the mailman delivering the mail.

Someone was here.

I hastily pressed the bookshelf back into the wall, dumped everything back into the desk drawer, and slid it shut. Then I grabbed the envelope and piece of paper addressed to me. Confident I had left everything else as I found it, I ran to the back door, locked the doorknob lock from the inside, and slipped out.

Lucy had stopped barking. She must have scared away whoever was here.

I debated about whether or not to go back inside. Was it worth the risk of leaving and possibly losing the files? Or staying and risking the loss of something even worse... like my life?

Okay, reality check. Maybe somebody bad had been out to get Schaeffer, but *I* didn't know anything worth killing over. *Deep breath.* The worst that could happen is that I might get caught breaking and entering, and then I'd just have to lawyer myself out of jail. No biggie. I could do that in my sleep. But it would take time, and that was a luxury I really didn't have.

I decided to leave and come back later. I would park farther away and watch the house from a distance to make sure no one was there.

I left through the same door I'd come in, locking it again behind me. Then I slid into the driver's seat of my car. Lucy hopped into my lap and started licking my face madly.

"Good dog," I whispered. "You told 'em, didn't you?"

I didn't wait for her to settle down before sliding the key into the ignition and starting the car. I twisted my wrist with maximum force and jerked the car into reverse, pressing down on the gas pedal as hard as I dared.

In a few moments, I was out of the driveway and humming down the street.

Even though I kept manically checking my rearview mirrors, I saw no one. I took the long route home, driving through three different neighborhoods, out to the river and back before I satisfied myself that I wasn't being followed.

When I got home, Detective Nash was waiting for me on my doorstep. Oy.

CHAPTER 8

I parked the car, grabbed Lucy, and walked toward him as nonchalantly as I possibly could.

"Is this a social call?" I asked.

He didn't smile. His expression didn't change.

"Put your dog inside and shut the door."

I did, and let me tell you, Lucy wasn't happy about it. She barked and whimpered up a storm. Apparently she was not a fan of the great Jensen Nash. I was starting to wonder who was. Apart from his amazing looks, he didn't seem to have a lot of other appealing qualities.

"Turn around and put your hands behind your back," Nash said.

Whoa. "Wait a minute," I said.

Nash fingered his handcuffs. "You have the right to remain silent."

"About what?" I demanded.

"Anything you say can and will be used against you in a court of law."

I didn't turn around. "I'm familiar with my rights," I said. "I waive them because I haven't done anything wrong."

Nash sighed. "You can drop the act. I know you just broke into Schaeffer's house."

D'oh! *Busted!* But how? And if he was certain of that fact, why was he here now instead of there, then? I was absolutely positive I had replaced everything exactly the way I found it. He couldn't possibly be certain it was me, or even that anyone had been there at all. I thought fast, trying to figure out how to react, what to say.

I settled on busting out with a hearty, faked belly laugh. Miles and I were both practiced up on our fake laughs, seeing as how sometimes we needed Dick to believe that he truly was the funniest attorney on the planet. This, of course, happened only when we really wanted or needed something from him. The rest of the time, we just tried to avoid him as much as we could.

"Where on earth would you get an idea like that?" I said. "Listen, I know it's been a long day for both of us, and we've both been drinking. . ."

"It's no good, Chloe. I *know* you were there."

I didn't flinch. "You are mistaken," I said through my teeth.

Nash leaned forward, his gaze piercing my own. I refused to look away, maintaining eye contact.

His lips came within inches of my face. I felt a certain electricity zoom up my spine against my will. It ought to be criminal for any one man to possess the amount of sex appeal Nash had. I was temporarily mesmerized.

"I was not mistaken," Nash insisted. His fingers encircled my left wrist slowly. His hands were hot but not sweaty, his grasp gentle but firm. "The neighbors called because they saw a car. When I got there, the car was gone, but I went inside, and I could smell your perfume," he said.

His warm breath, smelling of spearmint, caressed my face in a way that felt disturbingly intimate.

"Detective Nash." I gingerly pulled my wrist away from his grasp. "Are you trying to tell me you are going to arrest me because you walked into Schaeffer's house and smelled my scent? You know I spent a fair amount of time there, right?"

Nash's fingers found my other wrist. "Ms. Taylor, are you trying to tell me you think I don't know the difference between the smell of fresh perfume and the faint scent that's left behind hours after a woman has been gone?"

"I—"

"If so, you have greatly underestimated both my intelligence and my personal charm."

I slowly pulled my other wrist out of his grasp.

"It's a commercial perfume. Anybody could have walked in wearing it."

"Not just anyone in this town wears $500 Michael Kors perfume." Nash rested his hand on my shoulder and gently tried to turn me around.

I pulled away, the spell broken. I was angry now—for many reasons, not the least of which was discovering that Nash was women-wise enough to know that I had paid $500 for my perfume back in the days when I actually had money. Men weren't supposed to know those kinds of things. And if they did, they were *definitely* not to be trusted.

"*Do. Not. Touch. Me.*" I flung his arm away from me. "How stupid do you think I am? You haven't got a warrant."

"But I have probable cause."

"You saw nothing. We are not at the scene. The opportunity for arrest without a warrant has passed."

"I'll have a warrant in five minutes."

"That's five more minutes you have to wait before cuffing me. And if you so much as *try* it before then, I'll have myself out of your custody on procedural grounds so fast it'll make your head spin."

Nash lifted his hands and spread them, palms out. The traditional "hands-up, don't shoot" pose.

Inside, Lucy sensed I was in trouble and started up a steady stream of growling.

"You're freaking my dog out," I said, in an attempt to change the subject.

"I hear," he said.

"Well, stop it."

"What do you want me to do?"

"I want you to get lost."

Naturally, he didn't move. His harsh façade finally cracked into the beginnings of a grin, but just barely. Time to try another tactic. The roots of an idea were beginning to creep into my consciousness. Maybe if I worked things exactly right, I could come out of this not only unscathed, but actually ahead. I drew a deep breath.

"Listen to me, and listen good," I said. "A man is dead. You're looking for evidence to put someone away, and besides the deceased and the killers, I'm the only person who knows where that evidence is."

The momentary softness I had seen in Nash's features instantly disappeared. "I'm listening."

"I'm not admitting anything, but hypothetically, what if I told you that I know exactly where Schaeffer's file boxes are, and that ten of them are missing?"

"Hypothetically?" he asked.

I nodded. "Hypothetically."

"Well then, hypothetically, I'd wait for my warrant to come in, and then I'd arrest you and take you back to the station and interrogate you until you told me what I wanted to know."

"And hypothetically," I said, "what if I told you you don't have time to do that?"

"And why wouldn't I have time?"

"Because the files will be gone before the night is out if you don't go to Schaeffer's house and get them right now."

I wasn't sure I believed this myself, but it seemed like my best shot at both getting out of this sticky situation and getting an armed escort back to Schaeffer's place.

"What makes you think that?"

The building blocks of the case for going back in immediately assembled themselves in my mind even as I spoke. While I had previously written Dr. Schaeffer's paranoid tendencies off as the actions of an academic eccentric, perhaps there really was a piece of sensitive information in the files I didn't know about that someone else was after. That theory made sense under the circumstances. After all, PetroPlex fought the kind of toxicity and safety negligence claims I brought against them every day, and no one had turned up dead before. And since there were file boxes left, there was no guarantee that whoever was in Schaeffer's house before wouldn't be back—and the sooner the better.

"Those boxes contain crucial evidence against PetroPlex. And I know for a fact that all forty of them were at Schaeffer's house for his last-minute review the night he was murdered. I also know for a fact that he kept the boxes hidden in a secret place, because he was almost clinically paranoid."

"Okay," Nash said. "And how would you know there are now ten of those boxes missing?"

"I don't," I lied. "I only hypothetically know, remember?"

Nash shrugged. "Okay, whatever."

"If there are ten boxes missing from the secret place, that means someone else knows the secret. They'll be back for the rest of the boxes as soon as they can. I'm guessing you ran them off responding to the murder scene—or was it a torture scene? And you kept them away with crime scene personnel crawling all over the place. But now that your people are gone and it's dark, they'll be back fast—before your people find the boxes first."

"How do you know my people are gone?"

"It's dark."

"Crime scene techs work in the dark."

"I have a feeling," I said.

"Uh huh." Nash shifted his weight and ran his fingers through his hair. "Where is the secret place? Or wait. Let me guess. You can't tell me. You have to show me."

"Yep." I nodded as innocently as possible.

"You're just prolonging the inevitable," he said. "Don't think this is going to get you out of an arrest. I'm going to get my warrant any minute."

I was seriously on the verge of losing my temper. "Fine. Go ahead. Arrest me. You'll just be wasting time on me you could be devoting to Schaeffer's case. You know I'll have myself lawyered out of your custody in no time."

"We'll see about that."

"So are we going, or what?"

Nash wanted to say no. I could see that even through his all but expressionless face. But he wouldn't.

He stopped short of saying yes, instead turning towards his car and motioning for me to follow. I did.

He opened the back door for me.

"I don't think so," I said, sliding into the front.

He sighed, but thankfully, that was the extent of his protest.

CHAPTER 9

When Anna Delmont got home with the pizza, the poker game was well underway. She now faced a dilemma. What should she serve it on? On the one hand, it was just an informal poker game. On the other hand, the police chief, the mayor, and a couple of bigwigs from PetroPlex (who she knew only by reputation) were all sitting in there. If she walked in with paper plates, would they think she was uncouth? Her silver-rimmed china was certainly overkill, but maybe her Pottery Barn dishware would be okay. She settled on the Pottery Barn dishes, stacked some up in a neat pile on a serving tray, placed the pizzas beside them, and carried the whole thing in.

"'Bout time," Joe Bob said.

Foul, acrid cigar smoke filled her living room. The biggest cigar was perched between Joe Bob's own teeth. Anna could hardly believe her eyes. While Joe Bob often smoked in the house, he usually confined the activity to his study. The two of them had had this standing compromise forever. He had never, ever contaminated her living room before, and how here he was, smoking it up, and using her heirloom cut crystal bowl as an ash tray. And he wasn't the only one smoking either. Dick Richardson, Chief Scott, and the PetroPlex executives were smoking too.

"For crying out loud!" Anna said in exasperation. "I am *never* going to get this smell out of the drapes!"

Delmont shrugged. "You're the one who's been pestering me to host the game here. We play poker, we smoke cigars, and we drink whiskey. Three of life's simple pleasures. That's the way it is."

"Except for me," Judge Hooper said. "I don't smoke."

"Until tonight," Dick said.

Anna noticed that Dick had been fiddling with something in his pocket. Something he clearly didn't want anyone else to see. But she was too distressed about the cigar smoke to dwell on it too much.

"Come on, Judge," Dick said. "Everybody needs a vice. Lemme show you how it's done."

Dick crammed a cigar into Judge Hooper's mouth, flicked a flame into life, and lit the end.

"Okay, now suck," Dick said.

Judge Hooper did, and promptly began hacking up a storm.

"Don't tell him to suck," Joe Bob said. "He ain't some fairy like your fancypants paralegal. It's more like a manly puff."

Judge Hooper rested the cigar in the bowl and took a swig of whiskey to calm his cough. "Anna dear," he said. "Have you met Gerald Fitz and Frederick Lewis?" He gestured to the two bigwigs from PetroPlex.

"Not officially," Anna said. "I heard of you before though, of course."

The two men politely stood and shook Anna's hand. Lewis was a puny-looking guy with dark hair, which he wore in a deeply-parted comb-over that did little to disguise an advanced state of baldness. Fitz was a middle-aged guy with a sour face. He looked like a real curmudgeon.

"Pleased to meet you," Lewis said stiffly, in a manner that suggested he clearly wasn't.

"Likewise," Fitz said. His voice sounded like he'd eaten sandpaper for lunch, breakfast, and dinner every day of his entire life.

"And I don't believe I got the chance to say hello when I walked in, either." Mayor Fillion, a tall, lean man with a kind smile and wavy gray hair, stood and shook her hand. "You're looking mighty pretty this evening, Anna. Are you doing something different with your hair?"

Even though Anna knew he was almost literally blowing smoke up her skirt, she flushed with pleasure nevertheless. "I been to one of those Aveda salons in Houston recently," she said. "Joe Bob sent me on an overnight beauty spa trip just last week."

"I'll bet he does that all the time," Dick said, giving Joe Bob a knowing look. "That must be how you stay looking so good."

Anna barely registered the kick Joe Bob delivered to Dick under the table. "He does," she said. "He is so good to me."

Joe Bob buried his face in his whiskey glass and took a deep swig. He banged the empty glass back down on the table and glared at Anna. "You're holding up the game," he said.

Anna walked over to the bar to grab the whiskey decanter so she could refill Joe Bob's glass.

Mayor Fillion flipped over a card from the deck and added it to the four that were already face up on the table. Anna knew they were playing Texas Hold 'em, and she had a pretty good understanding of how it all worked, but she didn't fully understand the intricacies of the game. The cards on the table were the ace of spades, the ace of diamonds, the jack of clubs, the ten of hearts, and the two of clubs.

Fitz grunted and pushed his sizable stack of chips towards the center of the table. The entire stack. "All in."

Several of the other men swore.

"Fold," Lewis and Chief Scott said simultaneously.

"Me too." The mayor flopped his two cards on the table face down and swept them aside.

"I'm out," Hooper said, attempting to take another drag on the cigar, only to wind up coughing violently.

Joe Bob stared at Fitz intently before also folding.

That left only Dick.

Anna could feel the tension in the room. She didn't know how much money each chip represented, but judging from the expressions on each man's face, it must have been a lot.

Dick leaned forward and stared Fitz down. "You're bluffing."

"If that's what you think, call the bluff," Fitz said. His face was a stone.

Dick hesitated.

"Come on," Fitz said. "What're you afraid of? If you win the hand, you can buy yourself another new car."

Anna's eyes widened. She had been right. There was *a lot* of money on the table. She knew how Dick loved new cars, and she secretly rooted for him to win the hand. After all, he had defended her slot machine centerpiece.

"If I don't, I'm really gonna pressure you to make it up to me with a good settlement on the Gracie Miller case," Dick said.

Fitz laughed. "Why would I do that? Your expert witness is dead, and that rookie lawyer you've got handling things is in over her head."

"Hey, she got a continuance out of your buddy Delmont over there today." Dick jerked his finger toward Joe Bob. "I think she's doin' okay."

Fitz turned to Joe Bob and regarded him evenly. "Word on the grapevine is her argument was unusually compelling."

Joe Bob cleared his throat uncomfortably. "Hey, I can't get your back *every* time," he told Fitz. "That wouldn't be fair to Dick, ya know."

Fitz shrugged. "Don't worry about that. Dick has no problem taking care of himself. Isn't that right, Dick?"

Dick eyed his own stack of chips, which was roughly the same size as Fitz's. "Yeah, I do a pretty good job of looking out for the ol' Number One, if I don't say so myself."

Mayor Fillion laughed and slapped him on the back. "Do you ever. If I didn't know any better, I'd say it was you running this town instead of me."

"Don't be ridiculous," Dick said. "Everybody knows it's PetroPlex running the town, ain't that right?" He eyed both Lewis and Fitz.

Lewis rolled his eyes and took a drink.

Fitz just ignored him. "So come on, already," he said. "What'll it be? In or out?"

Anna held her breath. Was Dick about to win enough money to buy a new car, or not? More importantly, how much did Joe Bob stand to lose or win playing for these kinds of stakes? She eyed his stack of chips in a way she hoped wasn't too obvious. It was sizable. Enough to remodel the kitchen, for example, which was a project she'd been wanting to talk to him about. She was glad he hadn't gone all in with Dick and Fitz.

Let's make a deal," Dick said.

"You and your deals," Joe Bob grumbled.

"There are no deals in poker," Fitz said. "Only the game."

"Nah, there's always a deal to be made," Dick said. "In life, in work, in poker—don't matter when."

"Whatever deals we've made in the past do not apply right now," Fitz said.

Anna stood watching the game, transfixed. She wondered what kind of deals Dick had made with Fitz in the past. He had such an imposing presence for such a little man. It wouldn't surprise her to hear that he could not only hold his own against the PetroPlex machine, but also use it to his advantage. He just seemed like that kind of guy.

"Nah, come on," Dick said. "I'm just talking about sweetening the pot a little. I call, and if I win, you owe me a favor one of these days. You win, and I'll not only turn over my entire stack of chips, but I'll double it. That'd be eighty grand in one hand for ya."

Anna gasped.

"That's mighty brave of you," Fitz said, "considering I'm sitting on pocket aces and there are another two in the river."

Dick remained unperturbed. "You ain't got pocket aces."

"You'll never know if you don't call right now."

"I can spot a bluff a mile away," Dick said. "You got 'bluff' written all over you."

"Go ahead. Call, then," Fitz said. He stared at Dick, unblinking.

Anna felt breathless. She didn't know how in the world Dick could possibly tell whether Fitz was bluffing or not. He didn't look nervous at all, which was amazing, considering Anna herself was practically biting her fingernails, and it wasn't even her money on the table!

A cell phone rang and shattered the tension in the air.

"Whose phone is that?" Fitz asked angrily.

Nobody fessed up immediately. After four or five rings, Judge Hooper said "Oh!" and looked embarrassed. He rearranged himself on his chair and fished a cell phone out of his pocket. He moved slowly, seeing as how he was old and slightly arthritic. "I forgot," he said. "My clerk got me one of these newfangled things. I ain't quite sure how to use it yet."

Joe Bob took the phone from him and pointed to a little envelope icon on the screen. "See that? It means you got a voice mail. Press this button to listen to what it says."

They all paused while Judge Hooper checked his voicemail. "Hmmm," he said. "My clerk says Detective Nash wants a warrant to arrest Chloe Taylor."

"*What?*" Dick thundered. "That's ridiculous! What for?"

"He says she broke into somebody's house. Somebody Schaeffer."

"Chloe would never do that," Dick said. "And even if she did, Schaeffer is our dead expert witness. She's been working with him around the clock. She practically lives there—probably has a key."

"I call B.S. on that," Joe Bob said. He had a look of manic excitement on his face. "Key or not, it's a crime scene, and if she's there, it's a break-in. Issue the warrant."

"Gimme a break," Dick said. "We all know Jensen Nash is an uptight, arrogant Yankee who would arrest an elderly widow for crossing the street the wrong way. You gotta take him off his high horse." Dick turned to Judge Hooper. "You remember Chloe? You met her at a City Council fundraiser a couple of weeks ago. Pretty little thing with long red hair, huge boobs, and a cute behind. She'd never do anything you'd disapprove of."

Judge Hooper nodded thoughtfully. "I don't see her as the breaking and entering type. Just to be safe, maybe I better talk to Detective Nash. And Chloe, too, if I can get her."

"Not before this hand is done," Fitz said. He looked at Dick. "So what'll it be?"

"Have we got our side deal?"

Fitz hesitated. "What kind of favor are you looking for?"

"Whatever I want," Dick said. "Whenever I call it in."

Fitz shrugged. "Okay fine. You're on."

Dick shoved his pile of chips into the center of the table right up next to Fitz's pile.

This was it. Anna clenched her fists in anticipation.

Fitz turned over a king and queen of diamonds triumphantly.

"Straight," he said. "I told you I wasn't bluffing."

Anna eyed Dick concernedly. He appeared worried. Was it an act?

"Crap," he said. "I coulda sworn you were putting me on. All I got is two pair." He turned over his cards to reveal that *he* had been sitting on pocket aces. "Two pair of *aces*, that is, otherwise known as four of a kind. Woooo ha! How you like *them* apples?"

Even Anna knew Dick's four aces beat Fitz's straight.

The men all pounded the table and leaned back, renewing the puffs on their cigars and laughing. Mayor Fillion slapped Dick on the back. "You owe him one now," he said to Fitz.

Fitz just sat there with the usual sour expression on his face.

"Now about returning that phone call," Dick said to Judge Hooper. "You gotta make this right."

Judge Hooper nodded and fumbled with the phone. Dick showed him how to dial out.

Anna refilled everyone's drinks and settled down on the sofa. Poker games sure were fun.

CHAPTER 10

Nash and I arrived at Schaeffer's, along with backup, in ten minutes.

It wasn't long before I realized I had talked myself into a situation that still wasn't going to help me very much. As soon as I showed Nash the file stash, he was just going to have his guys cart everything back to the evidence locker. What to do? What to do?

Once the house was clear, Nash ushered me inside.

"Where to?" he asked.

"Well," I said, "I was thinking. You and your guys are not trained to read the kind of research Schaeffer has been compiling. What are you going to do if you *can* get your hands on these documents? You won't know how to handle them."

"I'm sure we'll figure it out."

"Even if you do, we're talking about tens of thousands of sheets of paper. Time is of the essence. You'll need help sifting through the stacks."

"I think we can manage."

"What if you can't? What if there's a single sheet of paper in there with a smoking gun and you guys miss it? It's entirely possible. You don't know the context of the case like I do," I said. I hoped I wasn't sounding as desperate as I felt. "The key piece of information that provides motive and points straight to the murderer could be right under your nose, and you wouldn't know it because you don't have a good grasp of the bigger picture."

"Quit stalling and show me where the files are." Nash encircled my upper arm with his hand, preparing to forcibly usher me around the house if he had to.

I shook him off. "I will. But I'm telling you, just like you need my help to find the files, you need my help to go through them. I'm offering my services free of charge. We'll just take the boxes back to my house and I can—"

"We'll do no such thing." Nash's grip tightened on my arm. "Even if I decide to accept your help, the boxes are going back to the station."

"Okay, okay. Ease up on the grip, already." He did, but only slightly. I took a few steps toward Schaeffer's office. "So you'll consider my offer?"

"Don't push your luck."

Deciding to give up for now, I led Nash into Schaeffer's office, walked to the bookshelf, and pressed firmly in on the Arthur Conan Doyle book. Just like before, there was a soft click and a gap appeared between the bookshelf and the wall. I slid the shelf open wider to reveal the file boxes inside.

Nash's cell phone rang. "About time," he muttered. "That'll be my warrant."

Nash motioned for his guys to load up the boxes and then answered the phone.

"Nash," he said. "What? Yes, I can prove it." A pause. "Based on my own testimony, that's what." Another pause. "Trust me, I know." A look of incredulity spread over Nash's face. "Well, she's right here if you want to do it now."

Nash shifted positions uncomfortably, then handed the phone to me. "Judge Hooper wants to talk to you."

Hmm. Now this was an interesting development. I knew Judge Hooper in passing and had talked to him at various social functions before, but we were hardly on a first name basis.

I took the phone. "Hello?"

"Miss Taylor?" Judge Hooper's high-pitched, aged voice crackled through the poor cell phone connection.

"Yes, Judge Hooper?"

"Did you break into that nice Dr. Schaeffer's house tonight?"

"Well. . ." I said, not wanting to lie to a judge, even though I wasn't on the stand and technically wouldn't be committing perjury.

"Heh. Of course you didn't. I didn't figure a pretty little thing like you would. The very idea."

"You're very kind," I said.

"Nonsense." Judge Hooper lapsed into a coughing fit. "Gol' darned cigar," he said. "I'm too old for this. Hold on while I take a swig."

"Chloe?" Another voice shot across the airwaves and into my ear—a voice I was hoping not to hear until at least tomorrow.

"Dick?" I asked.

"Come tomorrow morning, you got a lot of explaining to do."

"According to Judge Hooper, I don't," I said.

"Good thing the Hold 'em game was tonight," he said, "or you'd be up a creek. Also a good thing Judge Hooper appreciates your perky little bee-hind, 'cause anybody else'd be in custody right about now."

"I owe you one?" I asked, hardly believing the good 'ol boys network in this town was working in my favor, for once. If only I could figure out how to exploit it all the time!

"Darn right, you do," Dick said.

"Hey listen," I said. "I hate to push my luck, but here's the deal." I told Dick about the files, carefully omitting the part where I broke in. "They're about to be impounded as evidence, which means we're going to have an awfully hard time reviewing them and making them available to a new expert in time for the next summary judgment hearing."

"Don't worry about it," Dick said. "Tell Nash to expect a call from the mayor. Where do you want the files?"

"My house?" I asked. "I don't think there's enough room in the office."

"Sure. Fine."

I could hardly believe my luck. It was all I could do to keep from dancing around the room in glee. "Who's winning?" I asked, remembering the game.

"I am, of course."

Of course.

"I want you on those files tonight," Dick said. "Call Miles. Pull an all-nighter."

"Okay," I said.

"And holler at me tomorrow morning."

"You got it."

Dick hung up. I handed the phone back to Nash sheepishly. "You're not getting a warrant tonight. I'm sorry to ruin your fun," I said.

Nash actually almost scowled. "No you're not."

His phone rang again.

"That'll be the mayor," I said.

"The *mayor?* Who *are* you people?" Nash picked up the phone. "Hello sir," he said. There was a pause. "But sir. . ." Another pause. "Yes sir."

Nash's half-scowl turned into a full-on glare as he hung up the phone. I didn't like the look on his face, but at least, for once, I knew what he was thinking.

CHAPTER 11

Joe Bob Delmont sat alone in his study, clipping his toe nails, drinking whiskey, and puffing on one last cigar before bed. He could hear Anna clunking around in the living room as she cleaned up the mess and put things away for the night. What a fiasco. All that paraphernalia for one lousy poker game. How embarrassing. He felt like she'd emasculated him with all the girly décor.

And on top of that, it had sure been hard to get any work done with Anna nosing around. They'd had to be extra careful letting the money exchange hands. The city was low on funds, so Mayor Fillion had levied a minimal pollution fine against PetroPlex. This always meant Fitz would pay the fine, and then during poker games he'd "lose" hands to the Mayor and to Delmont. In exchange, Delmont and the Mayor would look the other way when it came to actually enforcing the regulatory codes.

And when election time came around, the two of them always had PetroPlex in their campaign funding corner.

Only tonight, Delmont hadn't expected Dick's big win. There was something funny about that guy. Delmont had only invited him to the poker games on the theory that it was best to keep your friends close and your enemies closer. What baffled him was that the bigwigs at PetroPlex didn't seem to regard him as the enemy at all.

Fitz was forever cutting settlement deals with Dick. Dick could make PetroPlex bleed money, and it was like Fitz didn't even care. Delmont figured when you ran a company that made millions of dollars an hour, dropping settlement checks of several hundred thousand here and there wouldn't really make a dent in the budget. And maybe it was better that way. The fact that Dick was actually settling cases allowed Delmont to stay under the radar in his dealings with PetroPlex. The more Dick settled, the less Delmont had to worry about handing down obviously biased rulings. It just looked better all around.

The real problem was Chloe Taylor. She could never seem to come to settlement terms with Fitz. They were all going to have to figure out what to do about that. Delmont never would have thought she had blackmail in her, but sure enough. And now here she was breaking into people's homes. If she couldn't be handled, she'd have to be eliminated. She was already way too close to finding out what Schaeffer knew, and if that happened, they were all sunk.

They'd all been forced to end the poker game after Dick took all of Fitz's money. If that alone hadn't killed the night, Judge Hooper's phone call to Nash and Chloe sure had.

It was sheer rotten luck that Chloe had been able to recover the bulk of Schaeffer's files before he'd been able to get to them first. Schaeffer had required a lot of unofficial persuasion before he had given up the location of that secret room, and even then, it was so full they couldn't cart all the stuff out before Nash and the crime scene techs had arrived on the scene. Nash was a problem—one they'd really have to consider how to address as they moved forward.

The only bright spot in the situation was that Dick and Mayor Fillion's maneuvering meant the files would be a lot easier to deal with at Chloe's house than they would be in an evidence locker. Now there were many more options, but time was of the essence. The files had to be recovered or destroyed before Chloe and Nash learned anything damaging.

Even though Delmont had been expecting the phone call, the actual ring startled him so that he jumped, spilling his drink and cutting his toe with the clippers. He just felt on edge. It had been that kind of night.

He pitched the clippers across the room and jerked the phone to his ear.

"What?"

"You thinking what I'm thinking?"

"If you're thinking about Chloe and Nash reading all those files, yeah, I'm thinking what you're thinking."

"This information leak is getting a little out of control. We've got to nip it in the bud. Can you handle Taylor?"

"I'm sick of handling things for you people," Delmont said. "Why can't you put your guys on it?"

"They're pursuing other avenues right now."

"What other avenues?"

"We have an ex-employee who could also be a problem. We believe he was working with Schaeffer. He's got a computer virus he's threatening to release that would wreak havoc on our system."

"*What*? How come this is the first I've heard of this?"

"Do I really have to give you the speech about a "need to know" basis and all that?"

Delmont swore. "Look, I told you, I don't want any more surprises."

"Don't worry about it. If you can't get on it tonight, I'll find someone else. But I'm just gonna warn you, I'm gonna tell them to do whatever they need to do to stop the leak on your side and end this thing right now. *Whatever* they need to do. Do I make myself clear?"

Delmont didn't like the sound of that, but he didn't know what else he could do at the moment. He couldn't leave the house himself under Anna's watchful eye, and Chief Scott was so drunk he'd had to walk home. "Fine," Delmont said. "You're clear."

Delmont hung up the phone, wondering if he should be worried. These folks were capable of anything and getting a little too cocky. There were sure to be problems if they weren't careful.

CHAPTER 12

Nash decided he would escort both me and the files back to my house. He also decided he would pull an all-nighter right along with me and Miles as we went through the files.

"That's unnecessary," I said.

"I insist," Nash insisted.

"I don't want you in my house."

"You don't have a choice."

I groaned. "Fine."

Can't win 'em all, and even if I could, I figured it might eventually work in my favor to go ahead and let Nash feel like he'd muscled his way in on something.

Miles was already waiting for us by the time we got back to my place. I opened the door, and Nash's guys hauled everything in and left.

Lucy was happy to see Miles. He scooped her up and she licked his face like it was made of roast chicken. But she shied away from Nash. I think she sensed his tension. She could always tell when someone was in a bad mood.

Nash whistled softly when he saw my furniture. It was all designer, all oversized, and all very expensive. It clearly didn't belong in my shabby little rent house.

The house felt even smaller with three people and thirty boxes of documents crammed into the living room. Miles and Nash shoved the sofa and arm chairs up against the wall to make a little bit of room and scooted the dining room table into the middle of the space. It was long and heavy and barely fit in the house. I'd had to take it apart to get it through the door when I moved in.

I also hauled a couple of card tables out of the closet and set them up adjacent to the larger table. Then we supplemented them with my coffee table and a couple of glass end tables and settled down to work.

"I was thinking about the benzene statistics you were telling me about earlier," Nash said. "What kind of exposures are we dealing with here in the city of Kettle?"

I choked back a smug smile. I had gotten to him earlier—at least a little. Good. "Take this one PetroPlex refinery." I nodded out the window to the specter of its glowing lights. "Every single day, this one refinery turns almost twelve-and-a-half million gallons of crude oil into six and-a-half million gallons of gasoline, two million gallons of diesel, and two million gallons of jet fuel. At the end of the day, this process will have also produced over 1500 pounds of toxic chemicals, many of which evaporate into the air or leak into groundwater or otherwise get dumped. And let me remind you, that's all just in *one day.*"

"Okay," Nash said. "But people live right here. *You* live right here. Why would the government allow that to happen if they themselves have said it's not safe?"

"I can answer that," Miles said. "Congress didn't pass *The Clean Air Act* until 1970. In order to get it to pass at all, they had to grandfather in exceptions for all the refineries that were already in existence—most of which already had residential neighborhoods built in their backyards."

"And so," I said, "once these tougher restrictions were passed, oil companies stopped building refineries. Guess how many new refineries have been built in America since 1976?" I asked.

Nash looked at me through wary eyes. "How many?"

"*None.*" I folded my arms across my chest. "Big oil just hunkered down and focused on getting all they could out of their older, dirtier facilities, adding on to them as needed."

"So what you're telling me," Nash said, "Is that we have a whole lot of pollution regulations on the books that *don't even apply?*"

"Some of them apply, but large portions don't," I said. "Plus, the Federal Clean Air act leaves a lot of discretion for states to pass their own clean air laws, and Texas doesn't accept the federal act as the final authority. Don't get me wrong. There are newer laws and other provisions that apply, but they haven't been enforced very well. Or if they are enforced, Big Oil could care less. For example, Texas oil and gas drilling penalties for leaks of toxins into the ground water tend to be less than $3500."

"And let me tell you how Big Oil could care less about *that*," Miles said. "PetroPlex alone is so rich it makes one and a half million dollars of pure profit *every single hour.* You think they care about a bunch of piddly little $3500 fines? I don't think so! It would cost them more to prevent the leaks than it would to just pay the fines!"

Nash was starting to get agitated, by which I mean "agitated for Nash." His expression remained the same, but he got up and strolled over to the window, gazing into the night at PetroPlex's seemingly innocuous twinkling lights. "That is outrageous," he said evenly.

"The government *knows* oil and oil refineries are toxic to human life. In fact, the EPA recently reported that if you live within a thirty-mile radius of an oil refinery, you are being exposed to benzene concentrations in excess of *The Clean Air Act's* acceptable risk threshold."

"So why don't we just move the neighborhoods away from the oil refineries?" Nash asked. "It can't be that hard."

"Wrong," I said. "A full one-third of the United States population lives within a thirty-mile radius of at least one oil refinery."

Nash turned around. "What? A *third?* Are you sure?"

"Yep," I said. "And of course we can't just move the oil refineries themselves, because they are private businesses. And they'll never choose to move themselves since any new refinery facilities would be subject to more rigorous health and safety laws. That would cost a lot of money. They are way too invested in the status quo. Since they're sheltered by *The Clean Air Act's* grandfather clause, they're getting away with it."

"Big oil *could* clean up their act by improving their technology," Miles said, "but again, they just don't have a lot of incentive to actually do it. Sure, they get sued and fined all the time, but they are so rich that the settlements and fines don't really make a dent. They barely feel the pain at all. Instead, it's easier and cheaper for them to spend money trying to convince the public that oil is perfectly natural and safe."

"Take the BP Gulf Oil Disaster," I said. "The worst environmental disaster in this country's history. The media coverage revealed some of the methods PetroPlex and Big Oil use try to pull a fast one on the American people. When BP hired thousands of fishermen to help clean up the spill, they issued plastic clothing to prevent the oil from getting on workers' skin. But on CNN, Dr. Sanjay Gupta speculated they didn't issue respiratory equipment because they didn't want to create the impression that the spill was somehow unsafe. Remember, it only takes a few gallons of crude to offgass enough benzene to poison an entire football stadium. Imagine what the health risks of floating around in millions of gallons of the stuff without respiratory equipment would be."

Nash was starting to look a little nauseated.

"Remember how everyone was getting sick?" I asked. "BP's president tried to blame it on food poisoning. But according to Dr. Gupta, who was there on the scene at the time, most of their symptoms were respiratory. Nice try, huh?"

"And," Miles added, "remember all the reports about how BP required all of the local fisherman they hired to clean the spill up to sign non-disclosure paperwork? Basically BP put a gag order on them that forced them to keep quiet about what they saw and experienced while cleaning up the oil. And of course they had to sign them or not work. They couldn't fish—the waters were closed. So it was either starve or work under BP's gag order."

"And then at the same time," Miles said, "we had Texas government leaders trying to convince us that because oil is a natural substance, it's not toxic. I'll give you three guesses where that little tidbit of conventional wisdom originated."

"*And*," Miles said, "Texas Congressman Joe Barton even apologized to BP just because the Obama administration had the nerve to ask them to clean up their own mess. What does that tell you about oil and politics in the great state of Texas? Who do you think is really running the show here?"

Nash groaned.

I could tell I had his attention, so I pressed on. "You know," I said, "Mercury is natural too, but we don't bathe in it. There's not a giant mercury industry fueling our country's economy, so there's not a big debate about whether or not it's safe. We just know it's not safe and we avoid it. We don't touch it or eat it. We worry about eating fish that have been exposed to it. And yet, we touch, drink, and breathe toxic byproducts from oil all the time. We *cook and store our food* in pans and Tupperware made from petroleum products, for crying out loud. We eat fish that have been swimming around in the stuff."

"All right, but how does benzene poison people, specifically?" Nash asked. "I mean, is it poisonous to inhale, or eat, or what?"

"It's toxic whether it's inhaled, ingested, or absorbed through the skin," I said. "And by the way, it is *easily* absorbed through the skin. So anyone who was out on the beaches during or after the Gulf Oil Disaster dragging their bare hands through the oil and breathing the vapors was exposed."

"Wait," Miles said. "I don't want to derail your benzene speech, but I think you left out an important point. Remember how BP's president initially tried to pass off the Gulf spill as a small one? Well, in the grand scheme of things, at the point in time he made that statement, he actually had a pretty good argument to back it up."

Nash spun around, pulling his attention away from the sight of the looming oil refinery and laser focusing on Miles. "After all this, *now* you're trying to tell me it wasn't actually that bad?"

"No, no," Miles said. "It was bad. Don't get me wrong. But you have to consider it in the context of how much polluting and toxic exposure goes on *every single day* that no one seems to care about. At the time that statement was made, everyone was estimating a potential spill of around 11 million gallons, which is the size of the *EXXON Valdez* disaster. That seems like a lot of oil, right?"

"It doesn't *seem* like it," Nash said. "It *is*. By anyone's standards."

"Well," I said. "Hold on to your hat, because tankers, drivers and boaters spill more oil in inland waters every year than the *Valdez* spilled in the ocean. According to the National Academy of Science, leaking oil from US cars, trucks, and two-stroke engines dumps almost 19 million gallons of oil in our lakes and rivers every single year. In *inland freshwater* alone, we spilled 120 million gallons of oil between 1985 and 2003. People fish in that. Swim in it. Drink it. It's no wonder cancer is on the rise."

Nash's gaze shifted to his glass of ice water, which he regarded suspiciously.

"It's filtered," I said.

Nash's expression relaxed a little bit.

"But your shower water is not," I said. "And we know there are plenty of groundwater contaminations in this area, which means you have no idea what you absorb through your skin every day."

Nash groaned. "This is all fascinating," he said sourly, "but what's it got to do with all this?" He gestured expansively at the mountains of documents piled up against my wall.

"This is all the data we have that proves toxicity," I said. "This is what Schaeffer was going to testify about—he was going to use all this data to try to prove that PetroPlex knowingly poisoned my client by failing to provide safety equipment and failing to limit toxic exposure. My client worked in the refinery's benzene unit for 30 years, and there were leaks all the time, according to this data. Probably most of it is stuff that is public record, or results of private air monitoring tests. Schaeffer was finishing up his report the night he was killed, so I *hope* to high Heaven the report is in here somewhere, because I haven't seen the final draft yet.

"But this sounds like all standard law suit stuff," Nash said. "PetroPlex has seen these kinds of claims before. What do you think is in here that's actually worth killing over?"

"I don't know. Maybe before the night is out, we'll find out." I smiled. "So. Who wants coffee?"

Nash sighed. "I *hate* all-nighters. Make mine a double."

***

Over coffee, we hatched a plan of attack for combing through the documents. Each of us would take a stack and work for an hour. We agreed to compare notes at the top of each hour.

At 3 a.m. we stopped for our fifth break.

"Anything yet?" I asked the two guys.

"I've got nothing," Nash said.

"I've seen it all before," Miles said, "which I know sounds melodramatic and jaded, but really, I've seen this all before."

"Maybe the reason only ten boxes were missing is because the killers got the ten boxes they wanted," Nash said, looking pointedly at me. "In which case, you really risked a lot to break into a crime scene for nothing."

"I only hypothetically broke in, remember?" I said, shifting uncomfortably in my chair.

This was news to Miles. "Wait, what? You broke in? You lifted all this stuff? Is that how we wound up with it?"

"*Hypothetically*," I emphasized.

"Look, Chloe," Miles said. "If you wanted to spend the night with two gorgeous guys, you wouldn't have to break the law to do it."

"Hardy har har," I said. "There's got to be something here. There's no way that whoever took the first ten boxes and killed Schaeffer would have had time to cherry pick before police arrived. If there's really nothing here, it's big time sorry luck."

"No sign of the final draft of Schaeffer's report?"

"No sign," I said. "Nash?"

"I'm not sure I'd recognize it if I saw it."

"Duh," Miles said. "It would have Schaeffer's name on it and be labeled 'Final Report.' Get with the program."

Nash remained unperturbed. "I'm just saying, a lot of this stuff is highly technical. I don't really understand it."

"And that's what PetroPlex is counting on," I said. "Public records aren't dangerous if they're so hyper-technical that the average Joe can't understand them. *Which* is why finding a good expert witness is critical. The witness is the translator. Frankly, I wouldn't trust myself to translate this data on the record without screwing something up and losing the case in the process."

Exhaustion was starting to catch up with me. I took another shot of coffee to ward it off and dove into the next box. The first file I pulled out contained not a stack of looseleaf papers, but a book. An appointment book. *Schaeffer's appointment book.*

"Hey, look at this," I said, opening it up to the current week. I saw a lot of time blocked out with my name on it. But I also saw several appointment blocks labeled "C.G."

Miles swiped the book away from me. "C.G? Who the Rita Hayworth is C. G?" he said.

"Beats me. C.G. could be anyone."

"How could he be meeting with some secret person right under our noses?"

"More importantly," I asked, "if it had anything to do with the case, why would he keep it secret from *us?*"

"Maybe it didn't have anything to do with the case. Maybe it's a relative or something," Nash said.

I shook my head. "He doesn't live here full time. He bought that house because he wanted to study the refinery. He's only in town for a few weeks at a time. And when he's here, all he does is work. It's not like he's super active in the Kettle social circles. It's got to be related to the case."

Out of the corner of my eye I saw five simultaneous bright flashes that started small, grew larger, and ended with the sound of breaking glass and an unnaturally loud *fwoooooooot!*

The Molotov cocktails smashed through my windows and into the dining room table and all the surrounding stacks of paper with no more warning than that.

Miles' hair gel was one of the first things to ignite. "My hair! They got my haaaaaaaaaair!"

I glanced frantically around for my dog. "Lucy! Save Lucy!"

All I could see were flames. Flames in my house. Flames in Schaeffer's files. Flames on my body. My shirt was burning.

Nash was on me in an instant, using the full length of his body to kill the fire. His muscles were hard. Chiseled. Not soft enough to fully press in and douse the flames for lack of oxygen supply.

He ripped my shirt completely off and gathered me into his arms urgently.

I thought of the original *Gone with the Wind* poster print that was hanging in my home office—Rhett clutching a half-clothed Scarlett in a protective but intimate embrace, framed in the backdrop of Atlanta burning.

My home. Burning.

I felt no pain. Only Nash's strength as he carried me out of the flames.

Delirious, I wondered in that moment if he would kiss me.

Unthinking, absent of any kind of rational thought, I lifted my chin and let my eyelids go slack, waiting, even hoping for, the sensation of his mouth on mine. In my diminished field of vision, I saw his lips. Strong. Hard. Steeled by heady determination and. . . something else? They moved. Sound came out.

"Miles! The book! Get the appointment book!"

Not what I had been expecting to hear.

And then the relative coolness of the night air enveloped me as Nash kicked out my front door and carried me onto the lawn, half naked. I could feel the breeze between my breasts. I could smell a mixture of smoke, early morning dew, and heavy refinery tar.

I was vaguely aware of Old Lady Ellason from next door standing in her lawn, clutching her curlers and screaming.

I heard the screech of tires speeding away in the distance.

And then, nothing.

CHAPTER 13

This time, when Delmont's phone rang, it woke up his wife. She rolled over and jabbed him in the ribs. He groaned. Seemed like all she ever did anymore was poke and prod and nag him. *Joe Bob, do this. Joe Bob, do that. Joe Bob, let me throw a poker party. Joe Bob, let me remodel the kitchen.* Nag, nag, nag. And as far as getting any action in the sack, forget it. Thank goodness he had his sweet little side number to rely on for that. At least until Chloe Taylor had ruined it for him.

His wife poked him again. "Pick up the phone already!"

Delmont groggily rolled over and reached for it.

He maneuvered himself out of bed and into the hallway before picking it up.

"You better have good news," Delmont said. "What happened?"

"We torched the girl's place. She and Nash and the town girly man had everything out on the dining room table when we got there."

"How much did they get through?"

"I don't know," said the voice on the other end of the line. "At any rate, it's gone now."

"Did you kill anyone?"

"I don't think so. An ambulance took the girl to the hospital, but she'll probably make it. Her clothes were on fire. You should have seen Nash rip her shirt off. It was almost like he was looking for an excuse to do it. Can't say I blame him, either. It'll be a real crime if we have to put that girl down."

"Yeah, well, if we have to, we have to," Delmont said. He wouldn't be sorry if she were gone, although he didn't want to be the one to off her.

"We're switching out counsel on the case. If it turns out that she knows anything she shouldn't, the new lawyer will find out and let us know."

"How can you be sure of that?" Delmont asked. "She's no idiot."

"The new counsel knows her. Well."

"How well?"

"Just trust me on this one."

The line went dead. Delmont was irritated, but he was also ready to get back to sleep. He shuffled to the bedroom and got into bed. Too bad his wife was still in it, snoring up a storm. Maybe it was about time to trade her in for a new model, he thought sleepily.

Surely there were some thugs at PetroPlex who could take care of that, too.

CHAPTER 14

I woke up in the hospital. Miles and Nash were both sitting by my bed. The first thing I saw was Lucy, unscathed and asleep in Miles's lap. I breathed a sigh of relief.

The second thing I saw was Miles's hair. There were only a few scorched patches left.

My eyes were barely open, but I started giggling. I felt a little delirious. Drugged. "I told you, Miles," I choked out.

Miles smacked Nash, who was dozing, on the arm. "She's awake," he said.

"I always told you," I said.

"Told me what?" Miles asked.

"That you use too much hair product. That stuff is all flammable, you know."

"Chloe!" Miles said. "You shut your mouth right now! You get hit by a homemade bomb, and the first thing you talk about afterwards is my hair? My *hair?* I will never forgive you for this."

"Your hair makes Ryan Seacrest's 'do' look like the Geico caveman's" I said.

That one made the very sleepy Jensen Nash actually crack a grin.

I weakly slapped Nash on the knee. "Doesn't it?" I said. "Doesn't it? Miles's hair is a friggin' sculpture. It ought to be on display at the Guggenheim."

"Chloe Taylor," Miles said again, momentarily choked up. "That's the nicest thing anyone's ever said to me! I might have to marry you for that one. Unfortunately, I'm now going to have to shave it off. Will you still find me attractive with a shaved head?"

"Of course," I said. "But now I know you're not safe. Your hair is apparently a Molotov Cocktail *magnet*. I really have to stay away from Molotov Cocktail *magnets*. What are you going to do about that?"

Miles shrugged. "Some risks are acceptable."

"And the smell," I said. "Miles, you reek. *Eau de burnt hair* is not your signature scent."

"Cripes, Chloe, ease up. I haven't had time to go home and take a shower, you know. And by the way, you don't look so good, yourself. Hospital gown peach is *so* not your color."

"You were lucky, though," Nash said softly. "Only a few minor burns on your torso. The doctors think you only passed out from the shock. "

Oh, nooooooooooo. That was so not like me. Fainting like a Victorian-era woman just because of a few flaming projectiles? With *no shirt* on? How would I ever live *that* down? Forever after, in court I would be the lawyer who passed out naked when the heat was on. I'd be a walking target. Defense attorneys would be placing bets about who could get me to faint first. Hearings would now be more of a nightmare than usual. So not good. I felt myself flush.

"It could have been a lot worse if I hadn't been able to get your shirt off so quickly," Nash said.

"Oh yeah," I snapped. "That would have been a *whole* lot worse."

"Don't worry," Nash said. "You have nothing to be ashamed of.

Miles fanned himself. "Ooooh!" Is it heating up in here!"

Nash actually had the decency to look embarrassed. "That's not what I meant."

I was quickly regaining full consciousness. "Really?" I asked? "What exactly did you mean?"

Nash was saved from a forthcoming cross examination by the nurse, who had come in to change my bandages. The nurse sent the guys outside while she did her business. I peered at the changing process through one eye. It really didn't look so bad. I had sustained worse from cooking. But then, maybe that was more of a reflection on my cooking skills than on the actual state of the burns.

The nurse finished up, and Nash and Miles resumed their places at my bedside.

"I'm tired," I said. "What time is it?"

"Five-thirty a.m.," Miles answered.

"How's my house?" I asked.

Nash carefully avoided my gaze. "The initial reports from the fire department don't sound good."

"Did they get all the files?"

"I think they got the whole house," Nash said.

I sighed. "Well, at least I had rental insurance." Assuming the policy was current and paid up. Crap. I really needed to make some money soon. Now, on top of everything else, I had *hospital* bills to pay. And of course Dick didn't provide health insurance.

Despite the vast amount of designer footwear and other expensive items I had amassed during my wealthier days, I wasn't too worried about losing my actual stuff. I wasn't materialistic. I had just bought all that stuff to keep up appearances. Lawyers tend to judge the quality of other lawyers by what they wear, drive, and possess in general. Louboutins were more of an intimidation tactic for me than must-have fashion.

"Don't worry," Miles said. "You can stay with me. You can use my shampoo and conditioner. I won't need it now."

"What about clothes?" I asked. "Can I borrow your clothes? I like that one shirt that's kind of sheer. You can't get away with wearing that around here, anyway."

"Whatever you need," Miles said altruistically, fingers clasped in front of his chest in a choirboy pose.

Nash rolled his eyes. "I'll *also* see what I can rustle up from the county's local shelter," he said.

Miles looked offended. "Hey, don't hate on the sheer shirt."

"I wasn't hating," Nash said. "I was just thinking about minor inconveniences like judges, who may appreciate sheer clothing but not condone it in the courtroom."

I sighed. "It's late," I said. "Don't worry about me. I'll be fine. Why don't you go home and come back in the morning? In the later morning, I mean. There's nothing else we can do right now anyway."

Miles and Nash both put up a weak protest, but I could tell they were tired and wanted to leave.

"Don't worry about me," I said. "Really. I think I'm going to be okay."

Miles stood up and kissed me on the forehead. "I'll come by and spring you out as soon as I can."

"Leave Lucy here," I said.

"I don't think we can do that. Hospital regulations. I had to practically bribe intake just to get her in this room." Miles scooped her up and held her over the bed. She wagged her tail and licked my face tentatively. I gave her a big kiss goodbye.

"Don't worry," Miles said. "I'll take good care of her."

"Let her sleep in your bed," I said.

"Okay," Miles said.

"If she sheds, maybe some hair will wind up on your head."

Miles scratched Lucy behind her ears. "I knew you were good for something," he said in a cooing "talking to dogs" voice. "I just didn't know for what until now."

My eyelids sank shut as they both shuffled out in exhaustion.

***

Miles arrived back at the hospital at ten a.m. with crisp, clean clothes, a bottle of vanilla-scented spritzer, and a freshly shaved head.

"Wow," I said. "Who are you?"

Miles groaned. "Shut it. I feel like a skinhead."

"And you look like one, too," I chirped. Despite the circumstances, I was in kind of a good mood. The lidocaine gel the doctor had prescribed for my burns kept them from hurting, and plus, we were definitely onto something. If PetroPlex was behind the violence (which I was 95% sure they were), and if I could find out whatever little piece of information they thought might be worth killing over, I could use it as leverage to get a quick, high settlement and a very large paycheck for myself just in the nick of time—maybe even before summary judgment. Assuming I could simultaneously keep myself out of harm's way, that is. Maybe if the info were *really* good, I could get a high enough settlement to get out of this town and start my own law firm. How great would that be?

"Get dressed," Miles said, tossing the clothes on the bed. Jeans, a tank, and the sheer shirt I had admired. Ugh. I was willing to bet the jeans didn't fit my behind. I could never find jeans to fit my curvy behind. If they did, they were always too loose at my waist, which was petite.

There was something in his face I didn't like.

"What's wrong?" I asked.

He hesitated. I immediately jumped to the worst possible conclusion.

"Lucy!" I gasped.

"No, no," he said.

"Then what?" I started to get up.

Miles put his hand on my shoulder and gently pushed me back down.

"Actually, you might want to stay sitting down for this."

What on earth? "Spill it," I said.

Miles took a deep breath and gazed up at the ceiling, then closed his eyes as though gathering the strength to spit out what he was about to say. "PetroPlex has replaced their lead counsel in this case," he finally said.

I felt relieved. "Is that all?" I said. "Holy cow, I thought you were going to tell me something terrible."

"With Dorian Saks," he finished.

"*What!*" I was instantly out of the bed. "As in Dorian Saks, my *ex fiancé?*"

Miles cowered in the corner. "I'm afraid so."

"As in, Dorian Saks, diamond ring big enough to have its own zip code, mansion in Highland Park, never having to eat Ramen noodles *ever again* Dorian Saks?"

"You eat *Ramen*?" Miles asked, horrified.

"Never mind," I said, trying to calm down.

"There's more. Dorian wants to meet with you this afternoon." Miles ducked for cover.

"*Whaaaaaaaaaaaaaaaaaaaaaaaaaaat!*" I clawed at my hair, my face. "He's already *in town*? PetroPlex did this on purpose!"

"I'm sure that's true."

"And he didn't care. Anything for a buck."

"Maybe he wanted to see you again."

"I don't care! I don't care! I don't want to see him! *Ever again!*"

Miles tentatively crept out of his corner and patted my back softly. "I'll go with you."

"And *what?*" I could feel my head floating through the ceiling. I could see my own body. This couldn't be. This could never happen. Part of the reason I was okay with living in Kettle,

Texas was because I knew it was a place in which Dorian Saks would never, *ever* set foot.

And yet, he was here. Here! How could this be? How could I *work* with him in the picture?

A worried nurse poked her head in the door.

"Don't worry," Miles assured her. "Trial lawyer antics."

She disappeared hurriedly, no doubt repulsed. Medical people hate trial lawyers. Something about medical malpractice and frivolous suits.

"You didn't tell him about the fire, did you? Say you didn't tell him about the fire."

"No, I didn't tell him."

"If he finds out about the fire, he'll know I'm destitute, and he'll use it as leverage against me."

"That's why I didn't tell him."

"What if he finds out anyway? I can't do this. I can't talk to him. Miles, we have to get rid of him somehow!"

"Chloe, calm down. I'll go with you."

"No flipping way. No! You don't know him. You've never seen how he works. You'll be in love with him in five seconds."

Miles stared at me, aghast. "I could never!"

"You won't be able to help it." I said. "I don't know if *I* can help falling in love with him all over again. It's good I packed up and moved here, really. What if I were still there? What if he had sucked me back in?"

"You're smarter than that. Tougher than that."

"Am I?"

Secretly, I knew I wasn't. I always tried to project a strong persona, but I was all soft romantic jelly inside. I cared about my career, but all I *really* wanted was for Prince Charming to come along, scoop me up, and take me away. Didn't every girl? Maybe we didn't all expect or even want happily every afters, but secretly. . . *secretly*. . . we tough girls wanted the prince. If only for a moment.

"I can't go. I have nothing to wear. I need a suit. A designer suit! Something intimidating—something I can't buy within a one-hundred-mile radius of here."

"You don't," Miles insisted. "You are not your clothes. You are *you*, which is way more than the sum of your parts."

I was hyperventilating. "I can't do it," I said. "Tell him I can't meet him today."

Miles shook me. "Chloe, we don't have time for games. Summary judgment hearing in a *week*, remember? I told him you'd meet him at Caliente at three."

I checked the clock on the wall. "That is *five hours* from now. How am I going to get to Houston and back in five hours?"

"You are *not* going to Houston."

"Galleria," I said. "I need Galleria. And the Aveda Spa. I'm not fit to be seen."

"Chloe!" Miles shook me again, this time harder. Harder, I thought, than an un-discharged hospital patient should be shaken. "We haven't got time. And if you've been eating Ramen, you haven't got the money. I know it has to have been awhile since your last paycheck."

"I'll figure it out."

"Really?" Miles said. "I think you lost your credit cards in the fire."

He had a point. And they were maxed out anyway. "Loan it to me! Dick pays *you* salary."

Miles sighed. "You know I'd do anything for you Chloe, but you have to be realistic." He grinned. "You know it's just not feasible to make an Escada selection in the timeframe we have. Who can do that?"

I wanted to cry. I knew he was right. I was going to have to settle for the local Supercuts, Cover Girl from Walmart, and whatever form of clothing they had in the Rosethorn Ritzy Rags boutique. And then I would somehow also have to find a big enough gap in the space-time continuum to prep for the part of the meeting that really counted in the grand scheme of things—the legal part.

Now that all my evidence was up in smoke, I would really have to scramble to put on a good face. I was terrified Dorian would be able to see right through me—to know that I had absolutely nothing. We had been together long enough that he knew all my tells.

There would be no marriage to Dorian Saks. I got that. But I refused to accept the possibility that I also had no case. I had a case. People were dead. I had a case. Right?

CHAPTER 15

"No, no, no! All you ever wear is brown!" Miles said, in the middle of the Walmart make-up aisle. "Try violet. It will make your eyes pop, and it'll look *fabulous* with your hair."

I let Miles talk me into violet eye shadow and pale nude lip gloss before we went clothes shopping.

At the Ritzy Rags boutique, all they had was fringe, fringe, and more fringe, heavily accented with rhinestones and silver studs. I eventually settled on a relatively tame black silk jacket with only a little fringe on the sleeves and hem. I also selected a purple cami and black slacks to match. I had to select something high-cut to hide one of the burns. Once dressed, despite my injuries and fatigue, I felt like something of a lawyer again, even though the clothes were definitely not Escada quality.

At three o'clock, I was not as ready as I could have been, but I was as ready as I could possibly be in that moment, given the timeframe for preparation. I had hoped to stop by the station and drop in on Nash before now, but I hadn't had the chance.

Thankfully, I also had not had the chance to go by the office, which meant I had not yet been forced to explain myself to Dick Richardson, so there was something of a silver lining in the situation after all. Was it small of me to notice that he hadn't bothered to drop by the hospital?

I parted ways with Miles and drove into the Caliente lot, parking behind a clump of prickly pear cacti and a barbed wire fence. All of the grass was dead because of the July heat. I was probably the only person between here and Houston wearing long sleeves. I concentrated on not sweating.

Maybe Dorian would buy me a margarita. That would be nice. On that note, I took a deep breath and walked inside.

The interior of Caliente was poorly lit, which, when you thought about it, made sense. If you were *going* to order chicken-fried jalapeno rattlesnake, did you really want to see what it looked like right before you shoveled it down your throat?

The contrast between the bright light of the outdoors and the air-conditioned shade inside had me squinting. If I had not been so acutely attuned to the potential of his presence, I might not have immediately seen Dorian sitting in the bar. He had chosen the corner of the restaurant, his back against the intersection of two walls, perfectly positioned to take in everything going on inside and everyone who came in from outdoors—before they had a chance to even notice he was there. Strategic as always. He hadn't changed.

It was the motion of him rising to his feet that first caught my eye.

I caught my breath. I felt nauseated. Exhilarated. Disgusted. Attracted to him against my will.

Dorian wore a black suit, black shirt, no tie. He was exquisitely tailored head to toe and didn't look like he'd been out in the South Texas dust and heat at all. He'd grown his hair out a bit. It was lush and curly, falling with a studied carelessness over his perfectly proportioned brow and dazzling blue eyes. He was clean shaven. And when he saw me and smiled, the glint off his teeth put the Orbitz gum commercial models to shame.

I swallowed hard.

He rushed towards me and enveloped me in an all-too-familiar embrace.

I caught myself sinking into it for just a split second before jerking backwards.

"Don't touch me," I said. I didn't think I could handle it.

"Ahh, Chloe." He smelled like coffee and spice and everything nice. "Have some compassion and be kind to the man whose heart you've already broken. He placed both palms on either side of my face and kissed my forehead. "I've missed you."

"Well, I haven't missed *you*," I lied. "So tell me. Why on earth did the partners at Smith Knight decide to send you all the way down here?"

"It took a lot of convincing on my part, but I finally managed to persuade them it was in their best interests for them to let me see you again."

"I'll bet," I said.

Without looking away from me, Dorian called the waiter over and asked for a table in the back. We sat down, and Dorian ordered. "Two margaritas, *por favor*." He flashed his uber-white smile at me one more time and took my hand in his. "Or have you gotten tired of margaritas since I've seen you last?"

"I've gotten tired of plenty of things since then, including you." I whipped my hand away and turned to the waiter, irritated.

Fifty percent of my irritation stemmed from the fact that I really wanted a margarita and wasn't *about* to let him order one for me. The other fifty percent was reserved solely for Dorian and Dorian alone.

"No margarita for me. Make it a martini. Extra dirty." I turned back to Dorian and glared at him. "Just like you and your filthy, dirty, stinking, low-down, conniving tricks. You've got a lot of nerve, showing up here like this, but if you think I'm going to let you throw me off my game, you've got another think coming."

The waiter raised his eyebrows and faded away without a word.

"I wouldn't expect anything less," Dorian said. "In fact, that's one of the reasons I came down here. No other girl in Dallas can compete with your game."

"A hundred bucks says that's not what you tell *them* when you're in bed together."

Dorian shifted in his seat. I could see the wheels turning in his head as he calculated his next move. Probably he didn't appear studied to anyone else who might have been watching him at the moment, but I knew him. Everything he said and did was calculated, down to the precise trim of his fingernails and the sheen on the Rolex watch he inevitably wore, not because he especially liked Rolexes, but because he knew they impressed juries.

"There is no one else," Dorian said. "There never was."

"Right," I said. "She came to my office, remember?"

"I told you," Dorian said. "She was my secretary. I fired her. She was mad and trying to get back at me. None of it was true."

I slammed my fist down on the table, stood, and leaned over it, getting right in Dorian's face. *"I am not stupid,"* I whispered, too angry to trust my normal speaking voice. "Don't you *dare* insult my intelligence." I sat back down, slowly. "We both know you are a lying, cheating, sorry excuse for a man and that you are here not because of me, or because of any kind of sense of human loss or personal regret, but because of the chance to get your name on the biggest named client of your career. Counsel of Record for PetroPlex, Incorporated. Mister big man. Time 100. Man of the Year. I will not—*not,* I tell you—allow you to get away with pretending you are here for any other reason."

I searched his face as he digested this little speech, realizing in the pit of my stomach that I was hoping for, praying for, the slightest indication that what I said was not the truth—that he had come back for me after all.

His face was marble. Michelangelo's David marble. He didn't move, didn't give an inch.

I felt my own upper lip twitch against my will. How could a girl feel such a mix of hurt, anger, betrayal, heat, and attraction all at the same time and never let on? The universe had no right to expect it of me. It was too much. I felt myself drawn to him again, only this time the attraction was just as strong as the repulsion that pushed me away. I felt stuck, suspended in a limbo that could not sustain itself if either of us moved a millimeter forward or back.

After a long moment, I saw the muscles in his neck tighten as he swallowed, considering what to say. He leaned forward, his eyes boring into me, as though no one but the two of us were sitting there. "I don't think you have ever really understood any of my intentions, or me, at all."

This time I felt the twitch in the corner of my eye. So help me, if a tear squeezed itself out of the duct and down my cheek right now, I would die of shame. "I think," I whispered, my voice shaking, "that's what you tell yourself in order to be able to sleep at night. You are a liar to your core. You have the unique ability to deceive even your own soul."

"Or maybe it's you who've been deceiving yourself," he said. "Did you ever think you might be wrong? Did you ever even once consider the fact that your ego got in the way of a future that could have been truly great?"

"My ego? *My* ego?" I was finding my voice again. "Our issues were never about *me*. They were about you. You and *your* ego. You and how one woman just wasn't enough for the legendary Dorian Saks."

"I think that's what *you* tell *yourself* in order to be able to sleep at night," he countered.

We were locked in a battle of wills. If he had just admitted it, just broken down and admitted that he'd had an affair, that he was wrong, that he had loved me and slipped in a moment of weakness, I might have given into him.

Under those circumstances, I might even have taken him back, if he'd asked. But he didn't. He steadfastly refused to admit that anything had happened, that he was to blame. He was a paragon of defense-attorney glory, a fortress for his clients and a fortress for himself—a characteristic that equally fascinated and repulsed me.

"Why are you here?" I asked. "Really. What do you want? If you ever gave two cents about me, you will not pretend you are here for some romantic reconciliation or an ex-lover's tryst."

I could see the muscles in his jaw clench as he considered how to answer.

"The truth," I pressed. "I do not think it is possible to make it more clear that I am not interested in, nor will I fall for any more posturing, any more seduction, anything that is any part of your act and the hollow façade that is you, at all, anymore. Ever. So what is it? What's the truth?"

Dorian drew a long breath. The waiter arrived with our drinks. Seeing the almost tangible tension between us, he set them on the table without a word. I downed half my martini in one swallow as I waited.

Dorian cleared his throat. "Well," he said. "Since you put it that way."

I sensed that I had somehow hurt him. Somehow wounded his pride by doubting his sincerity, by failing to welcome him back into my life with even a grudging appreciation for the love we had once shared.

I did doubt his sincerity after all, didn't I? There was *no* chance that he could possibly be for real. If he had been for real, he would have come after me long before now. Right. *Right?*

"I suppose I'm here," Dorian said slowly, "because in a week there will be a motion for summary judgment, which you will not win."

"We'll see about that," I said.

"I am not here alone," Dorian said. "I came down with six junior associates and an unlimited, blank-check bankroll, which your puny three-person firm cannot possibly hope to compete with."

"You've always underestimated me," I said.

"This is not about you, Chloe. This thing is so much bigger than you it's beyond your comprehension. Even if, by some miracle, you manage to win at summary judgment, my client has enough money and enough power to drag this thing out so long Armageddon will happen sooner than you'll get to trial. I represent a client who has all but bankrupted the FTC, who has forced the government to drop cases after 20 years of trying for sheer lack of resources and staying power. The *government*, Chloe. Do you think you're bigger, badder, and tougher than Uncle Sam? Your boss might pass for wealthy down here, but he cannot stand up to the sheer size of what I am threatening, and neither can you. You and your boss and your perky little paralegal are only three people. We are Big Oil, the very foundation of these United States."

I downed the rest of my martini and gathered my courage. "Nice try," I said. "You ought to know by now that your jury voice doesn't work on me."

The thing is, it did, kind of. If I had been wearing boots, I'd be shaking in them.

"I'm going to say this once," Dorian said. "And only once. The offer is off the table as of six p.m. tonight, so I suggest you run it by your client."

"Spit it out," I said.

"Three hundred thousand."

I laughed, almost genuinely. "You didn't have to come all the way down here to insult me like that. A man died. Two men, actually, a fact about which I think you are acutely aware, otherwise you wouldn't be here. The case is worth at least a million, and you know it."

"Do I?" he asked. "Because from where I sit, your expert is dead, your case files are destroyed, and you only have a week to prepare for a new hearing. In other words, you haven't got a prayer." He paused. "Unless you're aware of something I'm not?"

Little alarm bells went off in my head. Was it possible that Dorian was even more evil than I had previously imagined? Or was it that *he* was involved in something bigger than even *he* thought was possible?

I leaned forward and searched his eyes. All I saw was the same old Dorian, whoever that was. "You're asking me if I have a bargaining chip?"

"I'm asking you what your leverage for a counter offer might be. I'm asking you why in the world you wouldn't take three-hundred and run."

I had to be careful here. If I let on that perhaps I knew something he didn't—something big enough to warrant a larger counter-offer—and that information got back to the people who had killed Schaeffer, things could get ugly for me. On the other hand, if I let on like I had no case, Dorian was liable to take the entire offer off the table altogether. After all, there was nothing in writing yet.

"I'm not authorized to take offers or make counters without first speaking to my client," I said.

I could feel Dorian searching my eyes just as intensely as I had searched his a moment ago. I wondered what he saw. If he saw even a hint of my stress or fear, I would be toast.

"The question is, can you and your client afford to refuse?" He looked me up and down. "I can't help but notice that you've downgraded your wardrobe."

I felt myself wilting with embarrassment. I *knew* I should have begged, borrowed or stolen a better suit before meeting him in person. It wasn't that Dorian was into fashion. My clothes were just another way for him to judge the appropriate amount for his opening offer. I was sure that was one of the reasons why he'd come down here in person instead of just phoning it in. He needed to gauge how well I was doing for myself in my new life with his own eyes. If I had appeared successful, he would have offered more. I silently cursed the house fire and the unknown persons who had caused it, hoping to high Heaven that Dorian would read the anger in my face as anger at him and not at the situation in general.

Dorian was done with me for now. He stood up and tossed a fifty dollar bill onto the table. Knowing him, it was the smallest bill he had in his wallet.

"Six p.m." He reached into his jacket pocket and pulled out his card. "And my number, in case you've forgotten it."

He leaned over and kissed me softly on the cheek, taking care to brush my earlobe and the curve of my chin with the tips of his fingers. I didn't turn toward him. Didn't move.

"You could have had it better than this," he whispered, and walked away.

I waited until he disappeared into the halo of daylight that pooled around him when he opened the doors to leave before I took the napkin out of my lap and started sopping up the sweat threatening to stain my collar.

I eyed the money on the table. I didn't want to take his money. But desperate times called for desperate measures. I asked the waiter to make change and walked out the door forty bucks richer.

CHAPTER 16

I called Gracie from the Caliente bar phone. I hadn't made up my mind whether or not to advise her to take the offer. According to Dick, the case was worth one to two million. It seemed like he was always settling similar cases in that dollar range. Of course, we already had in excess of six figures invested into the case, and we'd have to recoup our expenses before our client saw any money. And then Dick would take forty percent in fees of the two-hundred-grand that was left over, which didn't leave a whole lot of money for Gracie in the end. For all that she'd lost, a hundred grand take-home seemed like an insult.

I let the phone ring eleven times before hanging up. No one was home. I would have called her cell phone, except she didn't have one. She was almost sixty years old and living the small-town life—too old fashioned and entrenched in older days to bother with new-fangled contraptions like modern communications devices. I looked at my watch. It was already four o'clock.

I decided I'd drive back by my house and just check it out on the way back to the office. Maybe there was something left that I could salvage.

When I got there, I wished I hadn't bothered. Where there once was a house, now only three blackened pieces of wood jutted up from a large hole in the ground filled with ash. The house had been old—it had a pier and beam foundation.

Everything had been wood. I had lost everything but my car, which had not been parked in the garage because the house was so old and so small that it didn't have one to start with.

I truly now had virtually nothing except a set of wheels and the forty bucks in my pocket. Even the clothes on my back really belonged to Miles.

Now what?

For lack of a better place to go, I drove back to the office. I crept in softly, hoping to avoid Dick. I held my breath and tiptoed all the way from the front entrance to my office door, shutting it softly behind me. Miles was waiting for me, working at my desk.

"So?" Miles asked softly.

"He offered three hundred grand, good only until six p.m. tonight."

"That's ridiculous."

"I know. I called Gracie, but no one answered."

"What else did he say?"

"I don't want to talk about it."

"Oh, come on!" Miles was mad, and he was getting louder. "I lost my hair for you! The least you can do is not leave me hanging."

"Shhhhh! You'll bring Dick in here! I don't feel like explaining anything right now!"

Miles clapped his hand over his mouth. "Sorry," he whispered through his fingers.

"What'd I miss while I was away?"

"Dick's been in rare form, stomping around and yelling at anyone who gets in his way. I'm starting to think he has a soft spot for you, judging from the way he let the fire chief have it for not saving your house."

I knew better than that. "He's upset about the files, not me, you doofus."

Miles shrugged. "Plus, the mayor is all over him for 'facilitating the destruction of key evidence.'"

"The mayor's the one who gave the order to send the files to my house!"

"I know, but you wouldn't know that to listen to the mayor talk. He's obviously looking for a scapegoat."

"For crying out loud," I said. "Have you been able to make any headway on finding another expert witness?"

"Yeah, but they all want time to run their own air sampling tests, which you know could take a year or more. I did find a few who said they'd be willing to rely on Schaeffer's data, except now we don't have Schaeffer's data."

I did a forehead slap. "Ugh! I can't *believe* Dick was too cheap to make Xerox copies of it all!"

"Maybe if he didn't spend all his money on new cars, he'd have some left for your cases." Miles sighed. "I think it's time to face the fact that this case is dead, my dear. Just like Derrick. Just like Schaeffer."

"It's not dead. We have a three-hundred-grand settlement offer on the table. If it's the best we can do under the circumstances, it's the best we can do."

I whipped out my cell phone and dialed Gracie Miller's house again. Still no answer. "I think we might have to go over there and hunt her down. Want to go?"

"Yeah," Miles said. "Anything to get out of this joint."

Miles hopped up from my desk and cracked open my office door slowly. He pressed one eye to it to make sure the coast was clear. When he gave me the signal, we crept out.

***

Gracie's house appeared to be deserted. No car in the driveway, no lights on. We walked up to the front porch and knocked on the door anyway.

We waited. Nothing.

I knocked a little harder, but still there was no answer.

When I decided to upgrade from medium knocking to full-on fist pounding, the door swung wide open of its own accord. There was no one there.

"Gracie?" I called. "Mrs. Miller? It's me, Chloe!"

"And your favorite paralegal, Miles!" he sang out.

I looked around for Gracie's cat, named Cat—a friendly long-haired black and white mutt (if cats can be mutts) who had a dog complex. She always came running and rubbed against my legs when I visited, wanting me to scratch her behind the ears, but now, she was nowhere to be seen.

"Cat?" I called. "Here, kitty kitty kitty?" I made little kissing noises into the air, but still no Cat.

"Do you think she's gone?" Miles asked.

I poked my head into Gracie's bedroom. Clothes were strewn everywhere. The closet door was wide open, and it didn't look like there was much left in it. I went to the bathroom and opened her medicine cabinet. It was empty, too. And the litter box was gone.

"It looks like she packed up and left in a hurry!" I yelled at Miles.

Miles's voice came back to me from the kitchen. "Hey, come here! Look at this!"

I went into the kitchen to find Miles holding an envelope.

"It was taped to the refrigerator door," Miles said, handing it to me.

It had my name on it. Miles and I looked at each other, alarmed.

I opened it, pulled out a sheet of paper, and started to read aloud:

Dear Chloe,

I'm sorry I didn't call, but I couldn't, on account of I knew you'd try to stop me. I figure by the time you get worried enough to come around looking for me and find this note, I'll be long gone. I would have left it at your house, but I couldn't, on account of you ain't got a house no more. Everybody in this here town's talking about how that nice Dr. Schaeffer's dead, and how you'd be dead too if that nice detective hadn't been there to save you.

"Hey!" Miles interjected. "What about me? What am I, a hill of beans? I could have saved you too, for all they know!"

"Old lady Ellason is probably telling everyone Nash carried me out of the house naked. You can't blame 'em for not noticing you."

I continued to read.

It ain't my business what you were doing with that nice detective in your house at three in the morning without a shirt on, honey, but you take my advice and be more careful, you hear?

"Great," I said. "What'd I tell you? The Kettle tongues are all wagging."

"On the upside, it'll probably be really easy for you to get a date now, if you want one. Everyone will think you're easy."

I ignored him and kept reading.

A nice girl like you has no business attracting bad gossip. It's the last thing you need, especially with arsonists and killers out to get you. Anywhoo, I figured that since they killed Dr. Schaeffer, and since they tried to kill you, all this stuff might be related to my law suit and I might be next. Well, I can't wait around for that to happen. When this all settles down, and if you're still alive, we'll talk about what to do next. I'm sorry I can't tell you where I'm going, but I figure if I write it down in this letter, somebody bad might find it just as easy as you. I'm sorry honey. Take care of yourself, and we'll talk soon. Love, Gracie

I let loose with a string of expletives that might even have made HBO producers feel squeamish.

Miles, however, was unphased. "Wow, Chloe. I didn't even know you knew any of those words."

I ripped up the letter into a bunch of tiny bits, and then ripped the tiny bits into even tinier bits and threw the pieces over my head. A pretty obvious possibility had escaped me until now. All this time, I thought the violence was about the files. But what if it wasn't *just* about the files? What if it was about my life, too? After all, we hadn't found anything in the files that confirmed motive.

But why would anyone want to kill me? I didn't know anything worth killing for!

Maybe they didn't know that I didn't know.

Holy Mary, Mother of God. "We have to go see Nash," I said. "Now."

I raced back to my car, Miles hot on my heels. The tires screeched as I tore out of Gracie's parking lot and around the corner of the main road to the police station.

CHAPTER 17

"She thinks they're trying to kill me," I explained to Nash, my voice a little louder and a little higher pitched than I intended it to be. I wanted to stay cool, but my flesh burned and my insides felt like jelly. I needed to reapply lidocaine gel to my injured tissue, but I'd left it at Miles' house by accident this morning.

"Hmm," Nash said, leaning back and propping his boot-clad feet up on the desk. "I hadn't thought of that, but it's possible. After all, if there was incriminating evidence in those files, they can't be certain you're not aware of it too."

"But I'm not! I don't know anything!"

"That's not entirely true, is it?" Nash said. "You know lots of stuff. You sure schooled me last night on a few things."

"Yeah," I said. "But that's all public knowledge."

"Public record maybe, but not public knowledge." Nash took a sip out of the coffee cup on his desk. "But you're right. Killing you wouldn't make any of that information go away."

"What about me?" Miles asked. "I don't know just as much as she doesn't know. And I was in the house, too."

"Has anyone tried to kill either of you today?"

"Yeah," I said. "I'm pretty sure Dorian Saks tried to give me a heart attack on purpose this afternoon, and I'm not sure he's not going to get away with it."

"Dorian Saks?" Nash asked.

Miles rolled his eyes. "Her ex fiancé. New opposing counsel in the PetroPlex case. And a whole lot of other things, too, apparently. Don't ask."

"Don't tell," I said, prompting a second eye roll from Miles.

Nash rubbed his eyes with the base of his palms and yawned. If he were at all interested in my sordid romantic past, he sure didn't let on. "Well, it wouldn't hurt to arrange protective custody for the both of you."

I groaned. "Just what I need. A bunch of police types shadowing my every step, stirring up the gossip mill even more. I don't know if I can handle that."

"Well, if you don't want me around," Nash said, "all you have to do is say so. But I did save your life last night, and I might come in handy again."

My jaw dropped. "Wait, *you?* You're the protective custody detail?"

Nash's eyebrows raised. "Why, is that a problem?"

"Yes! I mean no!" Yes, it was a problem because the very last thought I'd had before passing out last night was about how his lips might feel on mine, and because now Dorian was in town, and the thought of having those kinds of feelings about two men at the same time was. . . well, a problem. But I hated Dorian.

I wasn't really sure yet how I felt about Jensen Nash. I didn't hate him, but the man was a stone. He seemed all but unattainable. And yet here he was offering to hang out with me around the clock. . . did that mean something? Maybe he was attainable after all? Ugh! Mental head slap! How could I even be thinking this way when there was someone out there potentially trying to kill me!

Nash lowered one eyebrow and cocked the other one. "So that's a... what? A yes? A no?"

"But... but you're a detective," I stammered. The last time I checked, detectives didn't do the kind of mindless schmoe jobs that required nothing more than two good feet and a gun. At least, not without a good reason. Nash's potential reasons sent fun little tingles up my spine.

"In case you haven't noticed, this is a small town, and we're kind of short on staff around here. A lot of people wear a lot of different hats. Don't read anything into it that's not there."

"I'm not," I lied.

"You sure?"

"Of course," I said. "I'm living with Miles now, so we're kind of a package deal."

I turned my head toward Miles just in time to see his face light up.

"Don't you go getting any ideas," I snapped.

"Sure, sure," Miles said, lifting his hands over his head and forming a halo with his fingers. "Nash is all yours."

Nash actually grinned. Oh dear. What was I about to get myself into?

"Can you find Gracie Miller?" I asked.

Nash laughed. "Your priorities are all wrong. If we find Gracie but not the killer, you'll potentially make money but not be alive to spend it."

"Is that really so much worse than being alive with no money to spend?" Miles asked.

"Money isn't everything," Nash said.

"It's not the money I care about," I said. "It's the food it might buy. I'm sick of Ramen."

"Can't blame you for that one," Miles said.

Nash pulled his feet off the desk, sat up in his chair, grabbed a handful of paper and plopped it front of me. "Schaeffer's phone records," he said. "There are over a hundred calls in the last week to a number registered to a Cameron Gilbert. The area code is 214, which puts the phone in Dallas."

That got my attention. "C.G!"

Nash nodded. "But there is no address listed with the number. Anywhere."

"How can you get a phone number without giving an address?" Miles asked.

"You can't," Nash said. "Unless it's one of those disposable cell phone numbers, which this is not. That's why this is interesting."

"It wasn't interesting before?" Miles asked.

Nash shrugged. "Well, it's more interesting now. The plot thickens, so to speak."

I drummed my fingernails on the desk as I scanned the list of Schaeffer's last phone calls. "So now what?"

"I have a call in to an old friend at the FBI," Nash said. "There's an address record somewhere, and he'll find it."

Nash's office door slammed open without warning. The police chief, Chief Scott, who I recognized from some judicial fund raising events, walked in. He stopped short when he saw me.

"Oh. Hello, Ms. Taylor. Nice to see ya," he said, in a way that made it clear that it certainly wasn't. He seemed anxious and in a hurry. Turning to Nash, he said, "I'm sorry to tell you this, especially with Ms. Taylor in the room—"

"And me," Miles said. "I'm Miles."

The Chief shifted his feet uncomfortably. He was the kind of down-home boy who found it more convenient to pretend that people like Miles didn't exist. "Pleased to meet 'cha," he said, without really looking in Miles' direction. "Anyway, I'm sorry to tell you this, but the Schaeffer case is out of our hands now. The FBI has taken over jurisdiction."

"First I've heard of it. Nobody told me," Nash said.

The Chief cleared his throat. "I'm telling you now."

"Where are the agents?" Nash asked. "Nobody's in town, that I'm aware of."

"I'm sure somebody will be in touch," the Chief said shortly, and slammed the door behind him as he left.

Nash looked thoughtful. I didn't have time to ask him what he was thinking before his phone rang.

He picked it up. "Nash." A pause. "Is that so?"

I watched him write a Dallas address on a stray envelope. "Thanks for the info, but I'm surprised you bothered to call me back. I hear you boys swiped the Schaeffer case from me. Yeah, Dr. Joseph Schaeffer—killed in his house here in Kettle a couple days ago. Maybe you can check your database and tell me who's running point? Thanks." Another pause. "Nobody? Are you sure?" A pause again. "Okay, buddy. Thanks. I owe you one." Nash hung up the phone, scratching his head.

"What?" I asked.

"The FBI has no record of this case in the database. It's not even on their radar."

"Holy Shinola," Miles said. "That means. . ."

"I have to talk to the Chief," Nash finished. He jumped up and tore down the hall to the Chief's office.

"I'm coming with you," I said, rushing after him, Miles trailing behind us both.

If the local police force was dumping Schaeffer's case on a bunch of imaginary FBI agents, I felt entitled to know why.

The Chief was already barricaded behind his closed office door by the time we got to his office. We busted in without knocking (which was getting to be something of a habit for me around here lately) and caught him pouring himself a glass of Jim Beam. His hands shook as he hurriedly put the glass and the bottle away.

Nash was fit to be tied. His face was red, his eyes were narrowed to rattlesnake slits, and a faint sheen of perspiration moistened his forehead. I could understand why he was angry, but it seemed like he was over-reacting just a tad. This was one of the first times I'd seen his emotions get the better of him. Maybe there was an actual person inside of him after all.

"You just lied to me," Nash said to the Chief, "and you're about to tell me why. The FBI is not on this case, and apparently neither am I, so I want to know who is."

"Shut the door," the Chief said.

Nash acted like he didn't hear him. "I have a friend at the FBI—"

"Shut the door!" the Chief hollered.

Miles shot out a hand and slammed the door, since Nash was still talking.

"—who was running down some phone numbers for me, and according to him, this case is not even in the FBI database."

Chief Scott swore. "Sit down," he said.

"Unnecessary," Nash said.

The Chief stood up and placed his hands on his desk, leaning over it towards us. There was anger on his face, but also fear. "Sit down!" he commanded in such stentorian tones that Miles and I didn't dare do anything but sit.

Nash, however, continued to stand. He stuck his pointer finger right in Chief Scott's face. "Talk," he said. "Now."

The Chief held his ground, glaring at Nash. "What I have to say to you had best not be heard by these two." He gestured at Miles and me.

Nash considered this for a moment and rejected it. "They stay."

I was kind of surprised to hear him say that, but then I realized Nash probably wanted witnesses for whatever was about to go down, which was just fine with me. I didn't intend to leave anyway.

"They go," the Chief said. "Or I tell you nothing."

"Oh, you'll tell me," Nash said, "because you haven't got a choice. I make one phone call, and you are out of here so fast your family won't know what hit you. I *know* you're lying about the FBI, and unless you're willing to shoot me dead right here and right now, in front of two citizens of Kettle, Texas, everyone else will know it too. What I want to know is *why*."

The Chief drew in his breath and cleared his throat not once, not twice, but three times before continuing. I think he knew he was cornered.

"What I am about to tell you does not leave this room," he said. "Agreed?"

"We'll see," Nash said.

"For Pete's sake, Nash, I'm not asking you, I'm telling you."

"You're not in a position to dictate."

Oooh boy. I had a feeling this was about to get good.

Chief Scott's face had bloomed as red as Nash's, and it was now considerably wet with perspiration. He was sweating like a potbellied pig. "If you so much as breathe a word of this, or act like you've let on at all, it's not only my career, but yours, too. And maybe your life, if you're not careful."

"Understood," Nash said.

The Chief's face screwed up into a tortured ball so that his mustache contracted and looked more like a hedgehog than a fashion statement. "I'm only even bothering to go out on a limb and tell you anything at all because I know your reputation and your history. God help me for hiring you anyway, knowing about all the corruption running this town. I wouldn't have, if anyone else had wanted the job. I'd hate to see you do something stupid and get yourself hurt."

My eyes widened. Nash had a reputation?

"I used to be like you," Chief Scott said. "Above reproach. Nothing could touch me. But you live here long enough, and all your secrets will out. Not to everyone. But to people who are in a position to hold 'em over your head sooner or later."

Miles and I shifted in our seats guiltily. I'm sure we were both thinking of Judge Delmont and his mistress. I actually had never even bothered to ask Miles how he'd gotten his hands on those photographs, but I made a mental note to do so the next time I had him one on one.

"I think it's the size of the town," the Chief continued. "You get to knowing everyone else here, and everyone else knows you, and you have a certain reputation to maintain. 'Specially if you're holding public office. Public opinion matters. It can make you or break you. Wreck your marriage. Destroy your kids. Ruin your life."

Nash mimicked the Chief's pose by placing his hands on the desk and leaning over it so that the two of them were face to face, only inches apart. "I don't care about your secrets or whatever part of your personal life you think you're protecting right now. What I care about is who told you to lie to me about the FBI's jurisdiction and why."

"If I tell you, son, you are gonna swear on a stack of Bibles that this information never leaves this room."

"We've covered this ground already as much as it's going to get covered. Out with it."

The Chief swallowed hard before continuing. "The problem is, son, there's billions of dollars at stake. And not just dollars. Lives. Two thousand people work at this PetroPlex refinery, and without it, there wouldn't even be a town. Now, I don't know what Schaeffer knew, and I don't want to know. I live my little life, draw my little paycheck, and go home at night to kiss my wife and tuck my kids in bed. That's the way I like it. So when the powers that be come down and tell me I haven't got a case, I haven't got a case."

"Who are the powers that be?" Nash demanded.

The Chief collapsed into his chair. "I don't think you need to know that."

Nash reached over the desk, grabbed Chief Scott's collar with his left hand and cocked his right fist, ready to strike.

"Who are the powers that be?"

The Chief was trembling. "Think about what you're doing, son. Think about what you're getting into."

"Tell me now, or I make the call."

The Chief didn't say anything.

"I'm going to count to three. One."

The Chief said nothing. Nash un-cocked his hand and threw the Chief back down into his chair. "Two."

The Chief still said nothing, looking as defiant as he possibly could. "Three."

Nash picked up the phone on the Chief's desk and started dialing.

The Chief jumped up and ripped the cord out of the wall. "Okay! Okay!" he said. "The mayor. It was Mayor Fillion!"

What?

"But that doesn't make any sense!" I said. "The mayor's a good guy! He's the one who released Schaeffer's files to my house, and. . ."

The full import of the situation hit me. If PetroPlex was after the files, nobody could have known the files had been moved from Schaeffer's house to mine, unless I was followed, or *unless the people who made the hit were affiliated with the people who knew where the files were.* Oh no. No. No. No.

No! I knew Kettle as a city was generally bass-ackwards and rife with small town politics, and I knew the judicial system here was corrupt, but I never really considered the possible extent of the corruption.

I looked at Miles. He was as white as a sheet, and I knew he could read my thoughts. How convenient for the mayor that he happened to be friends with Dick. How convenient that he was in a position to know everything that was happening at our firm. Where did that put Dick, I wondered? Was Dick somehow in cahoots, or just an innocent pawn? Who could we possibly trust? Did I dare talk to Dick about any of this?

Nash scooped the Chief's phone off the desk and threw it within a hair's breadth of his head. It smashed against the wall behind him and landed on the ground in pieces.

"Is Chloe's life in danger?" he demanded.

The Chief nodded.

"And Miles?"

The Chief nodded again.

Nash bolted from the room and Miles and I were right behind him.

Nash would have slammed the office door in my face if I hadn't caught it and deflected it back against his office's inner wall. Not that he meant to shut me out, I'm sure. I just happened to be in the path of his fury. The door popped off my hands, swung inward, and hit the inside surface of his wall with so much force that the doorknob slammed a hole in the drywall and lodged there, stuck.

Nash was out of control, and since we were talking about Mr. Stone-faced Nash, that was saying something. He grabbed a paperweight off his desk and smashed it on the floor. His pencil jar followed, along with his coffee cup, his computer keyboard, and a sorry looking half-wilted potted plant.

"Nash!" I said. "Jensen, *please!*"

The use of his first name caught his attention. I'd never called him that before.

He glared at me. "I am *Not. Doing. This. Again.*" He said. "Not for you. Not for Miles. Not for me. Not for anybody."

He looked around for something else to throw. I saw him eye the computer monitor and decide against it.

"I think you are," Miles said softly. "I think you are incapable of sitting by and watching innocent people get hurt when you know you can do something about it."

Miles was right. If there's one thing I'd learned about Nash in the last twenty-four hours, it was that he was hyper-attuned to doing the right thing. Always. He was so by the book you'd think he wrote it. But now that the book was out the window, his own set of rules applied, and I was pretty sure those rules wouldn't allow him to sit around twiddling his thumbs while Miles and I got ourselves killed.

"So," I said. "We can either stay here like sitting ducks and wait to get shot, blown up, or worse, or we can go to Dallas, find Cameron Gilbert, and try to straighten this mess out. Road trip, anyone?"

CHAPTER 18

Delmont didn't feel like going home for the evening, so when Chief Scott invited him out for some beers, he readily agreed. The two of them met up at Caliente and ordered the fried rattlesnake appetizer with a side order of frog legs and a couple of Coronas.

Chief Scott seemed anxious. His mustache twitched when he ordered his beer.

Delmont waited for the waiter to leave before he said anything about it. "Whassamatter with you? You look like a rabbit on speed. Take a deep breath or something."

Chief Scott leaned in toward Delmont. "It's the goldarned Schaeffer case. I don't know how much longer I can hold it together. I'm not used to having to cover my tracks all the time. It's a lot of work, you know. Just staying honest would be a whole lot easier. If you tell the truth, you never gotta remember nothing."

"What are you talking about?"

"Nash and Taylor were all over me, so I mighta let slip that the mayor told me to bury their case."

Delmont swore. "You got a screw loose or something? What the hell would make you go and do a fool thing like that?"

"I dunno! Nash had me cornered! What was I supposed to do?"

"Anything but implicate the mayor! And yourself! Next thing you know, they'll be knocking down *my* door!" Delmont whacked Scott upside the head. "You gotta pull it together, man!"

"I know, I know! It's just that I been trying to keep an eye on those two all afternoon, and I think they left town."

"What makes you think that?"

"I checked Nash's files, and he's gone off to track down some guy named Cameron Gilbert who has a Dallas phone number. I think Taylor and that fairy of a paralegal went with him. Nobody in town has seen 'em for awhile."

"What do you know about this Cameron Gilbert guy?"

"Nothing, except that he used to work for PetroPlex."

Delmont gritted his teeth. If he were a betting man, he'd bet his hat that Cameron was the name of the ex-employee with the computer virus he'd learned about last night. Nash and Taylor were getting a little too close for comfort.

"Listen," Delmont said. "You screwed up. You've been exposed. You gotta nip this thing in the bud right now."

"How am I gonna do that?" Scott wanted to know.

"First thing you gotta do is get 'em back in town. Put out an APB on 'em or something."

"And then what?"

"Don't worry about it. We'll figure it out then."

Chief Scott pondered the situation. "On what grounds am I gonna put out an APB?"

"It don't matter. Just make something up."

"I can't do that."

"The hell you can't. It's either that or sit back and let the two of them ruin our gravy train. You haven't got much of a choice in the matter anymore."

Chief Scott let his head fall into his hands. "My wife is gonna kill me."

"Not if you *take care* of things," Delmont said. "Man up, already! If you don't, you're likely to get yourself killed by *you know who*. I think it ought to be pretty obvious to you by now that they ain't afraid to put a bullet in the heads of people who cross 'em."

"How can you be so calm about this? This ain't what I signed up for, man. Not even close."

"You think they're paying you to sit on your keister? Get a grip. Nothing in life is free."

"One lie on top of another. This whole thing is about to come crumbling down."

Delmont grabbed Scott's chin with one hand and slapped him across the cheek a few times with the other. "Hey! Not unless you *let* it. Now get on the phone and put out an APB!"

Scott shoved Delmont's hands away from his face. "All right, all right! I'm puttin' out an APB. But I don't like it one bit."

"Nobody said you had to like it. Just *do* it."

Scott pulled out his cell phone and speed-dialed the station.

CHAPTER 19

We hit Austin before I felt like Nash had calmed down enough to broach the subject of what had just happened. None of us bothered to pack, really. Me, I had nothing anyway. Nash brought only the stack of paper containing Schaeffer's call records. We stopped by Miles' house to get Lucy and left. Miles grabbed a couple of shirts, a pair of jeans, and some face cream for himself while he was there, but that was it. Nash had taken a small armory from his office before commandeering my keys. He was driving my car. There was nowhere to go but Dallas.

Every twenty minutes or so, I'd call Gilbert's number, but I never really expected him to pick up. None of us did. The call didn't even go to voicemail. It just rang and rang and rang without ceasing.

The three of us were feeling pretty low, but Lucy was ecstatic, since of course her favorite thing in the whole world was riding in the car. She sat in my lap, front paws propped on the window, tongue lolling out happily.

I rode shotgun. I turned my head and looked at Nash. His neck was rigid, face set, staring straight ahead at the road.

"So, where ya from?" Miles asked Nash conversationally, hoping to diffuse the tense atmosphere.

"Chicago," he said.

"And you left Chicago for *Kettle?*"

Nash sighed. "There was a drug ring. It was funded by the mayor's biggest campaign contributor. I found the paper trail and threatened to blow the whistle. I got fired. Then my wife died. I left."

"Whoa," Miles said. "You're a *widower?*"

That was certainly news. Maybe that explained why he seemed so emotionally shut down all the time, and maybe even why he came to Kettle, Texas. Kettle, after all, was worlds away from Chicago. Maybe he had just wanted a complete and total change—a totally new start. Like me.

"How did your wife die?" I asked, tentatively.

"It was a car accident. Some guy came at her out of nowhere. She swerved and drove off a bridge."

While I was debating whether or not to ask him if he thought it was an accident, Miles plunged in where I feared to tread.

"And you think the death and the loss of your job were connected?"

"I can't prove it," Nash said. "But with no job, I had no resources. No recourse. And I was so devastated about my wife, all I wanted to do was get away."

"What about the media?" I asked. "You could have talked to the media."

"I tried. No one would listen. I was just one man with no proof. I wanted out. I wanted to go far, far away to live in the middle of nowhere, where life was quiet. Peaceful. Where nothing ever happened."

"So you moved to Kettle," I said, staring at the expansive blackness of the road ahead of us.

"It seemed like a good idea at the time. There was a job opening. It's warmer down here. Escaping Chicago winters didn't seem like such a bad idea. And I thought I could also escape big city corruption."

Little did *he* know. Was there corruption everywhere, I wondered? Was there no place left in America where decent, hard-working men and women could get ahead? How many cases like Nash's happened all the time? How much went unnoticed and uncommented on for sheer lack of proof?

I was trying not to panic, but I was worried about what came next. It seemed like Miles and I were in a no-win situation. We could either sit around and get killed for something we might know but didn't, or we could try to figure out what it was we didn't know and then use that information to. . . do something. But what? The vast chasm of uncertainty seemed as though it would engulf me at any moment. Conventional wisdom was wrong. What you don't know *can* hurt you.

And then there was Nash. What about Nash? What was he doing on this road trip? Was it a personal vendetta for him now? Did he see some kind of redemption in spearheading a campaign against corruption? Did he care about me in some way I wasn't fully aware of yet? I needed to know.

"And now what?" I asked Nash. "What are you doing out here with us?"

Nash remained silent for a moment. Finally, he said quietly, "No one else is dying on my watch, if I can help it."

I sensed that something in him had changed. He seemed different to me today than he was yesterday. He seemed a little more raw. A little more desperate. A little more dangerous. Yesterday, he would have combed his hair every day with nothing but fingers and spit if the Kettle regulation manual required it, but now... well, now I didn't know what he'd do.

"So what's the plan?" Miles asked.

Nash's hands were clenched hard on the steering wheel. "Do you know how to shoot?"

"As in, a *gun?*" Miles sounded horrified.

"Yes, 'as in a gun.' What else?"

"I don't know!" Miles said frantically. "Shoot pool, shoot the breeze? I don't do guns."

"Me neither," I said.

"You do now. I'm about to Sarah Palin you up."

I groaned. "Is that really necessary?"

"It's safer to prepare for the worst. After that, we're going to stop at a motel and get some rest. We're going to need it. Then tomorrow, we'll go try to find Cameron Gilbert."

"And what if we can't find him?" I asked. "Then what?"

"We'll cross that bridge when we get to it." Nash exited the freeway and pulled onto a deserted farm road, following it a little ways in and stopping at a dark, wide open field. There were no lights in sight, except for my car's high beams. Nash killed the ignition but left the headlights on. He popped the trunk, got out of the car, and hauled his arsenal out and set everything down on the ground in the wash of the headlights so we could see it.

Miles and I got out of the car and stood hesitantly at the edge of the car's glow. Nash picked up a petite gun and held it out in front of me by the handle, barrel down. "This is a Smith and Wesson 38 Plus AirLite. " He showed me the safety and how to load and unload the ammo, then he placed the gun in my hand. Moving around behind me, he placed his hands on mine and aimed the gun into the night, pointing it at a slight downward angle so that if it fired, the bullet wouldn't travel far before hitting the ground.

"Feel this little button right here?" he asked, positioning my thumb on a small nodule in the handle. "That's a laser sight. Hold it down." I did, and a small laser dot appeared on the ground a few yards away. "Now pull the trigger."

The sound didn't shock me as much as the kickback. It was such a little gun, and yet it slammed back into the crook of my hand so hard I recoiled, my back pressing into Nash's body, not altogether unpleasantly.

I heard his voice and felt his breath in my ear. "Good," he said. "That was easy, wasn't it?"

My already anxiously fast heartbeat quickened even more. It had been a very, very long time since I found myself this close to a man. Fully conscious, anyway. I don't think being carried out of a burning building after being hit with an explosive device really counted. I hadn't dated much since Dorian, and the dates I had been on seemed to all be just first dates.

Nash's chest was hard and warm. It felt safe. It felt like the only safe place in the universe for me right now. I lingered against it for a moment. He didn't push me away.

I turned to look at Miles, whose arms were crossed. He was grinning at me in a smug, knowing way.

Abruptly, I pulled away from Nash and picked up another gun, holding it barrel down as an offering to Miles. "Your turn," I said. "Were you paying attention?"

To my surprise, Miles steeled himself, took the gun, aimed, and shot immediately, without hesitation. When the shot rang out, he gasped and dropped the thing on the ground. "Holy Shinola! That thing has kick!"

Nash grinned. "What, you think I pack pea-shooters?"

"That's enough," Miles said. "We're done shooting for one night. Say we're done, please."

"We're done," Nash said. "No sense in wasting ammunition."

We got back in the car and drove until we reached Waxahachie, a small town just south of Dallas. We found a cheap motel right off the freeway and decided to stay there. Miles protested about the quality of the venue, but Nash insisted. He didn't want to leave real names. He paid cash and we settled down for the night—Miles in one bed, Lucy and me in another, and Nash on an extra blanket on the floor.

It wasn't long before Miles' breathing settled into a regular rhythm. Once in awhile, he'd let out a little snore. Nothing major. I couldn't hear Nash breathing at all.

I tossed and turned in my bed, which was hard as a rock. I stared at the red digital readout of the motel nightstand's clock, watching the minutes go by. After an hour and a half of not being able to get comfortable, I decided I'd get up and look for some extra pillows.

I tip-toed over to the closet and opened it up, but found nothing. There was nothing in any of the drawers, either. I grabbed my card key and headed for the door, intending to just go to the front desk and see if they had any extra pillows lying around. I wasn't optimistic—this didn't seem like the kind of place that stocked extra anything, but it was worth a chance.

Certainly better than just lying around staring at a clock in the dark.

I was still fully clothed, not having anything else to sleep in except for what I had worn that day, so I crept through the door and closed it softly behind me. Outside, the night air was warm and humid. It felt thick and oppressive as it closed in around me and leeched into my skin. I began walking toward the front desk, but stopped when I heard a soft click behind me. I turned around to find Nash standing in front of the door to our room.

"Can't sleep?" he asked.

"No," I said. "I guess I'm not the only one, huh?"

Nash shrugged. "Want to take a walk?"

"Why not?" I said.

I waited for Nash to join me. He drew closer, and we began walking down the road together. We were on the service road for I-35, and large trucks whipped past us, adding the stink of exhaust to the already close air.

"I'm really sorry to hear about your wife," I said.

Nash stared at the ground in front of him and put one foot in front of the other. "Thanks," he said.

"That must have been really hard."

"It was. She was an amazing woman."

"Tell me about her," I said, almost certain he would decline. But he surprised me. I don't know if it was the lateness of the hour or the exhaust fumes in the air that made him more talkative than usual, but he began to open up to me.

"We met in college. She was an art major, and sometimes the college would display her art at various places on campus. It always caught my eye. One day, I was standing in the student center admiring an abstract print with her name on it. She saw me and walked over. The first thing she said to me was, 'Terrible, isn't it?' I had no idea who she was. All I knew was that I loved this piece of art in front of me, and it seemed wrong to let a stranger bash it.

"I told her that if she thought that, she didn't have much of an eye for art. She countered by asking me what made me think I *did*. I told her I was no professional, but on a gut level, I knew good art when I saw it. That's when she introduced herself. I took her to dinner that very night, and we talked every day after that, right through our wedding and into the years that came afterward. We were together every single day until the day she died."

"You really loved her, didn't you?" I asked.

Nash nodded. "She was pregnant when her car went over the bridge."

"Oh, no." What a devastating blow that must have been. "How long ago did this happen?"

"About a year and a half ago," he said.

"I'm so sorry."

Nash didn't say anything in reply, and we walked in silence together for a few minutes. I had never been married, but the thought of what it must be like, finding the love of your life, and then losing that person all too soon, seemed horrifying. Losing a fiancé had been bad enough. It had been two years, and I still wasn't totally over it.

I could only imagine that Nash was almost certainly still hurting. If he seemed like he was hiding behind an emotional wall, maybe that was just his way of protecting himself. Maybe that's why he was here with me now. Maybe the corruption and betrayal by the city of Kettle felt like a re-hash of his past problems—a kind of déjà vu come to life.

And to lose a child—again, I was no expert, but I felt like that might be the worst pain of all. Especially knowing the death could have been prevented. That's the thing that would have kept me up at night if I were in Nash's shoes.

"So what about you?" Nash asked. "How are you holding up?"

"I'm okay," I said, feeling anything but. My career was falling down around me in flames, just like my house. I was alone in life, having loved and lost through no fault of my own. I had no money in my bank account and owned only the clothes on my back. Even my car would be repossessed if I didn't figure out some way to make the payments soon. I had lost just about everything. On the upside, that meant there wasn't a whole lot left to lose.

"I find that hard to believe, under the circumstances," Nash said.

"Well." I sighed. "There's not a lot we can do to change the situation, so we might as well accept it and move forward."

Nash kicked a pebble off the road into the ditch absentmindedly. "You remind me of my wife in that respect," he said.

Something inside me softened toward him. "How so?" I asked.

"She never let anything get her down. Even when it looked like my career was over, she stayed optimistic. She was strong, like you."

I didn't feel strong. I felt like a big ball of wuss that wanted to curl up in my bed and never get out. The thing was, I didn't even have a bed anymore, so that wasn't a viable option.

"Do you miss Chicago?" I asked.

"I miss the summers there. I miss walking by the lake with my wife."

I fought the urge to reach out and grab Nash's hand. I wanted to connect with him, to help him fill a part of his void and comfort him somehow, but I wasn't sure how he'd react if I did that. I had just met him, and after all, yesterday our relationship was such that he was going to arrest me. What could possibly make me think he would even *want* comfort from someone like me?

And *why* did I feel the need to comfort him in the first place? I was undeniably attracted to him physically, but I barely knew him. Maybe it was the lure of the strong, silent type. He was mysterious. And he was clearly a hero. He had carried me out of a burning building, for Pete's sake. Maybe I was just feeling the natural affection someone would feel for someone else who saved a life. Or maybe it was the fact that Nash would be safe. He was honest and upstanding almost to a fault. I felt like he was not the kind of guy who would betray a woman the way Dorian had betrayed me. He was trustworthy. He was what I needed in a man.

"You don't miss the Chicago winters, then?" I asked.

"The winters in Texas are much nicer. I don't miss the snow. So there's that."

I liked snow. But then, I'd never had to shovel it. When it snowed in Texas, everything shut down and we had a lovely, white holiday until it melted—usually the next day.

"I'm sorry about your house," Nash said.

"Me too," I said.

"You're probably not too accustomed to having nothing," he ventured.

"That's not true," I said. "I didn't have a lot of money growing up. I can live just as well without a lot of stuff as I can with it."

Nash leaned over and gave me a quick side-hug. Just a fast squeeze—nothing lingering. Nevertheless, I flushed.

"Atta girl," he said.

Thank goodness it was too dark for him to see the sheet of redness creeping up my face. Once again, I found myself debating about whether or not to take his hand. But my thoughts were interrupted by a sudden flash of red and blue lights.

A cop car passed us and came to a stop directly in front of us. A chunky policeman clambered out of the front seat and walked towards us. "Kind of late for a stroll down the boulevard, don't you think?

"We couldn't sleep," Nash said.

"You live around here?"

Nash shook his head. "We're staying at a motel up the road."

"I'm gonna need to see some i.d.," the cop said.

I looked at Nash. I hadn't brought any. The only thing I had on me was my motel room key. I produced it and said, "This is all I have. My wallet is back in the room."

Nash pulled out his own wallet, which thankfully he had on him. He flashed his driver's license and his badge.

"Detective Nash," the cop said. "I see." He looked at me. "You Chloe Taylor?"

Nash glanced at me in alarm.

"Yes," I said, hesitatingly.

The cop handed Nash back his wallet and badge. "I'm going to need the two of you to come with me."

"How come?" Nash demanded.

"I got an APB out for the two of you. You're persons of interest in a murder case going on in the city of Kettle."

"The Schaeffer case?" Nash said.

"That sounds about right." The cop, sensing resistance, was fingering the cuffs hanging from his belt.

"You can't be serious," Nash said. "That's *my* case. I'm the investigator on it. There must be some misunderstanding."

The cop seemed uncertain. "Hold on," he said. "Stay right there." He went back to his car and radioed in to the station.

"This can't be good," I said. "Do you think the Chief put out an APB on you?"

"On *us*," Nash said. "Which means he's feeling antsy about having told us about the mayor."

"What are we going to do?"

The cop got back out of his car and advanced toward us, hand on his gun.

"Follow my lead," Nash whispered.

The cop drew his gun on us.

Nash raised his hands in the air, and I followed suit.

"Ain't nothing I hate worse than a dirty cop," the policeman said. "Word is, the Schaeffer case *was* yours until the police chief figured out you were falsifying evidence. Now it's a matter for the FBI."

"The FBI has no record of the case," Nash said. "Call them. You'll see."

The cop didn't lower his gun. "You think I got the FBI on speed dial?"

"I'll give you the number," Nash said. "Seriously, just make the call."

"Yeah right." The cop inched slowly toward us. "I call a number *you* give me so you can hook me up with some shill who sings your praises. I don't think so. Turn around. Hands behind your back. Now!"

I glanced at Nash, waiting to see what he would do.

Nash lowered his hands slowly and put them behind his back. Then he turned around. I did the same, even though I felt uneasy about it. I didn't relish the idea of being remanded into Chief Scott's custody. Somehow, I didn't think I'd get out again unscathed.

"Down on the ground!" the cop said.

Nash hesitated.

"On the ground now, or I shoot!"

Nash dropped to his knees, and so did I.

Out of the corner of my eye, I could see the cop fast-step toward us. When he got close, he aimed the gun at me with one hand and whipped a cuff on Nash's wrist with the other.

Just as the cop was about to close the second bracelet, Nash whirled, and the loose cuff caught him in the crotch.

The cop doubled over. Nash's hand shot out and sliced into the cop's wrist. His gun went flying.

A surge of adrenaline shot through me, and I jumped to my feet, not certain what to do.

I almost couldn't believe my eyes when Nash found his own feet, raised both arms and brought them down again on the cop's head. This seemed so out of character for the ultra-straight-laced Nash.

The cop struggled to regain his balance, but Nash's blows put him on one knee.

Nash spun again and knocked the cop's one good foot out from under him. The cop went down, hitting the ground with a thud. He looked like he'd eaten one too many donuts in his day, and he was no match for Nash's innate quickness and athleticism.

Nash turned to me. "Get the gun."

The cop struggled, but Nash stomped a foot down on his back to keep him down.

I got the gun, but didn't want to point it at anybody, especially a cop. I held it, barrel down, in front of me.

Nash seemed to understand that I was afraid to shoot, so he held out his hand, motioning for me to give him the weapon. I did, and he pointed it at the cop's head. "I'm sorry about this, buddy," he said, "but you're interfering with my investigation. I really wouldn't be doing this if you'd given me any other choice."

"This ain't right," the cop gasped.

"Get the keys, Chloe," Nash said.

I bent down and retrieved the handcuff keys from the cop's belt.

"Car keys, too," Nash said.

I gave Nash an incredulous look, but did what he said. He held out his arm, and I unlocked the cuff that bound his right wrist. Then he took the cuffs from me and put them on the cop.

"Get in the car," Nash told me.

"The *police* car?" I asked, shocked.

"Do you see another car around here?" Nash said.

"I'll have your badge for this!" the cop hollered.

I felt rooted to the ground. Surely Nash wasn't serious.

"Car! Now!" Nash said urgently.

I picked up my feet and ran to the car, hopping into the shotgun position.

Nash backed away from the cop, gun still pointed at the guy's head. "You move, and I shoot," he told the cop.

I could hear the cop shouting curses at Nash, but he wasn't fool enough to try to get up off the ground. He must have sensed that Nash was serious.

Nash backed up all the way to the car and hopped in. Then he floored it, and we high-tailed it back to the motel.

"What are you *thinking?*" I said.

"I'm thinking that the last place I want to *ever* find myself is behind bars on the orders of a dirty cop. I've lost enough to these kinds of scumbags already. I'm not doing it again."

"This just seems so unlike you," I said.

"It looks bad, but we're still on the right side of things. We'll find Cameron Gilbert, recover Schaeffer's evidence, and then out all the corruption in Kettle."

"That's a long shot," I said.

"Maybe, but it's our only shot. Unless you really want to trust yourself in the hands of Chief Scott."

"Um, no," I said.

"I'll just need a good lawyer to help me straighten things out once we get to the other side of the action. You know one?" He shot me a sideways grin.

"No," I said firmly. I wouldn't touch a criminal cop-on-cop case with a twenty-foot pole.

"Come on! You can use the necessity defense. It's an easy win."

"There is no such thing as an easy win," I said.

Nash fish-tailed into the motel parking lot. As he pulled up to our room, he wrenched the dash cam off its perch, opened the car door, and smashed the camera into pieces on the ground. "Get Miles and Lucy," he said. "That cop saw your room key, so he knows where we are. We have to get out of here before that guy can get somewhere he can call backup."

"We're not taking the cop car, are we?"

"And have them spot us with their GPS system? I don't think so."

I hopped out of the car and raced to our motel room, Nash hot on my heels.

"Get up!" I told Miles.

Miles didn't budge.

I raced toward him and shook him. "I'm serious, Miles! Get up! We have to get out of here!"

Miles rolled over groggily. "I need my beauty rest. If I get up now, I'll have bags under my eyes all day."

Nash grabbed Miles' arm and flung him unceremoniously out of bed.

"Hey!" Miles protested.

"You want to ride in the car?" I asked Lucy. She immediately started prancing in circles and jumping up and down excitedly.

Nash grabbed my keys off the dresser, threw Miles' wallet at him, and ushered him forcibly out the door.

Lucy was out the door ahead of us, bucking up and down in front of my car. I opened the passenger-side door and she jumped in. I followed. Nash dumped Miles in the back seat, hopped in the driver's side, and took off.

CHAPTER 20

"Where are we going?" Miles asked groggily.

We were all exhausted. Only Lucy was perky and excited to get to ride in the car, no matter what time of night it was.

"To find Cameron, ASAP," Nash said.

I entered Cameron's address into my GPS and filled Miles in on what had just gone down, omitting the part about my personal conversation with Nash.

"Girl, you better be kidding me," Miles said. "You took down a *cop?*"

"Technically, Nash took down the cop, not me," I said.

"Wow," Miles told Nash. "I am totally going to have to change my definition of who I think you are."

"Well, that makes two of us," Nash said.

We were about forty miles outside of Dallas. I was starting to worry that Chief Scott might have had a line on where we were headed, since he had bothered to put out an APB that extended this far north. I voiced my concerns to Nash.

"He probably just issued a state-wide alert," Nash said. "Even if he knows we're looking for a guy named Cameron Gilbert, he won't be able to get the address unless he calls the FBI—and I don't think he's going to call the FBI because he knows they're the white hats in this situation. He won't want to stir up anything that could come back to bite him."

I wasn't so sure, but I was too tired to argue with Nash.

Driving up I-35 as we neared Dallas, I could see the shifting lights that decorated the Reunion Tower ball and the green quasi-neon glow of the Bank of America building. I had so many memories here. High school, law school, Dorian. Under any other circumstances, I'd feel relieved to be back.

Nearer to downtown, I started to realize I didn't really care for the direction in which we were headed. We exited I-35 just south of downtown and took a right into the hood, into an area of town I never, ever went—especially at night—and was wholly unfamiliar with.

There were no gas stations here. No grocery stores. Only boarded up buildings about twenty-five years overdue for new windows and fresh paint. Structures that passed for homes were scattered around what used to be commercial real estate and warehouses. It was like the zoning commission had completely ignored this area when planning the city. Occasionally, we'd drive past some guys who were out walking around for probably no good reason at this hour. They stared suspiciously at my shiny black Lexus. Lexus owners didn't usually drive around in this neighborhood, and especially not in the middle of the night.

"This doesn't feel right," Nash said.

"You're telling me. This place scares me more than Kettle."

My GPS dinged. "You have arrived," it said.

Nash pulled to a stop in front of an old, abandoned garage. Rusted-out cars littered the parking lot, and scrap metal was strewn about like post-modern confetti. "Guns out. You two stay here. I'll go check it out. Try to cover me, okay?"

I didn't feel good about it, but reluctantly agreed. I would have felt a lot better calling for backup or something, which of course, was out of the question under the circumstances. Not that I didn't trust Nash. It's just that he was only *one man* backed up by a chick in high heels and a gay guy who was apparently allergic to steel.

Nash left the keys in the ignition. I shut the car off and rolled down the windows so I could better hear what was happening in there, if anything. Then I took my gun and propped it gingerly on the window sill, careful to keep my fingers away from the trigger. I did press the laser sight button though, just to make sure I wasn't aiming the thing at Nash accidentally. I settled for pointing it well to Nash's right and held still, alert.

Miles refused to touch his. "It's all you, baby," he said, leaving his gun on the car seat beside him.

Lucy poked her head out the window and sniffed the air.

Nash crept towards the half-open sliding garage door. He was crouched low, a gun in each hand, wrists crossed. He swiveled back and forth as he moved in, covering himself as best he could. It was pretty clear that he didn't really trust us to do the job.

Beside me, Lucy stiffened and let out a low growl. I tried to soothe her by stroking her head with my free hand. "Shhhh, baby. Shhhh. It's okay."

Her growl got progressively louder. She refused to calm down. I followed her gaze to a stack of old tires off to the left of the garage and readjusted my laser sight in that direction, just in case.

Lucy started barking immediately before the shots rang out. Not mine. Someone else's. Behind me, Miles swore and ducked low in the back seat. I pulled Lucy down from the window, hunkered down, and hesitantly fired off a couple return shots at the tire stack. On the one hand, I didn't want to shoot anyone. On the other hand, I really didn't want to *get* shot. If I had to choose the lesser of two evils, I would choose the one that kept me alive every time.

I peered at the tire stacks and still didn't see anyone. The shots had stopped.

Nash had his back pressed against an inside wall, out of the line of sight of the tire stack. Edging his head around the corner, he saw my laser sight pointed at the tire stack and gave me a thumbs up.

A bullet from another direction slammed into the wall next to Nash's head, and he dropped to the ground and rolled out of sight. There was more than one shooter, and they apparently had us surrounded.

"Miles!" I yelled. "They're on both sides! Cover the right! I'll take the tire stack to the left!"

Miles picked up his gun, pointed it out the window, shut his eyes, and fired off three rounds. He squinted one eye open. "Did I hit anything?" he asked?

"I don't think so."

Lucy was in the floorboard growling up a storm. I could barely keep her down.

Another gunshot from the tire stacks distracted me. Lucy took advantage of my momentary lack of vigilance, leapt over me, and jumped out the window. She ran straight toward the tires.

"Lucy! No! *Noooooooooooooo!*"

I didn't even think. My protective instincts kicked in, and I jumped out of the car and ran straight for her, shooting at the tires the whole time. Miles remained in the car, screaming.

Lucy rounded the tire stack and pounced on a man. In the glow of the headlights, I could see that he was Hispanic and wore black pants and a black t-shirt. Lucy looked like she was about to rip the tendons out of his gun arm.

I lunged to get her away from him.

The man tried to grab me and simultaneously fight off Lucy at the same time. I resisted him. In the scuffle, my gun went off, and he went down with a sickening thud. I watched, horrified, as he stopped breathing.

Realizing that I'd just killed a man, my body went cold and my muscles went slack. I felt a wave of nausea. Oh no. This was bad, bad, bad! But there wasn't enough time for the emotional repercussions to really sink in. Lucy, who was still growling, whirled and leapt out of my arms at someone behind me.

Before I could see who she was growling at this time, a hand came down hard on my arm and my gun went flying. A muscular arm wrapped around my throat. My hands were powerless to dislodge it.

The man shook Lucy off. She hit the ground with a squeal and ran away. I couldn't turn my head to see where to. I prayed she wasn't badly hurt, but the fact that she'd given up on attacking this guy didn't bode well.

In the parking lot, Miles must have scrambled into the front seat and fired up the engine. Tires peeled and screeched on the concrete as he floored the car and sped toward us, hand out the window holding his weapon.

Now he was going to use his gun? To shoot the guy *behind* me, who had his arm around my throat and was using me as a human shield?

"Don't shoot!" I screamed. "Are you crazy? You'll hit me!"

Miles withdrew his gun arm and floored it, speeding toward me and my captor in the ultimate game of chicken.

The guy bought it.

He let me go and dove left as I flew right. Miles hit the brakes and fishtailed in front of me. "Get in!"

It nearly killed me to get in the car not knowing what had happened to Lucy, but I did anyway, praying I could save myself and find her later.

I dove through the window and Miles took off, but not before my attacker jumped on the hood.

For the first time, I was able to get a good look at the guy. He was white, skinny, lightly tanned, clean-shaven, and wore the same black pants and t-shirt as the other guy. I might have thought he was a cologne-ad model if I'd met him in the daylight under different circumstances.

"What do I do? What do I do?" Miles asked, clearly panicked.

"Keep driving!"

Right about this time, fatigue caught up with me and I started to shake. . . this on top of the nausea wracking my body as a reaction to the accidental killing of a few seconds ago. If I took time to think about what might be happening to Lucy and Nash, I would vomit, for sure.

We sped away from the broken down garage, desperately trying to figure out how to shake the guy off the hood.

Miles glanced over at me. "You don't look so good."

"I think I just killed a guy," I said.

"Are you okay?"

"I don't think so."

Miles rolled down my window. The opportunity was all I needed to put me over the edge. I leaned out and lost my breakfast.

"Chloe, you had to," Miles said. "If you hadn't killed him, he would have killed you first."

"It was an accident," I said, wiping my face. "I don't know. Maybe I could have gotten away."

Our current attacker had a grip on the top of the hood just below the windshield wipers, and he was muscling his way up to get whatever kind of foothold he could. To me, it looked like his black sneakers were getting pretty good traction on my paint job.

"What about this guy? How are we going to get away from him?"

"I don't know," I said. "Try to shake him off!"

I reached over and flipped on the brights. Immediately, I spotted a mini skateboard ramp on the sidewalk ahead. "The ramp! Hit the ramp!"

Miles swerved, and the left front wheel bounced up on the sidewalk and hit the ramp. The ramp, instead of putting air between my ground and the wheels, just splintered beneath the weight of the car.

The guy inched over to the driver's side, putting himself directly in Miles's line of vision.

"I can't see!" he yelled, and slammed on the brakes.

"No! You have to keep driving!" I grabbed the steering wheel. "Hit the gas! I'll steer!"

I yanked the wheel back and forth, trying to shake the guy off while Miles leaned out the window, trying to loosen his grip.

No luck. He held on like a leech, or one of those particularly disgusting suckerfishes.

The guy's hand jumped from the hood and grasped the side of Miles' window. His fingers curled inside.

"Roll up the window!"

Miles did, but the smooth electronic close was way too slow to catch the guy's fingers. His hand flew loose. For a minute, I thought he'd fall. But he caught himself again and held on with two hands on the neck of the hood.

I circled back around towards the garage. After all, we couldn't just leave Nash and Lucy there. Maybe Nash would see us coming and shoot this guy off my car. Better him than me. I didn't want another body on my conscience.

"More gas," I told Miles.

Miles put a little more foot into it, hands over his face, eyes closed. I gripped the wheel and steered for my life.

"Do something!" Miles said. "I can't hold him anymore!"

The garage loomed ahead. I didn't see Nash, but I had a plan.

I adjusted the steering wheel and aimed the car straight for the tire stack.

I just wanted to shake the guy off. Maybe the tires would cushion his landing.

The tire stack seemed to grow ever larger as I careened toward it. We were approaching way too fast.

"Less gas! Foot off the pedal!"

Miles didn't appear to hear me. The car didn't slow down.

I fought the urge to close my eyes. If I was about to kill myself, I wanted to see what the end of my life looked like. On the other hand, if I was about to kill another guy, I also didn't want to watch. I settled for shutting one eye and squinting the other one half open.

The car crashed into the tires, and I saw an explosion of white as the airbags deployed.

The man's body flipped backwards. He sailed over the sea of tires rolling away in every direction and landed on the cement with a *crack*.

A rogue tire rolled up over his arm, did a little spin, and came to rest, doughnuting his head.

In the dim light, I could barely make him out. But it was bright enough to spot a small pool of blood oozing out from underneath the tire.

I felt woozy. I had never so much as punched a man before, let alone killed one. And here I had killed two guys in the space of five minutes. I wasn't too worried about legal repercussions, assuming I ever got out of this alive. Clearly it was self defense. But the sense of permanent destruction, of having done something so intense and so final, something that could never be taken back, had already started to haunt me.

But even stronger than the urge to stop the violence was the urge to protect myself and find Lucy and Nash. I grabbed another gun from the back seat and got out of the car, positioning myself between an old, rusted-out Buick and my Lexus. Miles did the same. We hunkered down behind it waiting, watching for more shots.

After a minute or two, I decided the coast was clear. We were sitting ducks in the middle of the garage lot. If anyone was out there, they'd surely be shooting at us by now.

"Lucy!" I called. "Nash?"

Silence.

Nothing moved. I heard no sounds.

Not good. If Lucy were around, surely she'd have come running. I held on to one small hope. Lucy was afraid of loud noises. Sometimes, if it thundered, or if I set off the smoke detector while cooking, she'd run and hide and wouldn't come out no matter how much I called her. I could only hope that the gunfire and the car crash had scared her into hiding, where she'd be safe.

I was anxious for Nash, but less worried about him than Lucy. He had a gun, after all, and he knew how to use it.

I called out again. We waited for what seemed like ages.

A light popped on inside the garage.

Through the gaping front door, I saw a silhouette emerge. Nash.

I breathed a sigh of relief. Thank God! He was okay!

Nash walked slowly forward. He looked anxious, like maybe he was worried about us.

I rushed toward him to tell him we were all right.

Not until I crossed the threshold did I see the barrel of the gun pointed at his head. Too late.

CHAPTER 21

Delmont had escaped to his office at the break of dawn. He couldn't sleep, and the old battleax had burned breakfast again, anyway. No use staying around to eat *that*. Honestly. The woman couldn't cook, she was no good in bed, and she didn't make any money. To top it all off, PetroPlex had been ringing his phone so much lately he was worried she'd begin to suspect he was having an affair. If she started nagging him about it, he was done with her. No ifs, ands, or buts about it.

He started to think maybe it might be better just to *tell* his wife he was having an affair and get a divorce. That way he could beat Chloe Taylor to the punch. The only problem was, if he did that, the gossip mill would start running and all the town ladies would badmouth him. Then he'd never get elected again, no matter how much money PetroPlex put into his campaign. Much better the old ball and chain should meet with some kind of accident. It was either that or move to a state that appointed judges instead of holding elections for them. But then there'd be no PetroPlex kickback money, so that didn't seem like an option either.

Maybe an accident really would be best, but that wouldn't be without its own set of drawbacks. An accident would mean he'd be single again, and all the little old ladies would be inviting him to lunch and trying to fix him up with other respectable old maids who also couldn't cook, made no money, and were no good in bed, and that sounded like a real hassle.

Delmont sighed. No, he decided, it would be better just to stay married and keep a slut on the side.

Anyway, it's not like the old woman was good for absolutely *nothing*. She ran errands and stuff. As the morning progressed, Delmont felt more and more hungry, especially since breakfast had been ruined. Delmont figured she owed him a trip to the donut shop. Everybody loved it when his wife showed up with donuts. And it wasn't like she was doing anything else this morning. It's not like she had a job. Her job was taking care of him.

He picked up the phone to call her when it rang in his hand, startling him.

"What now?" Delmont said to the familiar voice.

"You'll never believe this, but the guys we've got on our ex-employee just found Nash and Taylor."

"You're kidding me."

"Nope. You can tell your friend Scott to cancel that APB."

"Where are they?"

"At an old car garage in Dallas. Did you know they were working with Gilbert?"

"Had no idea. Are you sure they are?" Delmont eyed his whiskey decanter. Was it too early in the day to start drinking?

"It's the only explanation that makes sense. Even though that Dorian Saks character got nothing out of her yesterday, that means she's gotta know something. If she knew enough to go after Gilbert, she knows about the virus. And if she knows about the virus, she knows about me and you and Scott and the rest. If she has Schaeffer's evidence and gives it to Gilbert, I don't have to tell you what will happen."

"So what are you gonna do?" Delmont asked.

"Get her to give up the evidence, turn over the virus, and lead us to Gilbert."

"What if she won't?"

"We'll be very persuasive."

Delmont had no doubt. "And then?"

"What do you mean 'and then?' You know very well what then."

"All right, but do it in Dallas. I'm sick of bodies showing up in this town. If I have to listen to Chief Scott moan and groan anymore about how things are about to go downhill, I'll go berserk. If things keep up like this, I'll be tempted to just blow the whistle myself and put him out of my misery."

"You mean *his* misery?"

"No, I mean *my* misery! Pay attention!"

"Look, I'm working pretty hard here to keep us both in the clear, and I've been going out of my way to keep you in the loop. The least you could do is show some gratitude."

"Maybe I don't want in your loop," Delmont said. "Maybe I'm sick of your loop. Don't get me wrong, I appreciate your concern and all, but you've really got to start being more careful. Things are getting out of control."

"Things are never out of *our* control. Forty billion a year buys a lot."

"You just keep telling yourself that. And you see to it that you keep your word on it."

Delmont hung up. Then he cleared a new line to call his wife. High time for those donuts.

CHAPTER 22

The sun was starting to come up, and the shadows were long and deep, which is why I hadn't seen the gunman earlier. He was a tall, lean man who wore a black suit with a white shirt and a black tie.

Two more men in black t-shirts, obviously black-suit-man's subordinates, stepped forward and flanked Nash, guns drawn, aiming for me and Miles. One of these guys had a shaved head, like Miles. The other one had a full head of dark hair and a respectable-enough looking face, but his forearms were covered in a solid mass of colorful tattoos, including a wide variety of skulls, dragons, and bloody daggers.

Black-suit man pressed a gun to Nash's temple, effectively holding him hostage. "Drop your weapons," the man said, "or you're all going to get hurt."

I looked at Nash for direction. He gave me a tense nod, so I tossed my gun on the ground. Beside me, Miles did the same.

I looked around desperately for Lucy, but didn't see her anywhere.

"Hands up," suit man said.

We raised our hands obediently.

Skinhead and tattoo guy pounced on us, guns drawn, trigger finger ready to shoot. Tattoo guy edged around behind me, put his arm around my throat, and flexed his muscles. I felt the squeeze on my neck and struggled to breathe. With his other hand, he pressed the barrel of his gun to my head. The steel cut into my scalp. The gun barrel was hot, as though the gun had recently been discharged.

I glanced over at Miles, who was now held captive in the same manner by Skinhead.

"Ease up, will you?" Miles said. "You're gonna leave an imprint."

Skinhead told him to shut up, using both "F" words in the space of one sentence.

Miles struggled, but he was no match for his captor. The guy was a half-head taller than him and much better built.

I looked back at Nash, who was frantically glancing all around us, presumably looking for anything that might give us an advantage. I waited for him to pull out some patented super-Nash move and regain control of the situation like he'd done before, but when his captor spun him around and cuffed his hands behind his back, I knew I couldn't count on Nash for a rescue this time.

My stomach churned at the thought of what might be coming next. I didn't know who these guys were or what they wanted. I wasn't ready to die, even though my career was in shambles and I had no house to go home to. I thought of Lucy. What had happened to her? What if I had lost her, too?

Black-suit guy jerked his head toward Miles and Nash, and skinhead walked forward. He spun Miles around and cuffed his hands behind his back, too.

Then black-suit guy turned to me and wrenched my hands behind my back. A pair of cold metal cuffs clicked into place.

Tattoo guy calmly walked over to two rickety folding-chairs by the wall, dragged them into the middle of the room, and unfolded them. Then black-suit guy yanked me toward one of them and shoved me into it. He stood back and aimed his gun at my head.

Miles looked terrified as tattoo guy manhandled him into the other chair.

Having run out of chairs, skinhead secured Nash to a metal support pole that was holding up the roof.

A dim light bulb feebly lit the dusty room. The far corners of the vast space were dark.

I felt like I might start hyperventilating, so I closed my eyes and concentrated on taking deep, slow breaths.

Suit man was having none of that. I felt slaps across my face. Suit man grasped my head in both his hands and roughly peeled my right eyelid open with his thumb. He examined my pupils. Satisfied that I wasn't going to pass out on him, he let go.

Under the light of the naked bulb, I was able to get a good look at suit man for the first time. He was white with dark brown eyes, dark hair, and a slightly crooked nose. No unusual marks. No disfiguring scars you'd typically associate with a villain or anything. He was pretty ordinary looking and wouldn't seem scary if I'd met him on the street. But in this situation, I don't mind admitting I was scared. I had seen enough TV to know that the fact that he hadn't covered his face probably didn't bode well for my chances of seeing tomorrow.

I eyed him and the two guys in black t-shirts warily. They certainly weren't cops. But they didn't look like run of the mill thugs, either. They seemed too clean-cut for a gang. They looked more like military, or private security.

Suit man crouched down in front of me and waited, to make sure I was focused and giving him my full attention. "Now," he said. "Where is Cameron Gilbert?"

My jaw dropped. "You're asking *me?*" I croaked. My mouth was dry. Throat parched. My head hurt, and my burns ached. "I haven't got the foggiest idea!"

I watched, horrified, as the man slid the spaghetti strap of my camisole off my shoulder and peeled it down to reveal my bandages.

He stuck his fingernail under the corner of one and ripped it off. I winced.

"Leave her alone," Nash said. "She's telling the truth. She doesn't know."

"I am *so* not cut out for this," Miles groaned.

Him? What about *me?* Sheesh.

Black suit man ignored him. "I think you do. Not only do I think you know where he is, I think you know what he knows."

"Believe me," I said, voice shaking, "I wish I knew both of those things, but I don't."

The man stood, grabbed my chin, and yanked it upwards. "I don't expect your friend Nash over there to know anything. You just brought him along for the ride. Your pet paralegal, maybe. But probably not. *You*, on the other hand. . .

"You know me?" I asked.

"Oh yes. I know you. We've had our eye on you for some time. You've spent hours with Schaeffer, and Schaeffer has spent hours with Gilbert, and now here you are on Gilbert's turf, which makes me think you've been working with him all along. I want to know where Gilbert is."

"Why didn't you ask Schaeffer that before you killed *him?*" I asked, now certain I was looking at the face of his murderer.

The man laughed—a laugh with no mirth. "I did. He gave me this address. After a little persuasion."

I glanced at Nash, who was carefully avoiding my gaze. He hadn't told me Schaeffer had been tortured. I had suspected as much, though. These thugs never would have found his file stash in the secret room if they hadn't used methods I could barely bring myself to contemplate.

My stomach churned as I contemplated our situation. Even if suit man tortured me, I couldn't give him any information because I didn't have it. How long would it take for him to give up and realize that I had no information to extract? What on earth did he plan to do with me between now and then? Several scenarios flashed through my brain, none of which seemed remotely palatable. I wondered if I should just start begging him to kill me now. Would it make any difference? Would it shorten the agony?

Nash struggled against his bonds. "She doesn't know anything, and even if she did, she has no evidence! You and your thugs destroyed all of Schaeffer's files when you burned her house down. You know that. You're wasting your time here."

The man in black cracked his knuckles. "Oh, I don't think so," he said. "We came here looking for Gilbert. Unfortunately, he's not here. But now, I have you, and you will lead me to Gilbert."

"I swear, we don't know where Gilbert is," I said.

"And yet here you are, so far from home."

"I came here looking for him just like you," I said. "We got the address from a friend." The futility of my protest seemed to fill the room. Who was I kidding? This guy was never going to buy it.

Black suit man slapped me across my face. "You think I'm stupid. You think I'm stupid, huh? You expect me to believe you drove all the way up here just to visit an empty building? Huh?"

He pressed his finger into my exposed burn, and I screamed bloody murder.

"Stop this! Stop this right now!" Nash said. "She doesn't know anything! We got the address and came here hoping to find answers. That's all."

I felt faint. My head lolled to one side. Beside me, Miles sat frozen, his face rigid with fear. I could feel the curtain drawing over my vision again.

Black suit man's palms slapped me back to consciousness.

"Maybe you didn't tell your friends," he said. "But you know."

"I don't know," I said. "I swear. You have to believe me."

"Where is the virus?" he asked.

The *what?* What on earth was he talking about? First Cameron, now some mysterious virus? I wondered just exactly how much I was supposed to know but didn't. What else? What else could there be?

"I don't know what you mean."

"Tell me," suit man said, "or I will rip out your fingernails one by one and bury them in the wounds in your chest."

The room swayed. I said nothing. What else was there to say? How could I possibly convince this crazy man of the truth?

"Pliers," the suit man said to his accomplice.

The guy in the black t-shirt lifted a pair of pliers and walked toward me, then circled around to my back. Out of the corner of my eye, I saw him crouch beside my tied hands, and I felt the pliers clamp down onto my right pinkie nail.

I squeezed my eyes shut, but not tight enough to hold back the tears.

"I swear," I said, trembling. "I don't know anything. Believe me, I wish I did. If I did, I would tell you. I really like my fingernails. I'd do just about anything to keep them."

"Last chance," suit man said.

The pliers tightened.

I felt them pull.

Just as I was about to be sick all down the front of my shirt, I heard a *zip, zip!* and saw suit man crumple to a heap on the ground in front of me.

I turned to look behind me and saw t-shirt man on the ground, too. Both men had bullet holes through their foreheads.

From out of nowhere, a red and brown mass of slobbering fur launched itself at me and started licking my face.

Lucy! My tears flowed faster than she could lick them away.

She was followed by a tall man with a shock of nearly white blonde hair and strikingly blue eyes.

"Hi," he said. "I'm Cameron Gilbert. I had the place under video surveillance and would have been here sooner, but there was a wreck on I-30. Is that your dog? She's cute. I found her hiding under a car out back."

CHAPTER 23

Cameron cut our ropes off and led us to his car, a Toyota Prius hybrid.

"Thought I had this place pretty well protected," he said. "I wiped the address out of most of the commercial and government databases. How'd you get it?"

"FBI," Nash answered.

A strange look passed across Cameron's face.

"What?" I asked.

"Oh nothing," Cameron said. "You just shouldn't have been able to get it from them. But what's done is done."

Nash looked suspicious. "How come you didn't pick up your phone when we called?"

"What number did you have?" Cameron asked.

Nash told him.

"I got rid of that number last week. Have to keep things fresh, you know."

"Who the heck are you," I asked, "and why is everyone out to get you?"

"I'm a computer programmer," he said. "I used to work for PetroPlex. I'll tell you everything, but first we've got to get out of here."

A computer programmer who was also a crack shot with a gun? I supposed it was possible. This was Texas, after all. Still, I was a little spooked. He had killed those guys a little too cleanly—a little too easily—for your average white-collar Joe. "Where are we going?" I asked.

Cameron grinned. "I could tell you, but then I'd have to kill you."

My stomach dropped.

Seeing the pallor in my face, Cameron said quickly, "I'm kidding! I'm kidding! Calm down."

Nash scowled. "Is that some kind of computer geek humor? Knock it off!"

Undaunted, Cameron started whistling a tune. He sure was cheerful for a guy with some very bad dudes after him. His easy slouch and old beat up jeans made him come off like a dude who was comfortable in his skin, no matter the circumstances. If a bunch of dead assassins on his property didn't get to him, I was guessing that not much would. But *why* would he be so nonchalant about it all? Did he kill people every day? Was it a smart move to actually get in the car with him?

He opened the car door for me. I eyed Nash, and Nash nodded. He seemed to be okay with Cameron. I supposed Cameron *did* save our lives after all, but why? If I didn't get in the car, I guess I'd never know, so I slid into shotgun while the guys settled down in the back.

"What about the, um, bodies?" I asked. "Are we just going to leave them for people to find? Couldn't that be. . . bad for you?"

"Did you *notice* the neighborhood?" Cameron said. "Three or four bodies aren't going to seem that out of place. The police will assume gang violence and close the case without a lot of investigation."

"But you just... *shot* them. Just like that," I said.

"It's amazing what you can learn to do in the name of self-preservation," Cameron said.

I wasn't so sure. I felt certain I'd be having nightmares about all the bodies that had piled up around me today for years to come.

"So you don't stay here much then?" Nash asked.

"I'm staying at a hotel downtown." Cameron put the car in gear and pulled away. "Sometimes the best place to hide is in plain sight."

"So why do you have this place at all?" Miles asked.

"The virus is hidden on a jump drive disguised as a wrench," Cameron said. "What better place to hide a wrench than at an old car garage in a neighborhood with virtually no computers? Even if anybody found the place, they'd never find the virus."

The virus again. What on earth? "How come everyone seems to assume I know what this virus is? I mean, if it's on a jump drive, I assume it's a computer virus and not your common cold variety, but seriously. What is this about?"

"First, let's get where we're going," Cameron said.

It didn't take us long to get downtown. Cameron had a suite at the Adolphus, a hotel so swanky it had a one-point-two million dollar Steinway Art Case piano in the lobby and a five star restaurant on the first floor. He led us into a room with soft gray carpet, elaborately-framed mirrors, shiny black polished modern furniture, and richly-textured drapes. The place was littered with computers and networking equipment, making the already modern décor look downright space age.

Miles let out a low whistle. "Computer programmers make this kind of money? Honey, I picked the wrong profession."

Cameron grinned. "Nah. My friend's the manager. He's been letting me crash."

"Nice," I said. I eyed the doors that led to the bedroom. I was tired and willing to bet this suite had one heck of a bed.

Forcing myself to wrest my attention away from the prospect of rest, I said, "So. About the virus."

"The virus," Cameron said, "is my personal insurance policy against PetroPlex."

"Huh?" I asked.

"Yeah. You know. Against the plot to manipulate the energy market."

"The *what?*" How come everyone assumed I knew so much information I didn't?

"Schaeffer didn't tell you? He said he was going to ask you for advice."

"If he was, he didn't get to it before somebody else got to him."

Cameron sighed. "Yeah, that's a real shame. If I'd been able to get the tapes from him in time, we might have been able to prevent all this."

Tapes? What tapes? More stuff I didn't know about. Unbelievable! This time I didn't even bother to say anything. I just gave Cameron a look.

He interpreted it correctly. "You don't know about the tapes either? Sheesh, what *do* you know?"

I felt kind of offended. I am smart. I know a lot of stuff. Only lately, it's just that I didn't seem to know the *right* stuff.

"We know that PetroPlex owns the Mayor of Kettle, the Police Chief, and at least one of the judges in town, but we don't know how or why."

"Hmmm," Cameron said. "That's news to me. The only conspiracies I know about are global. Tell me more."

Global? Oh, was that all? Good grief.

Nash, Miles, and I filled Cameron in on the events of the last forty-eight hours.

"Well," Cameron said, "I think it's pretty safe to say that PetroPlex bought all your town officials in order to get to Schaeffer. It's your bad luck that you picked him of all people as your expert, because now you're involved. And it seems to me that everyone, including me, is assuming you know more than you actually do. That's bad for you. Very bad."

I felt exasperated by the sheer weight of everything I didn't know but should. "Why? Why is it bad? What is this about? If somebody's out to get me, I feel like I at least deserve to know why."

Cameron settled into a sleek gray chair and interlaced his fingers. "Well, Schaeffer and I were working together to assemble evidence against PetroPlex. It was kind of funny how I met him. He was always nosing around the perimeters of the refinery taking air samples. The higher-ups kept trying to figure out a way to get rid of him, but he always stayed on public land, so there wasn't a lot they could do.

"At the time, a lot of people at PetroPlex, myself included, were suffering from chronic headaches and congestion. Watching Schaeffer snoop around made me start to wonder if maybe there was something in the air that PetroPlex wasn't warning employees about. So I decided one day that I'd take my lunch break and go downstairs and talk to him."

"And he talked to you?" I asked.

Cameron nodded.

I was surprised, knowing how reserved, academic, and secretive Schaeffer had been. On the other hand, Cameron didn't come off as a threatening kind of guy. His cheerful manner and ease of conversation did a lot to put people at ease—which was saying something, considering that we'd just met over the barrel of a gun. Even in this short time, my reservations about him seemed to be melting away.

"We struck up a conversation," Cameron continued, "and Schaeffer told me all about the dangers of benzene, toluene, and other chemicals that the refinery emitted every day. When I went back to my office, I decided I'd do a little cyber-snooping myself, just to see if I could find any evidence that the higher ups knew this stuff was floating around. Sure enough, I discovered that PetroPlex was willfully cutting corners and sacrificing safety for the sake of cutting costs and boosting profit margins."

"And how'd you feel about that?" I asked.

"Well, I was mad, of course," Cameron said, looking anything but. "I mean, here was this big company poisoning an entire community, and nobody seemed to know about it, or care. I decided I was going to do a large-scale media release that sent all our evidence digitally to all media outlets. I contacted Schaeffer to see if he wanted to pool his information with mine. He said yes, but urged me to wait until he had a complete set of data. He wanted the data to be as damning as possible before releasing it. He had a personal vendetta against PetroPlex because his father, who spent his life working at the Kettle refinery, died of benzene-induced cancer."

I was flabbergasted. "He never told me that," I said.

Cameron shrugged, as though it had been the most natural thing in the world for someone like Schaeffer to share his family secrets with him. "Anyway, at about that time, the refinery VP came to me and asked me to write a computer program that would disrupt trading on the energy market and artificially increase the price of oil. He said it was to be used only in the event of a financial emergency—but I knew better because I had been monitoring internal communications."

Whoa. That was more big news, to say the least. "So you didn't do it, right?" "Yeah, I did it, but only because I needed to buy time. I was getting a lot of inside information while working there, and the veep made it clear that I would get fired if I didn't do it.

"Anyway, while I was writing the program, I also wrote a virus designed to counteract the program. By the time I was done with both, Schaeffer and I had gathered just about all the evidence we needed. When I turned the program over to PetroPlex, I made my escape. Then I threatened to release the virus if they used my program or came after me at all. The virus manipulates the market so that the price of oil drops dramatically, and it also makes it impossible for the original program I wrote to work. See this laptop right here?" Cameron pointed to a laptop on the end table. "It's ready to go right now. All I have to do is hit 'enter' and the thing is loose."

"I thought it was hidden on a jump drive in a wrench," Nash said.

"That's the backup," Cameron explained. "The virus wouldn't be much good with the safety off now, would it? I have to be ready to launch at a moment's notice. But if something happened to me, Schaeffer knew where to find the backup."

"Let me get this straight," Miles said. "You're just sitting around with the trigger cocked, right out here in the open?"

Cameron nodded. "Moment's notice, like I said."

Miles stood and walked toward Cameron's laptop for a better look.

"Easy now," Cameron said. "Too close, and you have no idea what you'd be unleashing."

Miles backed off, but tripped over the laptop cord in the process.

Cameron's computer went crashing to the ground, along with the desk lamp, which landed on the "Enter" key and set off a shrill alarm.

Miles and Cameron both swore simultaneously.

"What did I do?" Miles said, backing himself all the way up against the opposite wall, as far from the offending machine as possible. "Can you undo it?"

For the first time since I'd met him, Cameron seemed perturbed. I couldn't believe he could so calmly shoot two guys in cold blood but freak out at the press of a mere button. And yet there it was, happening right in front of me.

"No, I can't undo it!" he said. "Once a virus is loose, it's loose!"

"Whatsamatter with you?" Miles said. "Leaving a thing like that out in the open! It's not my fault! I take no responsibility."

Cameron ignored him. He was rushing around the room, shutting laptops and dismantling wires. "Get your stuff! We have to get out of here!"

"Why?" Nash asked.

Cameron didn't give him a second glance. "Because PetroPlex will be able to trace the originating IP address of the virus to this location, and when they do, we don't want to be here, believe me. You've already been treated to the hospitality of their private security team once. You want to go there again?"

I knew I sure didn't.

"Everybody grab a computer and get to the car!" Cameron said.

Everybody grabbed a machine except for me. I grabbed Lucy instead, and we raced down to the parking garage and piled back into Cameron's Prius.

"Where are we going?" I asked.

"I don't know," Cameron said. "Away. Out of town."

"What happens now?" Miles wanted to know.

"You don't want to know. The markets crash. The price of gasoline drops."

"That's a good thing, right?" Miles asked. "Let's fill 'er up!"

"It's good up to a point," Cameron said. "PetroPlex will probably do something desperate to try to recover and prevent bankruptcy. I didn't intend to use this virus unless PetroPlex released my original program. The virus was designed to counteract the effects of the original program, not to destroy a functioning market."

"*Bankruptcy?*" Nash asked. He sounded skeptical.

"I don't think you understand the magnitude of what this thing will do. The financial markets are a very delicate balancing act that isn't that hard to disrupt."

Cameron peeled out of the parking garage. He drove fast—a little too fast. The buildings of downtown Dallas whipped past us.

"Dude!" Miles said. "Pedestrian!"

Cameron swerved around an idiot who was standing in the middle of Elm Street on the X that marked the spot where JFK had been assassinated. "Moron," he said, before pulling onto the freeway.

I was worried he was going to attract unwanted attention. I had an uneasy feeling in my chest.

"Slow it down some," I said. But it wasn't just Cameron's speed that was bothering me. All this stuff about the financial markets didn't make any sense. "If it's so easy to manipulate the energy market, how come someone hasn't done it already?"

"Who says they haven't?" Cameron asked. "Remember when the stock market lost a trillion dollars in a matter of minutes in May 2010 because of a computer glitch?"

I didn't, as I had long since pulled all the money I had in the stock market out and converted it to cash. And spent it. On Ramen. Ugh.

"I remember," Nash said.

"How is that possible?" Miles said. "I don't understand the financial markets."

Cameron eased his foot off the gas pedal some. "If you did, you'd be rich. If everybody knew what the people on Wall Street know, the country would look a whole lot different than it does today, I suspect."

"But you get it, right?" Miles asked. "Otherwise you couldn't have written the program."

"I know enough to be dangerous," Cameron said. "The energy market is a little different than the stock market. It works kind of like this. Oil is a commodity, right? So it's not traded on the stock market. It's historically been traded on the NYMEX, the New York Mercantile Exchange, which is the market where businesses buy and sell energy, metals and other commodities that people use every day. Trading is fast and furious. About a thousand transactions take place every minute. But when it comes to oil, the traders are not buying and selling actual oil. They are buying and selling contracts called futures contracts, which are agreements to accept delivery of oil in the future at a price set in the present."

"That sounds simple enough," Miles said.

I glanced at Nash. He was uneasily scanning the horizon, presumably looking for pursuers, cops, or anyone else we wanted to steer clear of.

Cameron glanced back at Miles. "It's not too complicated. It's basically just a bet on the future price of oil. Where it gets complicated is when all these other traders, called speculators, jump in. They're not interested in the actual oil. They're only interested in making bets on other people's bets. There are so many of them that less than one percent of crude oil and gasoline physically changes hands as a result of the buying and selling of all these contracts. The speculators could care less about the actual oil. They're just interested in betting on which direction the market will go. They buy the futures contracts intending to sell them before the actual oil gets delivered. They hope that if they bet right, they can cash out on the deal. Buy low, sell high. See?"

"I guess," Miles said.

"Theoretically," Cameron continued, "speculators are good for the market because they inject a lot of dough into it. A lot of cash keeps the market healthy. The problem is, excessive speculation can really inflate the price of oil. So if I release a program that makes it look like a lot of speculation is happening, the market would react and the price of oil would go up."

"Is that what your virus did?" I asked.

Cameron nodded. "Kind of. Only in reverse."

"All right," Nash said. "But the NYMEX is regulated by the government. Eventually they'll find the source of the computer program, you'll go to jail, and the market would correct itself. You're not worried about that at all?"

"Well, if the program were released on the NYMEX, that's probably true," Cameron said. "But remember, I said that oil futures contracts have *historically* been traded on the NYMEX. These days, fewer and fewer of them are actually traded there."

"What?" I asked. "Where else would they be traded? Not on the stock market."

"Cop," Nash said, pointing out a red and blue on the horizon.

"I'm slowing down," Cameron said. "Anyway, Chloe, you're right. They wouldn't be traded on the stock market, because that's regulated too. Think about this for a minute. Let's say you're one of the richest corporations in the world, and you feel like trading futures contracts on the NYMEX is good for your industry. But let's say you wanted a little more control over the trades without having to worry about a whole lot of regulation and government oversight. What would you do?"

"Establish a private market that isn't government-regulated," I said. "But that would require an act of Congress. It would be virtually impossible to pull off."

"Maybe for most people," Cameron said. "But not for Big Oil. Big Oil has deep pockets. George W. Bush has received more money in campaign contributions than any other political candidate in history. It got him the presidency, and some people have argued that in exchange, he went to war on Big Oil's behalf. According to certain other sources, the number two and three recipients of the most money paid in campaign contributions by Big Oil are Texas's very own senator Kay Bailey Hutchison and Senator Phil Graham."

"So you're saying Hutchison and Graham were bought?" I asked.

"Absolutely not. I'm just saying that it's naïve to think campaign contributions don't in some way inform the decisions politicians make—either directly or indirectly. Politicians naturally want to represent the interests of their constituents, especially if those constituents are in a position to help put them and keep them in office."

Behind me, Nash swore.

I caught a glimpse of red and blue flashing lights in Cameron's rear-view mirror. "I thought you slowed down!"

"I did!" Cameron said. "I'm not speeding!"

"What are we going to do?" I bit my lip. I didn't see how Nash could orchestrate some major getaway this time—not on a heavily populated freeway in broad daylight.

"Wait a minute," Nash said. "Don't panic."

Cameron's knuckles were white from gripping the wheel.

"Keep your speed steady," Nash said.

Cameron did.

Behind us, the cop car edged closer, then peeled around us and went after somebody else.

We all let out a collective exhale.

"I *hate* that!" Miles said.

He wasn't the only one.

"Yeah, that was close." Cameron relaxed his grip on the steering wheel a little. "Where were we? Oh yeah, senators and campaign funds. With that in mind, consider that in the year 2000, Phil Graham introduced a little law now referred to as "the Enron Loophole" into the Commodity Futures Modernization Act, which was signed into law by President Clinton."

"What's Enron got to do with the commodities exchange?" Nash wanted to know. "Or with oil, for that matter? Enron was not even an oil company."

"Hold your horses," Cameron said. "I'm about to tell you. The Enron Loophole is what made it possible for large corporations to establish private commodities exchanges."

"And trade any way they want without interference from government regulators!" Miles said triumphantly.

"Yep," Cameron said. "So today, thanks to the Enron Loophole, we have the Intercontinental Exchange, also known as the ICE—a private commodities trading market. Today, more oil futures contracts are traded on the ICE than are traded on the NYMEX."

"I've never even *heard* of the ICE," Nash said.

"And don't you think that's the way Big Oil wants it?" Cameron asked.

Wow. The enormity of what PetroPlex was involved in and able to pull off overwhelmed even me. I knew all about oil's toxicity and how many people it killed on a yearly basis. I knew about increased cancer rates and the rise of asthma. I knew about birth defects and minor spills, and major ones. But this? The creation and manipulation of completely private, totally unregulated energy markets? This was bigger than I'd ever even imagined.

Of course in a post Gulf-Oil Disaster environment, the whole world knew that oil was capable of ruining whole sections of the planet and killing not just wildlife, but people too. Even though I made a living railing against Big Oil, I had always kind of viewed oil as a necessary evil.

But in light of what I'd just learned, now Big Oil struck me as an evil more black than oil itself. The sheer size and money involved made them not only too big to fail, but too big to control. Instead, they were controlling us. They weren't just driving our economy and trying to influence government policy. They were controlling it. They were blatantly throwing money at political candidates who favored the policies they wanted and then sitting back and hoping for favors in return, thus corrupting—and potentially destroying—our whole system of democracy.

In light of those facts, all of a sudden it made sense to me why certain Texas political leaders were so strongly against government regulation. The party line was all about not letting government control invade private lives—but it was nothing but fear manipulation, all designed to distract the public and cause them to be blind to the real threat—the corporations whose vast amounts of money allowed them to pull the government's strings with the finesse of the most experienced puppeteers. Small government is one thing. But a government that's too small to control big business and protect its citizens is another. The implications for the future seemed ominous.

Cameron was thinking the same thing. "Yeah, we're on the run out of town now, but when you think about where this could lead and what it could mean for the country and the world, it kind of makes you want to pack up and head for the moon. Remember Enron? This loophole allowed Enron to create its own online energy futures exchange, which they did. Then from 2000-2002, their traders manipulated the energy markets and artificially inflated the price of energy on the West Coast. Since this whole exchange was unregulated, nobody knew what was going on until there were rolling blackouts, energy bills no one could afford to pay, school and business shutdowns, and deaths from heat exposure. Thousands of people lost their jobs, California's two largest utility companies declared bankruptcy, and the state lost billions of dollars. Meanwhile, Enron got rich at everyone else's expense."

"We have to do something," I said. "Can you imagine what would happen if trading on the ICE created the same situation, only this time with gasoline? People wouldn't be able to get to work. Businesses would shut down. Food wouldn't get delivered to grocery stores. There would be panic in the streets. Riots. Violence. Injuries."

"Right," Cameron said. "And no gas means no ambulances to take people to hospitals. And even if people still somehow managed to get there, it wouldn't be a safe environment. The hospitals wouldn't be able to get new sterile supplies, since many of those supplies are made out of plastic, which is made from crude oil. They wouldn't have the equipment they need to treat injuries. So people would be dying in the hospitals, starving on the streets, and shooting each other for gas or food. We are talking complete and total chaos and devastation caused by the unchecked greed of a few privileged people."

I groaned. "But what can we do to prevent this? Like you said, here we are on the run, with no resources and no plan. We are totally powerless!"

"We are not totally powerless," Cameron said. "We can collect evidence against them and release it to the press. We can make the public aware that there are flaws in the system that need to be corrected. We can demand campaign finance reform and push for stricter lobbyist controls. Nothing will ever change if the public doesn't rise up and take control of these core issues. Nothing else can guarantee the integrity of the system. That's why Schaeffer's and my press release was so important."

"Only now Schaeffer is dead," Nash said.

"Yeah," Cameron said, "which is a major problem for us because he was about to take delivery on a series of recorded conversations between PetroPlex executives that proved they were about to manipulate the markets and defraud the American people. Schaeffer had a connection with some inside guy at the Kettle refinery—a mole—I don't know who. The problem is, the recordings were all on analog audio tape from an old handheld recorder and weren't digital, so he couldn't email them to me. I sent him a cassette-to-digital converter, but he didn't know how to operate it, and neither did his inside guy, so he was going to ask you to show him how."

"Me?" I said, surprised.

"Yeah," Cameron said. "Apparently, he trusted you. But since you don't seem to know anything about the tapes, I guess he didn't get around to asking you yet."

"He didn't," I said. "Do you know where the tapes are?"

"Nope," Cameron said sheepishly. "I was kind of hoping *you* did, though."

Crap. I hadn't the first clue where the tapes were, obviously, and said so.

"Schaeffer may have gotten his hands on them before he died, or he may not have," Cameron said. "I don't know when the delivery was scheduled to take place. Without the tapes, I can't really prove the plot to manipulate the markets. I've hacked into the system and have been monitoring executive emails, but so far, no one has been stupid enough to put anything explicit in writing. They've been much more careful covering up evidence about the energy market plot than they ever were about safety violations."

That made sense. After all, the fines for safety violations were so negligible that they constituted a mere slap on the wrist. A global plot to manipulate the energy market and artificially drive up gasoline prices was a whole different ballpark, however.

I considered the implications of these missing tapes and what they meant for my case so far—or the shreds that were left of it. Apparently, it wasn't necessarily the paper files PetroPlex had been after. They could have been after something else entirely—namely, these tapes. Maybe they were worried about a transcript of the tapes? Or maybe they thought the tapes would be in the same place as the paper files.

So at last I knew what PetroPlex had been after and why my expert was dead. The question now was, what to do about it?

CHAPTER 24

We seemed to be in the clear and had all relaxed a little bit. Cameron flipped on the radio and surfed around for a news station. "Let's hope nothing's happening," he said.

"Like what?" Nash asked.

Cameron glanced back at him. "Did you not just see Miles release that virus?"

"It's not possible that something would have happened this quickly, is it?" Nash asked.

"Oh, it's possible," Cameron said. "The oil market is so volatile that if even one part of one refinery goes down for just a few minutes, the price of oil jumps up immediately. I've seen it jump six cents in a matter of minutes just because the Kettle PetroPlex refinery had a small malfunction that didn't take long to fix. I fixed it, in fact. It was a computer glitch."

"Six cents doesn't seem like a lot," Miles said.

"We are not talking about a change of six cents right now," Cameron said. "We are talking orders of magnitude beyond that. We are talking change in the order of magnitude similar to that computer glitch that dropped the stock market by a trillion dollars."

Nash was fishing Lucy off of Miles' lap so he could pet her. She seemed to be warming up to him a little. She licked his hand tentatively. "But this is good for consumers, right? For the little guy? Gas will be cheaper now, right? PetroPlex gas, anyway?

And since the virus is out, your original program won't work. Right?"

"Yes, but as I mentioned earlier, there are other things PetroPlex can do to combat the price drop."

"Like what?" I wanted to know.

"Like orchestrate a refinery failure, or worse, create a catastrophic explosion. Every time there's a refinery outage or an explosion, the price of oil goes back up and stays there until the problem is fixed. The reason it works this way is that American refineries run at 97% capacity. That means that when something goes wrong, there's not enough supply to meet demand. So the price jumps."

Cameron surfed past a station that was talking about PetroPlex.

"Wait!" I said. "Go back."

Cameron did. The radio DJ was reporting a twenty percent drop in gasoline prices and a market loss of 3000 points. And according to him, the numbers were steadily continuing to fall.

And then, there was more breaking news. "Wait," the DJ said. I'm now being told that an explosion rocked PetroPlex's largest oil refinery in Kettle, Texas, just moments ago. There are pictures coming in from eyewitnesses on the scene, but no official news media is on site yet. Our news copters are en route as we speak, and we hope to bring you more information shortly."

Nash, Miles, and I all exchanged stunned glances. "No," I said. "They wouldn't. It has to be a coincidence."

Only Cameron didn't seem shocked. He abruptly pulled the car over, fished out a laptop and opened it up. Then he popped in a mobile wireless card and waited for everything to come online. Miles and I watched silently while Nash nervously scanned our surroundings.

At first, all we saw was a white cursor on a black screen. Cameron began furiously typing a string of commands that looked like gibberish to me. Then before I knew it, he had pulled up a string of emails between PetroPlex executives. The word "explosion" was highlighted at various points in various messages. I inspected the dates and timestamps on all these emails. They were all real time.

"Hey, I know those names," I said. "Gerald Fitz—that's PetroPlex's regional president. He works out of the Kettle office. And Frederick Lewis—that's his VP of Quality Control. I deposed him last year."

"Fitz," Miles said. "Isn't that the guy who practically shut down the Dairy Queen a few months ago because the kitchen boy didn't put the right amount of candy in his daughter's Blizzard?"

"Yeah, that's him," Cameron said. Cameron screwed up his face and glared at all of us, preparing to do his best Fitz impression. "You call that a Blizzard?" he barked in a sandpapery voice. "Get out of my way, and I'll show you how to make a Blizzard!"

"Hey, that's pretty good!" I said. "You totally have him down! If I didn't know any better, I'd think you *were* him!"

Cameron shrugged and turned back to his computer screen. "Yeah, I used to do community theater."

I raised my eyebrows. This guy was full of surprises. Definitely not your run of the mill nerd.

Cameron executed another series of commands that appeared to bring up a string of emails all sent between the time Miles accidentally released the virus and the time of the explosion. One email in particular caught Cameron's eye, and he opened it full screen. It was from Gerald Fitz, and it was damning.

It was sent to Frederick Lewis and simply said, "Virus active. Light the fuse."

Wow. Cameron really *was* good. Perhaps it was possible we actually could accomplish something with a computer geek on our side.

"We need a plan," Nash said.

"We need the tapes," Cameron said.

We all looked at each other. There was only one place to go, and that was, unfortunately, straight back to Kettle.

CHAPTER 25

Delmont felt the blast from the refinery explosion and ran to the window in his chambers. He could see flames shooting high into the sky and a plume of black smoke billowing over the town.

He went back to his desk and furiously punched numbers into his phone.

As soon as the line connected, he started hollering. "What the hell just happened out there?

"Gilbert deployed the virus," said the voice on the other end.

"And the virus caused the explosion?"

"Not exactly. The virus was designed to dramatically drop the price of oil. Were you watching the financial tickers? There's no way we could have sustained that kind of a loss without suffering irreparable harm. We didn't have a choice."

"A choice about. . . wait a minute. Are you trying to tell me you blew up the refinery *on purpose?*"

"It was just a small explosion. Don't worry about it. We'll have it fixed in no time. In the meantime, fears about shortages will help stabilize market prices, and everyone will be okay."

"Listen, I don't like this," Delmont said. "You guys are really putting a strain on the system lately. I already gotta deal with the run-of-the-mill toxic torts cases that come through here, but now I got a dead guy on my hands, and you're also blowing yourselves up? How many injuries?"

"Minimal. I evacuated the area first."

"Are there *any* injuries? How many cases will I have to shut down now?"

"We're still waiting on preliminary reports."

Delmont swore. "This is getting old, you know. Real old. And I can only help you out so much without making people suspicious. How do you think it looks if thirty personal injury cases land on my desk and every single one of them gets thrown out? You better be ready to pay out some damages on at least some of the cases."

"Yeah, sure. Gotta make sure old Dick has enough money to ante up on Tuesday nights anyway."

"There's something about that guy that I don't trust."

"Don't worry about him. We've got him under control."

"You'd better," Delmont said.

He slammed the phone down on the receiver and turned back to the window to survey the damage.

CHAPTER 26

When Anna Delmont heard the explosion, she immediately jumped in the car and headed for town, which was located up on a hill and had the best view of the refinery. She never even considered the possibility that the explosion could have come from anywhere besides PetroPlex. There had been explosions in town before, and they all came from the same source.

She could see a number of her neighbors, also in their cars, driving hot on her tail. She dialed Joe Bob on his cell phone, but he didn't answer, which was irritating. It seemed like lately, he never answered her phone calls. This made it mighty hard for her to maintain her position as the go-to girl for all the town gossip. She didn't have any idea what was going on if her husband wouldn't give her the scoop.

Really, it was darn inconsiderate of him not to pick up the phone. After all, there had been an explosion! How could he be sure she hadn't been hurt in it? Didn't he care at all?

Anna gasped as a thought occurred to her. Maybe he wasn't picking up his phone because *he'd* been injured in the explosion. She dialed his cell again. Still no answer. Frantic, she called the courthouse clerk.

"Is Joe Bob in chambers?" she asked, her voice shaking slightly.

"Yes," the clerk said. "Everything's fine."

"Why isn't he picking up the phone?"

"Hold on," the clerk said, and presumably ducked around the corner to poke her head into Delmont's office. "I'm back. He's on the other line. The phone is ringing off the hook here. I'm sure he'll call you when he gets a chance."

Anna wasn't so sure about that. She thanked the clerk and hung up.

She pulled into the town square, along with a swarm of other rubberneckers who were dying to get a peek at the action without having to get too close to the source of the danger.

Although black smoke and flames shot from the refinery, most of the flames and smoke appeared to be coming from the safety flares that burned off excess chemicals if pressure in the system got too high. She could see a big, black hole in one of the walls, and smoke and flame belched from it periodically. For the most part, the firemen seemed to have the blaze under control already. This was definitely not the worst explosion she'd seen in this town. Most of the activity surrounding the refinery now was from paramedics, who were working to get injured people out of the building.

She looked around for familiar faces and spotted several of her lady friends. However, she didn't really want to talk to them because they'd be asking her for the details about what happened, and since Joe Bob hadn't bothered to call her back and fill her in, she didn't know. She hated feeling so out of the loop.

When she spotted Dick Richardson, though, she didn't hesitate to shove her way through the crowd toward him. After all, *he* might know something.

He was holding binoculars to his eyes, trying to catch sight of who they were bringing out of the refinery on stretchers.

She sidled up to him. "Hi, Dick," she said.

He barely gave her a second glance. Instead, he shoved the binoculars in her face. "Look through here. Is that Jason Wheedly they're pulling out of there?"

Anna took the binoculars and looked. She recognized the youth, who she knew from church, immediately. "Yep, that's him," she said. "Poor thing. He looks pretty tore up."

Dick nodded and wrote "Jason Wheedly" at the top of his notepad, along with a dollar sign and the notation "300-600k."

"Who else is coming out of there?" Dick asked.

He sounded frantic. Anna thought it was so nice of him to show such concern for his fellow citizens. She wished Joe Bob would sometimes act like he cared two cents about somebody besides himself. Maybe she should have married a man like Dick instead of marrying Joe Bob. Dick obviously had plenty of money and could have supported her in style, plus he seemed genuinely caring. Here he was, all worried about townspeople he didn't even know! It was a touching scene.

Anna peered through the binoculars again. "Why, that right there's Ellie Marvin's son."

"What's his name?" Dick asked eagerly.

"John," she said. "He's a nice boy. He married that lovely girl, Julie Carpenter from across the creek."

Dick grabbed the binoculars. "He looks pretty rough, too."

Anna watched him scrawl "John Marvin" on his scratch pad, along with some other numerical notations.

"Ain't you just the sweetest thing," she said to Dick.

"Oh yeah?" Dick said, the binoculars pressed once again to his face. "Why's that?"

"It's just so nice to see a man taking such an interest in the community. It's a wonder you're still single. I can't believe some woman hasn't already snatched you up."

Anna appraised Dick and thought that he might be a good match for her friend, Widow Schumacher. Widow Judy Schumacher was short, just like Dick, and she had a strong personality, too. Plus, she had expensive tastes, and Anna knew the widow's life insurance policy was darn near about to give out. It'd be good to get her hitched up to someone who could take care of her like Dick could. It seemed somehow unnatural for a man and a woman not to be enjoying the sanctity of marriage together when there was no reason to prevent it.

Dick kept dialing Chief Scott's number on the cell phone, but just like Joe Bob, Chief Scott wasn't answering.

"Do you know how all this happened?" Anna asked.

"I would if that good-for-nothing Chief Scott would pick up his gol-darned phone," Dick said. "Worthless S.O.B."

"Joe Bob ain't answering his phone either," Anna said.

"I'll bet he's not." Dick pressed the binoculars to his eyes again and squinted, forming little fleshy mounds around the eyepieces. "You know this guy?" He passed the binoculars to Anna again.

"Sure enough," Anna said, and filled him in on the details. They went through the binocular exchange routine a few more times, with Anna confirming the names of injury victims and Dick making notations.

Just then, Anna heard somebody calling her name.

Speak of the devil! She turned around to find Widow Schumacher waving at her. Anna motioned for her to come on over.

"How'd all this happen?" the widow's cheeks were flushed with all the excitement, and Anna decided that made her appear pretty attractive. It would be the perfect time to introduce her to Dick. And then who knew what might happen? They might fall in love and live happily ever after, just like she and Joe Bob had!

"I'm not sure yet," Anna said, "but this here's the man to tell you." She tugged on Dick's arm to get his attention. "Dick, this here's Judy Schumacher. I been meaning to introduce you two for some time."

This was obviously a lie, as the idea had just occurred to her, but it seemed like it wouldn't hurt anything if she'd said so. "Judy's a widow, so she's single just like you," Anna told Dick.

Dick glanced back over his shoulder at the refinery. "Is that so?" he said.

"I was thinking I might invite you two over for dinner with me and Joe Bob one night next week. How does that sound?"

Dick backed away. "I'd love to, he said, but my case load is about to get really busy."

"Well, what about right now?" Anna asked. "You're not doing anything but standing out here rubbernecking with the rest of us! Let's head over to Caliente and get acquainted."

"Sure, sure," Dick said. "It's just that I gotta get to the hospital." He cleared his throat. "Right now," he added. With that, he turned and fled.

Widow Schumacher looked flabbergasted.

"Oh, don't take it the wrong way," Anna said. "He's such a good man. You should have seen the way he was fussing over everyone who got carried out of there. For the life of me, I never seen a man who cared so much about the good of other people."

She'd set up a dinner later.

CHAPTER 27

Miles wanted to stop by his house to pick up some fresh clothes and his special designer shaving cream, but Cameron and Nash convinced him that probably wouldn't be a good idea.

In the end, we decided to set up shop in Gracie Miller's root cellar. Since my client was M.I.A. and probably wasn't returning any time soon, it seemed like as good a place as any. Plus, if she did unexpectedly return, I'd be able to deliver Dorian's settlement offer the minute she walked in the door.

Gracie had her root cellar pretty well equipped as a storm shelter. Canned food was stashed everywhere, and there were even cots for when hurricanes came through and spun off tornadoes. The door to the root cellar was hidden behind a wood shed and wasn't visible from the street. Anybody who might be looking for it would have to know it was there. The only reason *I* knew it was there was because Derrick had been working down there one day when he collapsed. Gracie had called the hospital, then she had called me.

We got electricity from an old generator Gracie had in the shed above-ground. Of course, Cameron knew how to turn it on and make sure it kept working. He set up his computer network, hacked into PetroPlex again, and we were back in business.

"Check this out," Cameron said, pulling up a string of documents that had my name scattered throughout. "PetroPlex was corresponding about you, which is why I thought you had the tapes."

I scanned the documents. *Chloe Taylor. . . evidence. . . Schaeffer. . . threat. . . recover. . . eliminate. . .* all words that didn't bode well for me.

"What about me?" Miles asked. "Anything about me?"

Cameron ran a quick and dirty search for Miles' name. Nothing came up. Then he ran a search for "Taylor's paralegal" and got all kinds of hits.

"Great," Miles said. "I never knew my name was 'Taylor's paralegal.' I feel like I have a whole new identity now."

I patted him on the back, jovially. "Look at it this way. At least you still have your house and your car."

"Yeah, but not my hair," he said. "I maybe would trade my house and car for my hair. Especially right now, seeing as how I'm not using either of them."

"Well, nobody's looking at your hair right now either except for us, and we like you anyway." I stuck my hand out and massaged his crown. "Even though you have that really weird bump right there that makes you look like a conehead."

Miles moaned. "Don't hate on the bump. That's brain in there. A big brain."

"I don't know," I said. "I think you might just be a bonehead." I punched him playfully in the arm, and he went over to lie on a cot and sulk. Lucy followed him and curled up on his stomach.

Nash was concerned with more important things. He leaned over Cameron, staring into his computer screen. "Can you pull up anything that might relate to the tapes?"

"I've been reading through stuff for days," Cameron said. "The amount of documents these guys generate on a daily basis would suffocate a horse. They know Schaeffer had something on them, but they're not sure what, and they don't seem to know about the tapes. I don't think they're aware of the mole or that any recordings were made at all."

"What makes you think that?" Nash asked.

"There are no hits on a search for 'recordings' or 'tapes,' and I've been reading all the executive level correspondence for weeks. I haven't noticed any kind of obscure references to any recordings of any kind. The only thing I can find is a few references to Schaeffer's files."

"Anything that specifically orders a recovery?" I asked.

"No," Cameron said. "But I didn't know about the connections with all the local officials until you guys told me your story today. The good news there is that PetroPlex uses a digital IP PBX phone system."

"Okay," I said, feeling like I should know what that meant, but again, I had no clue.

"That means I can hack into the phone system and retrieve the phone records," Cameron explained.

"Cool." Sounded good to me, even if I wasn't exactly sure how it worked.

Nash sat down in front of another computer. "Let me see if my login to the City of Kettle's system still works." He typed a few characters, paused, and typed some more. "Yep," he said. "They never were very good at staying on top of their computer network. Most of the guys at the department wouldn't know a computer from a hole in the ground."

"It could be a trap," Cameron said, alarmed. "They could be waiting for you to log in so they can trace your IP address."

"Trust me, not gonna happen," Nash said. "I've seen the way they operate down there, and it takes a week to get a new email account set up. They are simply not equipped."

Cameron didn't look so sure. "Just hurry up and log out as soon as you can. Maybe nobody will notice a little activity blip."

Nash did some fast typing, printed out a list of phone numbers, and logged off.

He handed the list to Cameron. "Here are the phone numbers for the mayor, the police chief, and Judge Joe Bob Delmont. We know for sure they are involved in some kind of local conspiracy. Can you cross reference them against PetroPlex's database?"

Cameron nodded eagerly and went to work. Before long, he had a list of times and dates pulled up. There were at least a hundred calls to and from Delmont and the refinery president in the last week. There were half as many to Mayor Fillion, and a handful to Chief Scott. The calls to Chief Scott were all placed within the last three days, which was interesting.

"Can you pull up the actual phone calls?" Nash asked.

Cameron shook his head. "I've already scanned for sound files and didn't find anything relevant."

"So how does this help us?" I asked. "From where I sit, all I can see is that we've confirmed what we already knew before— PetroPlex is dirty, and so are Delmont, Fillion, and Scott. So what? Now what? What about the mole? You said Schaeffer had an inside guy. Haven't your scans turned up anything on this guy or any other leads on the tapes at all?"

Cameron shook his head again. "No. As far as I can tell, PetroPlex is not aware they have a mole. And like I said, I'm not sure they know about the tapes either. I only know what I read on the network, so if they don't know, I don't know. "

"One more reason why Schaeffer was key," I said.

A snoring symphony wafted from the cot in the corner. Lucy and Miles were both sleeping up a storm.

"How can he sleep at a time like this?" Nash asked.

I shrugged. I couldn't say I blamed them. I knew I, for one, was plenty tired. "Losing hair is stressful," I said. "Maybe he just needed some rest."

"It'll grow back," Nash said. "It's not the end of the world."

"Yeah, but you're a straight guy," I said. "You wouldn't understand. Anyway, back to the problem at hand. To sum up, a bunch of people are dead, my house is gone, my car is destroyed, we're in hiding, and PetroPlex is hunting us all because they think we have something we don't. And to top it all off, there's no one to call for help, thanks to the APB our friendly local law enforcement put out. Where does that leave us?"

"With two options," Cameron said.

"Find the mole or find the tapes," Nash finished.

"Yep." Cameron leaned back from the computer, interlaced his fingers, and stretched his hands over his head. "That means some of us have to leave the hole." He looked pointedly at Nash and me.

"I'm not going back out there," I said.

Typically, I don't think of myself as a coward, but the thought of more car chases, more bullets, more potential torture, and more killings had me scared. I had already lost so much. I didn't want to lose the only things I had left—my health and my life. And if I never witnessed another shooting again, well, that would be okay with me, too.

I forced myself to ignore a wave of nausea as visions of the two men I had killed finagled themselves onto my mental movie screen. I wondered how long it would be before that particular film stopped showing in my mind.

Nash put his hand on my shoulder. "Chloe, we have to find the tapes. It's the only way forward. We can't stay in Gracie's root cellar forever."

"I can stay here and continue scanning the network," Cameron said. "Maybe something will turn up. In the meantime, it would be a good idea to go search Schaeffer's house. Maybe you'll find something."

"I don't know," I said. "I've been over it pretty thoroughly before and didn't find anything."

Nash's grip on my shoulder tightened.

"Hypothetically, I mean." I sighed.

"Hypothetically my arse," Nash said.

"So are you arresting me?" I looked up into his eyes. Instead of finding the usual unreadable mask, I saw something akin to affection. Or was that my imagination? My heart skipped a beat.

"Not today," he said.

"Well, that's something, I guess." I turned to look at Miles and Lucy sleeping on the cot. It was past 11:00 P.M. I would have given my right arm to sleep right now, too. It had been a very long twenty-four hours. "Should we wake them up?"

"No," Nash said, looking at his watch and yawning. "I think we can handle this one on our own."

CHAPTER 28

Under cover of darkness, we returned to Schaeffer's house. We parked around the block and walked through the alleyways to his back door. The house was still surrounded with crime scene tape. Schaeffer tried the doorknob.

"Locked." He stood still and looked at me.

"What are you looking at me for?" I asked.

"Haven't you got a key?" he said.

I shook my head.

He raised one eyebrow.

I sighed. "Gimme your credit card, and I'll see what I can do."

Nash rolled his eyes and pulled out his wallet, handing me a Visa Platinum. "That's my good card," he said. "Don't ruin it."

"I'll do my best."

Fortunately, once again, the police had only bothered to lock one of the myriad locks, so my picking job was relatively easy.

"Where did you learn how to do that?" Nash asked, once we were inside.

"Google," I said. "Where else? Don't you know how to do it?"

"Yes, but it was a lot more fun watching you try it." Nash took his credit card back from me and put it in his wallet. "Next you'll be making bombs, I suppose."

"Give me a little credit," I said. "I'm not really a bomb kind of girl."

"So what kind of girl are you?" In the darkness, he seemed even taller than usual, his muscular torso framed in the moonlight pooling the window.

"Lately, I'm not sure," I said. "I used to be the kind of girl who kicked butt and took names. These days. . ." I trailed off. What was I supposed to say? That I was scared? Vulnerable? Tired of fighting? If Nash admired my supposed strength, I didn't want to rob him of his illusion. I didn't want to give my true self away.

Nash stepped slowly towards me. His arms encircled my waist, and he pulled me close. "It's going to be okay, Chloe."

I felt the muscles in his torso flex as he gently rubbed my back. And his arms—his arms were so strong, so sure, so safe. I was so surprised, I let my hands hang limp by my sides for a few moments before I melted into him and grabbed him tight, hanging on for dear life. I needed a refuge so badly. A rock. An anchor. Something to hold on to when everything else was gone.

And I felt for him and the losses in his own life. I was so grateful that he'd come to Kettle and that he had somehow found it within himself to help me in my fight. Where would I be without him?

Either dead or sitting in Chief Scott's jail, that's where.

Against my will, a sob escaped from somewhere deep in my chest. "How do you know everything will be okay? How can you possibly say that?"

His hands found my hair and gently stroked it. "I have a feeling," he said.

"I didn't think you were a feelings kind of guy."

He let his fingers trace the contours of my cheek before wiping away an unwilled tear. "Oh, I have feelings." His voice sounded soft. Tender, even.

"I can never tell what you're thinking," I breathed. "I can never read you."

"No? Can you read this?" He tilted my chin up and his lips brushed mine—softly at first, then harder. I felt light and floaty. My lips moved in perfect rhythm with his while my hands explored the muscles in his back, shoulders, and arms.

Schaeffer's house and the tapes and PetroPlex seemed a million miles away. Nash was an island oasis of sanity in a sea of chaos, and I was content to shipwreck on his shore.

Nash pulled away.

I was breathless, left wanting more.

"I owe you an apology," Nash said.

"What for?"

"For the way I treated you when we first met."

"You were doing your job," I said.

"I was, but I was doing it rudely. I confess I had certain. . . preconceptions about you."

I ran my hand up and down the hollow in his chest. "Such as?"

"Such as thinking you were a greedy, shallow plaintiff's attorney who didn't care about anything but designer shoes and handbags and the next big win."

"And what do you think now?"

Nash touched his forehead to mine and stroked my cheek. He didn't answer verbally. Instead, he kissed me again, and waves of bliss flowed over my body. The sensation was everything I'd imagined before I'd passed out in front of my burning house—and then some. For the first time in a long time, I felt wholly and completely appreciated for the entirety of my body, brain, and soul. And when he kissed me, I felt as though it was more than a physical kiss. It felt as though his whole being joined mine, intertwined with my spirit, and sent our collective consciousness spiraling into the air in a joyful dance of freedom and joy, youth and optimism.

Nash broke away. "Are you okay?"

"Yes," I breathed. I was better than okay.

"Too fast?" he asked.

I shook my head. A little out of left field, yes, but not unappreciated.

"I just wanted to. . . do that now. . . in case. . ."

In case he didn't have the chance to do it at all. I lowered my face and pulled away. Suddenly, I was back in Schaeffer's house, and I was acutely aware of that fact.

Nash pulled me close again. "Not the ideal circumstances for a first kiss," Nash said. "I'm sorry."

"It would have been better with margaritas," I agreed.

Nash laughed. "And enough time for me to kiss you properly."

My heart fluttered.

"Well, maybe later," I said reluctantly. "For now. . . what? We didn't really come here with a plan."

Nash kissed me quickly one more time. "The plan is to look around. How did you find the file boxes the first time you were here?"

"Schaeffer had a false-bottomed drawer that he'd told me about. I opened it up and found an envelope with my name on it. It contained a piece of paper with a cryptic message, so I had to decipher it and follow the clues until I found the trigger that opened the secret wall."

Nash clicked on his flashlight and I followed suit. We went into Schaeffer's study, found *The Adventures of Sherlock Holmes*, and pushed the book in towards the wall. Just like before, there was a soft click and the shelf popped open.

We slid it back and walked into the now empty chamber.

"There's nothing here," I said.

"Are you sure?" Nash asked. "If I really wanted to hide something, I would double hide it."

"Like a hiding place in a hiding place?"

"Exactly."

"Makes sense to me," I said. "It's as good a place to start looking as any."

We began methodically shining our flashlights over the walls inside the hidden chamber, looking for anything that might indicate a chamber within a chamber. The walls were bare brick—the same that was used on the exterior of the house—so we had to search carefully for cracks and suspicious spots.

We were about halfway down the north side of the room without finding anything when we heard the soft click of a doorknob and the creak of a hinge. I froze.

Nash quickly slid the shelving unit almost closed. I knew he didn't want to shut it all the way because we didn't really see a lever we could press to get out once we were stuck on the inside. I shuddered. The implications of *that* ran through my head, and I imagined all kinds of sinister prisoner scenarios. I had to forcibly shut down those thoughts and attune myself to what was happening outside. I pressed my eyeball to the crack in the shelf and waited. Nash hovered over me, his eye also pressed to the door.

It wasn't long before a swimming ball of light bobbed into view and started hopping around the room. When my eyes adjusted and I could finally see who was holding the flashlight, I couldn't believe who I saw.

The very sight of him made me *livid*.

Unafraid—perhaps stupidly so—I swung open the bookcase and flipped on the overhead light. Nash swore under his breath, but stayed hidden.

"Dorian Saks!" I said. "What the *hell!*"

Dorian Blinked in the light. "Chloe? Chloe!" He rushed towards me and enveloped me in that same old, familiar embrace. "I can't believe it! I thought you were—"

He didn't bother to tell me what he thought I was. Instead, his lips clamped on to mine in a savage, hungry greeting. And Nash was watching from the shadows. Oh boy.

I shoved him away, but he was like a leech, back on me, refusing to let go. I struggled against him as he poured out what were apparently great feelings of relief.

"I heard about your house, and then you were gone, and I kept trying to call you, to call your office! And nobody knew where you were! And I just thought, *I can't lose her again!*"

"Again!" I said. "You never got me back, you moron! Let me go!"

Dorian let go of my body and gripped my face in his palms, his eyes boring into mine. "What's wrong? The other day at Caliente—"

"You slapped me in the face with an offer I couldn't refuse!" I said.

"I was trying to take care of you, Chloe. I know it can't have been easy down here. Do you think anyone else would have offered you as much?"

I shoved his hands away. The *nerve* of this guy! And the *timing!* Ugh! I could only imagine what must be going through Nash's mind. "The offer was laughable, and you know it," I said.

"You always were a fiery little redhead. It's what I love about you. There's no one else in the world like you."

Dorian's eyes appeared to mist up so that they glistened slightly. If I hadn't known he possessed the ability to create this effect at will in front of juries, I might have been slightly swayed.

"Come home with me," he said. "I've missed you too much."

"You are out of your ever-loving mind if you think I'm going anywhere with you!"

"Why the sudden change of heart?" Dorian asked earnestly. "The other day at Caliente, I could tell your feelings were still there. I came over the next day to talk to you, but your house was burnt to a crisp and Dick had no idea where you were. I've been frantic ever since."

He embraced me again, forcing his lips on mine.

What was once familiar and comforting was now repulsive. How could I have ever even thought *twice* about taking this guy back? The energy I felt from Dorian was a completely different kind of energy than I felt from Nash.

Dorian was powerful and strong, but in a self-centered, egotistical sort of way. He would always be looking for better deals and greener pastures. Nash felt powerful and strong to me, but more selfless. More of just everything that was right and in tune with the universe.

Also, the thing about Dorian was, he was such a good liar that even now, I didn't know if he was really relieved to see me or just playing off the fact that he got caught snooping around somewhere he clearly shouldn't be. Maybe he really was relieved to see me. But maybe the whole "come home with me" routine was just a ploy to get me to leave with him so he could deliver me to PetroPlex. That would seem incredibly evil, even for Dorian, but the thing is, with him, you just never knew. Above all else, he loved money, and if the price were right. . .

I twisted my neck away from Dorian's face. "Nash!" I said. "What are you waiting for? Get him off me! Cuff him to something."

Dorian looked up, surprised.

Nash launched himself out of the hidden chamber and tackled Dorian, wrestling him to the ground.

"Who are *you?*" Dorian got his arm free and delivered a punch. Nash caught the punch and expertly twisted Dorian's arm back down. "Jensen Nash."

Dorian grunted under Nash's weight. "The cop?"

Nash rolled him over and cuffed his hands behind his back. "Detective."

Suddenly, Dorian was all smiles. "Oh, I apologize, officer. Thank goodness you're around. I don't know what I'd do if Chloe got hurt."

Nash rolled him over roughly and dragged him towards Schaeffer's heavy wooden desk.

"Dorian, *shut up*," I said.

Nash pulled out a second set of cuffs and double-cuffed him to the desk leg. Then he pulled Dorian's cell phone out of its holster and threw it against the wall so that it broke.

The desk leg was thicker in the middle than on both ends, which meant Dorian couldn't slide the cuff down to the bottom and underneath to get free. He'd have to pull the entire leg off the desk if he wanted to get away, and it was a pretty sturdy leg.

I turned towards Nash to thank him, but he refused to look at me.

My heart sank. I would have a lot of explaining to do here shortly, I was pretty sure.

Dorian. Trust him to show up at the worst possible time and ruin everything. Always.

"What are you doing here?" I demanded of Dorian.

"Trying to find you!" he said.

I resisted the urge to slap him. "You are *such* a liar. Did PetroPlex put you up to this, or are you just free-agenting, hoping to make a buck?"

"I don't know what you're talking about," he said.

"You know the rest of Schaeffer's files were burned to a crisp in my house, right? They're not here anymore."

"Schaeffer's files? What?"

"Oh come off it," I said.

"Chloe, I swear. I was here looking for you. God knows I couldn't get any cops in this town to do it for me. This town is the most backward place I've ever been in my life. I don't know how you've managed down here for so long."

"Why would you be looking for me *here?*"

"I didn't know where else to look. I'd already been to your office and to your paralegal's house and everywhere else in town. There's not many other places to look. Kettle's not that big, you know. I figured that since you spent a lot of time here, maybe I could find something that might give me a clue where you were."

I wasn't sure whether to buy it. He *sounded* sincere, but he *always* sounded sincere. It's what made him so good in front of a jury. He wouldn't be near as rich as he was if he also wasn't such a slick actor. I didn't know what to do.

I looked at Nash, who was still steadily not looking at me. I grabbed his arm and pulled him into the hallway.

"I don't know what to do," I whispered.

"Me neither," Nash said, still not meeting my eye. "Listen, about earlier—"

"No!" I said quickly. "No! "

"—I rushed into things. I barely know you. It was too early. My wife is still fresh for me, Dorian is obviously still fresh for you—"

I pulled his face square with mine. "Look at me!"

He looked.

"Dorian is ancient history. You can't believe anything he says. He is the world's smoothest liar."

"And how do I know you're not? You're a lawyer too, after all."

My heart started beating fast—too fast. "What? *What!* Are you serious? I have been to hell and back with you over the last two days! After everything that's happened, how can you even say something like that!"

"The guy seems pretty sincere. And you *were* engaged to him, after all."

"How did you know that?"

"Dorian Saks, right? Miles told me not to ask, remember?"

That seemed like ages ago. Wow, this guy didn't miss a thing. "Listen to me. The reason I broke up with him is because he was cheating with his secretary and no telling how many other women and lying about it. He is a trial attorney. He's an amazing actor. He has a gift for making you believe everything he says, but you can't. *You* can't. You just can't, okay?"

"We'll see," Nash said maddeningly.

"I'm telling you, I don't know why he's here," I said. "So we have a problem. If he's here on behalf of PetroPlex, we could give too much information away by continuing our search. We'd have to do it in front of him. It's not like we can call the cops to come get him. And as tempting as it would be for me to kill him right now, I'm just really not that kind of girl."

"But if we don't finish the search and leave him here, then he gets loose and maybe finds the tapes before we do."

"If he knows they exist," I said.

"Do you think he does?"

"I don't know what to think. But I wouldn't put it past him. The question is, do we risk letting him know we're looking for something important? What if we don't find them? What if Schaeffer didn't even have them yet?"

"I could interrogate him to try to figure out what he knows," Nash said.

"Trust me, you'd be wasting your time." I sighed. Goodness knows I'd tried every interrogation tactic in the book on him previously for personal reasons. "You've got no leverage, and he's a professional prevaricator. We'd be here all night and none the wiser by morning."

"I don't see how we have any choice but to finish the search."

"Okay," I whispered. "Let's see if we can find something to blindfold him, at least, in case we do find the tapes."

I crept into Schaeffer's bedroom and pulled a t-shirt out of his closet. I felt like I was violating some kind of unwritten rule, crossing some kind of line in rummaging through a dead man's bedroom, but necessity ruled.

We went back to Schaeffer's office and tied the shirt over Dorian's eyes.

"Come on, Chloe," Dorian said. "What is this? What are you doing here, anyway?"

"Working on my case," I said. "You think I'm going to let you beat me at summary judgment next week?

"After all that's happened, you're still worried about the *case?*" Dorian asked.

"Why? Should I be worried about something else?"

"I just thought. . . well, with Schaeffer dead, and your house burned down, and your client gone—"

"How do you know Gracie's gone?" I said quickly.

"Well, you didn't get back to me about the offer, did you?"

"And you went by her house, I'm guessing."

"I did, but—"

"That is a violation of ethics," I said. "Opposing counsel is not supposed to ever speak to the other side's client directly if that client also has an attorney. And you know what else is a violation of ethics? Snooping around in my expert witness's house for no good reason."

"I had a good reason, and you know it."

"What I know is that you weren't actually looking for me, so enlighten me. Please."

Nash and I had walked back over to the hidden chamber and continued our search of the walls. We found a few suspicious cracks, but no bricks that moved or came out of the wall, or pushed in and triggered any other hidden switches.

"What other reason could I possibly have for being here?" Dorian asked.

This was one of Dorian's signature tricks. He asked a question that seemed innocent but was really designed to get you to give away your position. I wasn't about to fall for it.

"You tell me," I said.

Dorian didn't say anything for a minute. Nash and I finished our search of the chamber without finding anything.

"Where to next?" he whispered.

"Desk," I said.

We went to the desk and started looking. Dorian squirmed as I pushed and pulled him in different directions to get the drawers out of the body of the desk.

"What are you looking for?" Dorian wanted to know.

"A jump drive," I lied. "It had Schaeffer's expert report on it, and I need it to retain another witness. Which, I might add, I'm having an awfully hard time doing in a week, especially under the circumstances. How about a Rule Eleven agreement for a continuance?"

"Why bother with that?" Dorian said. "Just take the settlement offer."

"I can't do that without a client, and you know it."

Nash paused in sorting through the contents of his drawer and looked up. "Are you two seriously negotiating the case right now?"

"Way I like it," I said. "If only I could always negotiate with opposing counsel tied up and blindfolded. It would make getting a settlement a lot easier."

"I didn't know you were kinky like that," Dorian said. "How come you never told me?"

"Shut up," I said. "You know what I meant. You want to agree to a continuance, or not?"

"If I do, will you uncuff me?" Dorian asked.

"Maybe, but I wouldn't count on it."

I had been through three drawers and found no more false bottoms, no tapes, no mysterious messages, no nothing. Nash looked like he was in about the same shape. We moved back to the bookshelf and started looking behind books. We also randomly opened some and paged through, hoping to find some pieces of paper lodged in there, or a secret hole cut in the paper, or something.

Who were we kidding? There must be hundreds, maybe thousands of books on these shelves, which spanned the whole length of the wall. And the rest of the house was large and equally full of stuff. We couldn't possibly hope to do a thorough search in the time we had with Dorian in the way.

I could tell by the look on Nash's face that he was probably thinking the same thing. Nevertheless, we plowed through.

"As a gesture of good faith, I agree to a continuance," Dorian said. "Do you think a month will be long enough for you to find your client and make the settlement offer?"

"I don't know," I said. "I don't know where she went."

"Well, I agree to a month."

"That's fine," I said. "I agree that if I find her, I'll tell her you made a ridiculous offer and counsel her to refuse it."

Dorian shifted positions by the desk. "Okay, Chloe. Time to get real. This little verbal sparring match has been fun and all, but let's be frank. You don't really have a leg to stand on in this case. You don't even have an expert witness. In fact, right now, you don't even have a client. If she never comes back, I can have the case dismissed for lack of prosecution."

"Is that a threat?" I asked, still paging frantically through the books on the shelf.

"If you're asking me if I'll file the motion, absolutely. It's just business."

"And what if your client just offs her, instead. Wouldn't that be much easier?"

"Now you're being ridiculous." Dorian shifted positions again. I could tell he was getting uncomfortable—physically, if not mentally.

"Am I?" I asked. "I think you know better than that."

"I'm not sure what you're implying," he said, "but I don't like the sound of it. It sounds like a defamation suit to me."

"Another threat?" I asked. "You're really working hard to get me to come back home with you now, aren't you?"

"At this point, I think it seems safe to say that's not going to happen," Dorian said. "If you were just looking for a jump drive with an expert report on it, you wouldn't have me cuffed to the desk and blindfolded, would you?"

Nash abruptly slammed the book he was paging through back into the shelf, and Dorian jumped when he heard the sound. Good. I was glad Dorian was jumpy.

Nash moved over to the sofa cushions. I headed to the fireplace and lifted an iron shovel from the rack. Instead of bashing Dorian's head in, which felt like an attractive option for me at the moment, I opted to poke through some very old ashes from last winter.

"If you were really looking for *me*," I said to Dorian, "*you* wouldn't be here in the middle of the night, would you?"

Dorian sighed and shifted positions again. "What did Schaeffer have?"

So he really was wise to the situation after all. I was glad I hadn't expected any less.

"What do you mean?" I stalled.

"Do me a favor. You cut the crap, and I will too. I know you're here looking for it, just like everyone else has been. This place is like Grand Central Station. You're lucky it was me here tonight instead of someone else. Unlike Delmont and the rest of them, I really do care about you."

"I don't for one second believe you give two cents about me, but how nice of you to stop pretending you have no idea what's going on."

I found nothing in the ashes and cast around for somewhere else to look instead. I settled on the piano and started with the bench. Nash had moved on to the chairs. I took comfort in the fact that Dorian had referred to the object of our search as 'it,' rather than 'them.' Maybe that meant he wasn't sure exactly what he was looking for.

"I know Delmont is in PetroPlex's pocket," Dorian said. "But I'm sure that was obvious even to you."

"I am so flattered by your estimation of my intelligence," I said sourly.

"And I know Schaeffer had something on PetroPlex. But I don't know what it was."

"Then what are you doing here?" I asked, moving on to search the piano's plate and fallboard.

"Hoping to find out," he said. "I don't like the emotional tenor at the refinery. Something has clearly gotten my client upset, but they're not talking about it. I can't adequately represent them if I'm not fully aware of what I'm dealing with."

"Oh, so you're just doing your job," I said. "Going above and beyond."

"It's the client of my career," Dorian said. "They can make me rich."

"You're already rich."

"Okay, richer," he said. "There's no such thing as too rich."

"Yeah, there is actually," I said. "When you're so rich you can turn the government into your own personal marionette, that's too rich."

"That's capitalism."

"Yes, but *democracy* is better. What good is unchecked capitalism if it threatens democracy? There have to be checks and balances."

"So you're a socialist now?" Dorian asked.

"Nope," I said. "I'm a moderate. In all things moderation. I know you're not too familiar with the Good Book, but that's actually Biblical, you know."

The piano was clean. Nash had finished searching the chairs.

"Now what?" Nash said.

"I'll take the bedrooms, you take the kitchen."

Nash nodded and headed for the hallway.

"By the way," I said to Dorian, "I know you're dedicated to your career, but I still think you know more than you're letting on."

"Which implies that you do too."

"Get comfortable," I said. "You're in for a long night. Maybe the crime scene techs will let you out in the morning."

I slammed the door behind me. Dorian didn't even bother to call after me. He knew better.

Our search of the rest of the house turned up nothing.

Not knowing what else to do, we left Dorian there and headed back to Gracie's root cellar.

CHAPTER 29

I tried repeatedly to start up a conversation with Nash on the way back to the root cellar, but Nash refused to bite. He met my attempts at friendly chatter with stonewall silence.

"Okay, can we talk about this?" I finally asked.

"What's to talk about?"

"What's *not* to talk about? Listen, about Dorian. . ."

"Don't worry about it," Nash said. "Like I said, I can see that Dorian is still fresh for you. I shouldn't have. . . done what I did."

"Arrrgh!" I said. "Dorian is *not* fresh. Dorian is two years ago."

"You're still angry, which means it's fresh."

"You know what makes me angry? Do you? You! You make me angry! Who are you to tell me how I feel? You have *no idea* what's going on inside my head! How dare you think you know everything there is to know about me! How dare you say the things you just said and do the things you just did and back off immediately! You have no right to jerk me around like that!"

"I'm sorry," he said. "Maybe if you had made it clear that you were still emotionally involved with your ex—"

"I'm not! Why can't you understand that?"

"He kissed you. He seemed to think he had the right to do it. Why would he act that way without a reason?"

"He had a reason," I said. "He thought he could cover the fact that he was up to no good by pretending he still cared about me. That's all you saw."

"That's not what it looked like."

"I don't care what it looked like! I'm telling you what it *was!*"

"Well, what about me?" Nash asked. "Maybe *I'm* not ready. Did you ever think of that?"

"*You're* the one who kissed *me*. I didn't kiss you. So don't go making this all my fault when you're the one who started it."

Nash said nothing.

I felt bad for snapping at him, but seriously. This was not my fault. If he hadn't been ready, he should never have rushed it. I wouldn't have pushed him, as much as I might have wanted to.

I was starting to think that maybe he had trust issues, thanks to his past. Like, maybe having been driven from his home town by corruption only to find himself in the midst of even more corruption, he had a hard time believing that anyone's motives could be pure and good—even mine. Maybe he felt that if he let his guard down for one second, he'd be burned again. That seemed possible.

"You can *trust* me," I said.

Nash still said nothing.

"For real, it's okay," I said.

I looked over at him. He didn't turn his head. He refused to respond.

"You have to talk to me some time, you know. It's going to be a rotten day in the root cellar otherwise."

I saw a muscle in his jaw clench, but other than that, I got no response.

Despite further attempts to get him to talk, he gave me the silent treatment all the way back to Gracie's.

When we crawled down the stairway, I tried to bury my feelings of frustration and appear cheerful. I called out, "Lucy! I'm home!"

Miles' voice came back to me with a Cuban accent. "You've got some 'splainin to do!"

Lucy launched herself at me, tail wagging, tongue hanging out. She bucked up and down, happy to see me. I scooped her up and gave her a kiss.

"How could you go off and leave me like that?" Miles said.

"You wanted to come?" I asked. "I thought you wanted to get your beauty rest."

"Of course I didn't want to go," Miles said. "But you might have at least said goodbye. These days, who knows if you're ever coming back?"

"Nice," I said. "Thanks for reminding me."

"Did you find the tapes?" Cameron wanted to know.

"No," I said. "We looked everywhere and couldn't find a thing."

Miles was looking Nash and his sour expression up and down. "Geez, whatsamatter with *you?*" he asked.

"Nothing," Nash said.

"We ran into Dorian at Schaeffer's house, and now Nash is all pissed off and giving me the silent treatment." I put Lucy down and she ran back over to Miles.

"*Ooooooooooooooohhhhhh,*" said Miles knowingly.

Nash rolled his eyes.

I filled them both in on the situation at Schaeffer's and turned to Cameron. "Did you have any luck back here?"

"Actually, I think I found something," Cameron said.

"What have you got?" Nash asked.

"I found an email from Gerald Fitz to Mayor Fillion expressing concerns about the loyalty of his VP."

"Lewis?" I asked.

"Yeah," Cameron said, excitedly. "Think about it. If the insider were Frederick Lewis, he would have more access to Fitz than anyone else at the company. It would have been easy for him to make recordings of private conversations. It fits."

"So what do we do about it?" I asked.

"We talk to him," Nash said.

"Wow," I said. "Are you sure you're capable of doing that? I mean, it involves actual *speech* and all." I knew I shouldn't have been so acerbic, but I was really tired and the filters on my mouth weren't operating at maximum capacity.

Nash ignored me. "I say we all get some sleep and see if we can catch him at his house before he leaves for work in the morning."

Mister big man. Laying down the plan. Ordinarily, I might not have been irritated, but now, I was. "Who says you get to make all the rules?" I asked. "Who says me and Miles and Cameron don't get a say?"

"Rawrrr," Miles said, making a cat noise and holding up claws. "Somebody needs a nap."

Cameron's eyebrows raised at this exchange, but he didn't say anything.

"Okay, Chloe," Nash said patronizingly. "What would *you* like to do?"

I really didn't have a better plan. "I say we go catch him at his house before he leaves for work in the morning and see if he'll talk to us."

Nash sighed. "Fine," he said. "That's just fine with me."

With that, he stalked over to a cot and went to sleep.

***

In the morning, Miles refused to get up. He lifted one eyelid, muttered something about the dangers of sleep deficits, and said "goodbye." That was it. So I figured he wasn't going.

Cameron was still monitoring data, looking for anything else that might be helpful. Nobody thought that one person should go to Lewis's house alone, so that left me and Nash, together alone again.

We pulled up to our destination at 6:30 A.M.

Frederick Lewis lived in one of the biggest houses in Kettle—an old Victorian-style mansion with white lace trim on country blue siding and a perfectly manicured lawn. It was set in the middle of a massive estate, surrounded by acres and acres of land. No neighbors. What a luxury *that* would be! A covered patio surrounded the entire house, and the patio itself was surrounded by magnificent rose bushes that were all in bloom.

I inhaled deeply. I loved the scent of roses. They were by far my favorite flower. So romantic. The very thought of romance brought back all the memories from the night before, and I glared at Nash.

"What?" he asked.

I just turned away. Two could play the silent treatment game.

I had borrowed some clothes from Gracie's closet this morning. They were way too big and much frumpier than I would have preferred, but I had been wearing the black suit pants and purple cami for two days, and they were starting to reek.

Standing in front of the door, Nash spun me around and felt for the gun tucked into my pants at the small of my back.

"Safety's off," he said, shortly. "Heads up."

I nodded.

He checked his own weapon and rang the doorbell.

We waited, but no one answered.

We knocked, and waited some more, then knocked louder and waited again.

Finally, Lewis answered the door. He was unshaven and in his bathrobe. His eyes widened when he saw me.

"Chloe! Wow! Come in." I took this as a good sign and shot Nash a glance to communicate my feelings about it.

We walked in and let Lewis lead us to a plush, Victorian-styled living room with ornate chairs, velvet drapes, and everything—obviously styled with a woman's touch. And yet, I didn't hear anyone else in the house.

"Who is your friend?" Lewis asked.

Nash extended his arm for a handshake. "Detective Jensen Nash."

"Oh yes," Lewis said. "I know you by reputation, of course. I'm afraid my wife is out of town visiting her mother, otherwise there would be coffee ready."

"We're fine," I said.

"Good, good," Lewis said. "Glad to hear it. That you're okay, in general, I mean."

Nash frowned. Lewis seemed a little nervous, but that didn't strike me as unnatural under the circumstances. It was very early in the morning, and we had surprised him, after all.

"So what brings you here this morning?" Lewis asked.

Nash started to say something, but I put my hand on his knee, letting him know I'd handle it.

"I think you know," I said.

"Yes, well, if it's about the case, Dorian has full authority to—"

"It's not about the case," I said. "Well, kind of, it is, I guess."

"Schaeffer's info. . ." Lewis said uncertainly.

"Yes. We know about his inside guy and the tapes. It's okay. We're on your side and here to help."

"Chloe—" Nash said.

Lewis cut him off. "Right. The tapes. I have the tapes."

I let out a big sigh of relief. "Thank goodness."

"Do you know what's on them?" Lewis asked.

"Chloe," Nash started again, but I waved him off.

"No," I said. "Your guys killed Schaeffer before he could even tell me about them."

"My guys?"

"Well, not *your* guys, obviously, but PetroPlex. The bad guys. Once we get the tapes to Cameron, he'll be able to get them converted to digital and distributed to the press, and then we can all get the heck out of Dodge."

"Cameron Gilbert?" Lewis asked. "You're working with him?"

I nodded.

Lewis let out a low whistle. "That guy is a computer *genius*," he said.

"I know."

"Did he mean to unleash the virus? Do you know how many problems that caused?"

"No, that was an accident," I said, "and it wasn't Cameron's fault. I'm sorry if it put you in any hot water."

Nash jumped in again. "Chloe, we need to talk. Outside. Now."

I continued to ignore him. Heh. This silent treatment thing was totally working for me. We'd just see how much *he* liked it.

Lewis swallowed. "No hot water," he said hurriedly. "Did anyone see you come here?"

"No," I said. "It's so early. Nobody was out."

Lewis nodded. "Okay," he said. "Why don't I go upstairs and get the tapes for you so you can get out of here before anyone notices. I'll just be right back."

Lewis disappeared up an ornate staircase.

"Are you out of your mind?" Nash whispered. "Have you got any idea how much information you just gave away?"

I debated about whether or not to answer him. In the end, I decided that right now, defending myself was more important than continuing to play some childish game. "You have to give information to get it," I whispered back. "And besides that, he's got the tapes. It all worked out. We got what we wanted."

At that moment, a little red laser dot appeared right in the middle of Nash's forehead.

I groaned.

"What?" Nash asked. "Have I got something on my face?"

Without moving my head, I shifted my eyes towards the staircase. Nash followed suit.

"Chloe Taylor," Nash said. "You talk *way* too much. From now on, I'll do all the talking."

"Well, wouldn't that be a refreshing change," I said.

"Stand up slowly," Lewis said from the staircase.

We complied. "Slowly take out your weapons and put them on the ground in front of you."

"We're unarmed," Nash said.

"Give me a break," Lewis said. "This is Texas. Guns out, or I shoot first and ask questions later."

Nash slowly pulled his gun out of his jacket and put it on the carpet in front of him.

"Chloe, you're next," Lewis said. "Move slowly, or I shoot your boyfriend."

"He's *not* my boyfriend," I said, inching my right arm around to the small of my back. I pulled out my gun and put it on the ground in front of me, then returned to the standard hands-up, don't shoot position.

"Kick the guns behind you."

We did.

"Now Chloe," Lewis said. "I want you to take the detective's handcuffs and cuff him to the stair railing over here. Then I want you to take his second set and handcuff yourself also."

I sighed. "He doesn't have any handcuffs," I said.

The laser dot moved an inch to the left of Nash's face, and Lewis fired.

"Do it!" he said. "Or you're both dead!"

"No handcuffs, I swear!" I said, eyes shut. "We kind of left them on Dorian Saks last night. He's stuck at Schaeffer's house right now."

Lewis fired his gun again. This time, Nash flinched.

"What have you got to gain by shooting us?" Nash said. "Thanks to Chloe and her big mouth here, it should be pretty obvious by now that we've got nothing on you or your company. You shoot us, then you have to deal with two bodies, a lot of blood, stains on the carpet. Your wife'll be mad, and the police will be tromping all through your house, and it'll just be a big hassle. Plus, what if they try you for murder? You let us go now, and you don't have to worry about any of that."

"I can't take that risk," Lewis said. "If Schaeffer had a mole, and the mole finds you, things could get ugly."

"That's a big if," I said. "We have no idea who the mole might be, if he even really exists at all. All we have is Schaeffer's word on that."

"You could be lying."

"Of *course* we're not lying," Nash said. "If we had any idea who the mole actually was, we certainly wouldn't be *here*. You know we thought you were the mole. Look, it ought to be pretty obvious to you by now that we are no threat."

Lewis didn't look so sure. Holding his gun steady in one hand, he pulled an iPhone out of the pocket of his robe and speed dialed someone. The call connected.

"Hey, I know it's early," he said into the phone, "but you'll never guess who turned up on my doorstep this morning." A pause. "Chloe Taylor and Cop Nash. Yeah, they think I'm some kind of company mole and that I have some tapes that Schaeffer was going to use as evidence against us. Large scale press release. They're working with Gilbert."

Another pause. "I know," he said. "It's Gilbert that's the most dangerous." Another pause. "Okay, when I find him, I'll let you know."

Lewis hung up.

I grasped at straws. "They don't trust you, you know," I said. "Cameron intercepted an email from Fitz that questioned your loyalty."

"Chloe," Nash said. "Shut *up*."

"That is why I am going to make you take me to Cameron Gilbert so I can get rid of him."

"We're not taking you to Gilbert," Nash said.

"You are," Lewis said, and just like that, he shot Nash in the foot.

Nash crumpled to the ground.

"Stop! Stop!" I fell to the ground beside Nash, pulling off his shoe and trying to staunch the flow of blood.

Crap! This was all my fault! I was tired. Despite the few hours of sleep I'd had last night, I felt like I hadn't slept in days.

I just hadn't been thinking straight. I thought I had seen an end in sight and rushed in way too fast. I should have been more careful.

It looked like Lewis had hit the very end of Nash's big toe—a flesh wound. That was better than if he'd shattered some bones, but even under the circumstances, I knew Nash had to be in tremendous pain.

"Help him up," Lewis said. "Get him to the car, or his kneecap is next. After that, it's *your* foot. Then your knee. And so on."

Nash was apparently unwilling to risk any more gunshots. "Car," he said, throwing his arm around my shoulder. "Now."

"But Nash—"

"Trust me," he said.

Well, that was a tall order coming from someone who clearly had trust issues that he was taking out on little ol' me. But what choice did I have? I grabbed his arm and helped him up.

Together, we did a kind of three-legged limp towards the front door and out to the car. Lewis grabbed a roll of gardening twine from the front porch, and once we were at the car, he ordered me to tie Nash's hands behind his back. I did so, trying to keep the knots loose.

Lewis checked the knots and tightened them up, all the while keeping his gun's laser sight trained on me.

Once he was satisfied with the knots, he waved the gun towards the driver's seat. "Drive," he told me.

I got behind the wheel, and Lewis got in the seat behind me, holding the gun to my head.

"Where do I go?" I whispered to Nash.

"I can *hear* you, you know," Lewis said.

"Take him to Cameron," Nash said.

"Really?" I asked.

"Yes, really," Nash said.

Lewis pressed the gun into my head even harder.

I turned the key in the ignition and put the car in gear, heading towards town, not towards Gracie's root cellar. Surely Nash didn't *really* mean take him to Cameron. I wondered how long I could keep up the deception before Lewis got suspicious. Did he have a whole lot of experience with this whole hostage driving thing? Surely not, I hoped.

I had only gone a couple of miles when I noticed that someone was following us. It was a black car with heavily tinted windows. Impossible to see who was inside.

"Where are we going?" Lewis demanded.

"To Cameron," I said. "Like you want."

"Where is that?"

I had a feeling there was going to be one heck of a gun bruise on my scalp if I lived to tell about it.

"Ease off the barrel, will you? You're giving me a headache. "

Lewis eased off the pressure, but only a little. "Tell me where we're going, or Nash gets it in the knee. Right here in the car."

I swallowed hard. "My office," I said. "Cameron's holed up in my office. We're almost there."

I had no idea what we were going to do when we got to my office, but I just didn't feel right about actually taking Lewis to the root cellar. I couldn't give Cameron up that easily. Plus, there were also Miles and Lucy to think about.

I checked the rearview mirror uneasily. The dark car was still following us. Lewis seemed to be oblivious.

"If you're lying to me," Lewis said, "you'll regret it."

"Not as much as you're about to regret waking up this morning," Nash said. He spun around in his seat and shot Lewis in the forehead.

I screamed and let go of the wheel, gripping my chest to make sure my heart hadn't popped right out. "Again? Again with the bullets in the head? *Really?*"

Nash reached out and steadied the wheel.

"I saw you leave your gun on Lewis's floor," I said.

"What, you think I only carry one gun? Good thing Lewis is obviously not a professional crook. A violent one, anyway," Nash amended. "He didn't even check for the knife in my back pocket, or my backup firearm."

"A knife, too?"

"How do you think I got my hands free? Nicked my finger though. Darn hard to maneuver a switchblade when you can't see what you're doing."

I shook my head. "Good Lord. You almost gave me a heart attack."

"You didn't really expect me to telegraph what I was about to do, did you?"

"I guess not," I said.

"You *guess* not?

"That's what I said."

Nash sighed.

"And now there's *another* body on our hands," I said. "These things are kind of starting to pile up." I was really going to have to start winning some cases so I could afford a therapist.

"Better them than you and me," Nash said.

He did have a fair point. Since the black car was still trailing along behind us, I thought it might be a good idea to bring it up.

"Somebody's following us," I said.

"I know. Keep driving."

"Where to?"

"Anywhere but back to Gracie's."

I drove downtown and past my office. Then I took a right turn and drove several blocks towards the court house. I swung around and drove past Caliente, the grocery store, and then back by the office again. The black car stayed on my tail. The car was *definitely* following us. This was too circuitous a route to be a coincidence.

I wished Kettle had some dark alleyways full of garbage cans and punks—the kind you can pull into during a high speed chase, swerve back and forth a couple times, and lose the tail. But Kettle was open and spacious and made for easy driving. I decided I needed to get out of town and into the countryside.

I hung a left at my office and took Opossum Road to the outskirts of town.

The black car stayed right behind me, following noiselessly along like an eerie shadow.

Nash flipped open the passenger's side vanity mirror and adjusted it so he could keep a close eye on the car.

"What do you think?" I asked.

"I think I wish I were driving," Nash said. "You drive like a girl."

I glanced sharply over at him, trying to figure out whether he'd said that with a hint of a grin, or if he was just being a jerk. I thought I maybe detected a hint of a grin, but I put the pedal to the metal anyway.

"I'll show you who drives like a girl," I said.

My back tires spun on the pavement, and to the serenade of screeching rubber, we were off.

A matching tire screech sounded behind me, and the black car stayed hot on our heels.

I fishtailed right onto Farm Road 1538, kicking up a cloud of dust behind me.

The black car followed suit, swerving right and then left, but still managing to keep up.

Nash flipped on the radio and turned it way up loud.

"What are you doing?" The noise of electric guitars and a heavy rhythm threatened to drown out my voice.

"Car chase music!" Nash yelled.

"Are you *serious?*"

"A little extra motivation!"

"I don't need extra motivation! Running for my life with a dead guy in the back seat is motivation enough!"

"Then what are you still doing out on the open road? You have to get off these long stretches, or we'll never lose this guy!"

I veered left onto a smaller two-lane road that led deeper into farmland area. At a hundred-and-ten miles an hour, I felt a little out of control of the car. If my tail was bothered by the speed, it didn't show. The car kept on keeping up.

"Fence post!" Nash hollered, pointing at a thick metal pipe lying across the road.

I couldn't swerve fast enough to miss it. It popped up under my car and hit the innards with a sickening thud, and then flew out behind me.

I watched my rearview mirror anxiously, hoping it would fly up and catch the pursuer in the windshield. It smacked into his grill and spun sideways, back to the side of the road.

I'd been watching the rear view mirror so anxiously I had forgotten to look where I was going.

"Cow!" Nash pointed at it, jabbing his finger toward it repeatedly. "Cow!"

I swung right off the road and narrowly avoided a deadly collision. I managed to steer through a hole in the fence into some open pasture. The car bumped and bounced across the dried up grass, kicking up a cloud of dust behind us. This definitely didn't *feel* better than the open road.

I checked the rear view mirror again.

The black car veered left around the cow and missed it on the other side. Then it hurtled through the hole in the fence right after us. Not good.

"You look forward, I'll look backward!" Nash yelled.

I raced farther into the pasture, keeping an eye out for more holes in the fence, looking for a way to get out. The field was huge, but surrounded by barbed wire. I was penned in.

The car bumped along the uneven ground as we sped along, half airborne. Lewis's body bounced around on the seat behind us like a lottery ball in the picker machine.

A herd of cattle loomed ahead of me. I honked my horn and they fanned out, creating a big wall of cow—the very opposite of what I had hoped would happen. I had *hoped* they would all run away and clear a space for me. I braced myself for impact.

Nash reached over and yanked the steering wheel right. We went into a spin.

"What are you doing? Let me drive, already!"

"I would, if you weren't trying to kill us! A cow through the windshield is *not* a good idea."

I fought frantically to get control of the spinning car. After two full turns, I straightened it out and swerved right.

The black car hit the brakes and made a cleaner turn. It edged in to try to cut us off.

I spun the wheel again and changed directions. The new route took me right into the wall of a barn.

Wooden siding crashed around us, and I narrowly missed a bale of hay.

A shovel handle speared my windshield and planted itself an inch to the right of my face in the padded headrest.

I shut my eyes tight as we went through the other side of the barn.

"Open your eyes!" Nash said.

I did, and discovered that we'd acquired a new hood ornament. A severed pair of longhorns, which had most likely been used as a barn door ornament, stuck upside down, horns first, into my hood.

The black car kept pace.

I squinted past the longhorns on my hood, scanning for a hole in the fence, and found one.

I floored it and headed straight towards the hole.

"You're going too fast!" Nash hollered over a thrumming electric guitar baseline. "You're going to miss the road!"

Too late, I hit the brakes. I sailed through the hole in the fence, across the road, and into a stretch of barbed wire.

We both ducked as the wire dislodged the longhorns and slingshotted them into the windshield. Miraculously, they glanced off the shovel tip before bouncing into the windshield and cracking the glass even more.

I felt like I was driving blind. "I can't see!"

Nash reached over and grabbed the handle of the shovel, giving it a good yank. Once again, I shut my eyes—this time, against the waterfall of glass coming down on me.

I heard Nash bash out the rest of the windshield and toss the shovel behind us. It landed with a thump.

Since the rearview mirror was now gone, I twisted my head around for a look at what was going on behind me. The black car swerved around the shovel and kept pace.

"I told you, you look forward, I'll look back!" Nash said.

Returning my attention to the pasture, I spotted a cattle crossing, which provided a break in the barbed wire fence, and sped towards it. "Can't you shoot this guy or something?"

"I only have five bullets," Nash said, "and it's a handgun!"

"So?"

"So, accuracy is already low at this range, and you're bouncing the car so much I'd never hit him!"

"Let me get back on the pavement!"

I slowed up a bit as I reached the cattle crossing and fishtailed back onto actual pavement. It was a one-lane road with no paint and no curbs. The edges of the pavement just crumbled out into the dirt. Obviously not a public street.

Nash twisted in his seat and pointed the gun backwards. He shot once.

Our back window shattered, but he didn't appear to have hit the black car.

The black car slowed pace a little and hung farther back.

"Hit his tires!" I said.

"What do you think I'm aiming for? Slow down a little! He's falling back."

I slowed, but the black car did too, keeping pace, but also keeping its distance.

The Texas countryside was nothing but wide open spaces, which meant this guy could hang a half a mile back and still be able to see us. I didn't see how we were going to be able to lose him under the circumstances.

"We've got to get him closer or I won't hit him!" Nash said. "Speed up some, and when I say 'go,' slam on the brakes. Got it?"

"Got it!" I floored the accelerator again and heard the echo of the black car's engine straining to keep up.

We zoomed along on the blacktop. I waited for Nash's signal.

"*Go!*" he said.

I punched the brake with both feet and hung onto the steering wheel, trying to keep the car moving in a straight line.

I heard the black car screeching behind us.

Nash fired off three shots.

"Did you get him?" I twisted around to look.

"I don't think so!" Nash said. "Go! *Go!*"

I put the pedal to the metal again.

"Dude!" I said. "You're a cop! You're supposed to be able to shoot better than this!"

"It's not as easy as it looks in the movies!" he said. "I'd like to see *you* try to hit the broad side of a barn at high speed, let alone a five inch wide span of rubber."

"Try again!" I said.

"I only have one bullet left. We need to hang onto it until it's our very last resort. Keep driving."

I leaned forward in my seat, scanning the land in front of me for any advantage over our pursuer.

Smack.

A giant bug hit me right in the center of the forehead. Bug guts dripped down into my eyes.

Nash laughed and reached over and wiped it off.

"You wouldn't be laughing if that had just happened to you," I said.

Splat.

Now Nash was wiping bug guts off his cheek. He stopped laughing.

"See?" I said. "How unfair is it that the car behind us still has its windshield?"

On the horizon, the road changed color. As we sped towards it, I saw that the pavement ended and the road turned to dirt. When I hit the end of the pavement, a cloud of dust kicked up around the car. Nash and I struggled to breathe, coughing uncontrollably.

"Grass!" Nash choked out. "Get on the grass!"

I jerked the wheel to the right and we were bumping along in the grass again.

That gave us a distinct disadvantage, as the car behind us was able to keep up its speed on the dirt road. It gained on us.

Nash readied his gun.

The car drew closer.

Nash fired just as I hit a bump. His bullet went wide, and he swore. "You could have told me you were about to hit that!"

"I couldn't see it! It was covered with grass!"

Nash faced forward again. "Creek!"

"I see it!" I said. "We have to jump it!" I turned the radio up.

"Are you crazy? You're driving a Toyota hybrid, not the General Lee!"

"I can make it!" I said, pressing harder on the gas.

"There's no incline! Stop!"

It was way too late to stop.

The car careened over the edge of the creek bank.

We were airborne for only a couple of yards.

The car chassis crashed down on the rocky bank, bounced twice, and spun to a stop in the shallow water.

My torso slammed into the steering wheel as the airbags deployed. Nash slammed forward into the dash and groaned. Lewis's body thumped against our seatbacks and crumpled into a heap in the floor. His arm twisted through the seats and his dead hand came to rest between us on top of the cup holders. Eww.

Behind us, a little man in a suit stepped out of the black car.

"Taylor?" he called. "Is that you? Why haven't you been answering your cell phone?"

I turned to get a better look at the guy.

It was Dick.

He scrambled down the creek bank and popped his head in my window. "Are you okay?" he asked.

I nodded.

He patted me on the shoulder. "That's good. I was afraid I wouldn't be able to catch you. So how do you like my new car? That window tint is something else, isn't it? It's supposed to keep the heat out in the summertime. Works real good, too!"

***

"What are you *doing* here?" I demanded. "You could have killed us!"

"Calm down, Taylor," Dick said. "I've been trying to get you on your cell for two days."

"It burned in the fire," I said.

"Well, hellfire and tarnation." Dick reached a hand into his suit jacket pocket and pulled out a little baggie containing eight or ten mini analog tapes. "It's just that I thought you might want to get a hold of these."

I stared, aghast, at the tapes. "*You?*" I said. "*You're* the inside guy?"

Nash let out a low whistle.

"But I *hate* you," I said.

"Which is the way I wanted it," Dick replied. "Didn't need you all up in my business at the office. You'da been likely to get yourself hurt. And me too. Wouldn't of hired you in the first place if I could have handled all the business myself."

Dick helped us out of the car and onto the creek bank, where he inspected Nash's wounded foot. "You need to get to the hospital," Dick said.

Nash waved him off. "No, no. It's just a flesh wound. I'll be okay. We have to get back."

"You working with Cameron Gilbert?" Dick asked.

I massaged the muscles in my neck, which were rapidly stiffening up. "How did you know?"

"Deductive reasonin,'" Dick said. "Lawyer's toolkit. I was on my way into the office this morning when I noticed the hybrid. Not many of those around here, and you know how I like cars. So I took a closer look to see who was driving, and well, I'd recognize your red head anywhere. Then I saw Frederick Lewis sticking a gun to you in the back seat, so I started following you.

"I knew you didn't know anything worth killing for on your own, because PetroPlex had recovered Schaeffer's paper files and burned the rest down with your house, and I had the tapes. The other big threat to PetroPlex is Gilbert, and I knew he'd released the virus."

"That was an accident," Nash said.

"Is that so?" Dick asked. "Can't see as how that really matters. The damage was done. Anyway, since Lewis was forcing you to drive somewhere, I figured it was most likely to wherever Gilbert's hiding out. The hybrid's Gilbert's, isn't it?"

I nodded.

"I been trying to find Gilbert ever since Schaeffer got killed, but that sorry S.O.B. is a darn sight hard to find, and he's the only person I know and trust who has a full press contact list and the technology to blast all the info out."

I frowned. "You mean, *email?*" I asked sourly.

"Whatever," Dick said. "You kids and all these newfangled computers. I don't know how it all works."

"Why didn't you come to me with the tapes before?" I asked.

"I knew you didn't know anything, and I didn't want to involve you," Dick said. "PetroPlex already had you on the radar, and if you got any more active, I was afraid you might come to harm. I didn't know you were working with Gilbert."

"We weren't, until two days ago," Nash said. "How'd you get the tapes?"

"Wait," I said. "Let me guess. Poker games?"

"Yep," Dick said. "At first I just tried to get in real good with all these guys hoping to make settlements easier. It got a lot easier than I thought."

Dick told us about all the deals that happened over the poker table.

"Then," he said, "the Miller case cropped up and Schaeffer came to town and started nosing around. Next thing you know, he was hanging out with Cameron Gilbert, and then Gilbert quit his job and disappeared. Lewis and Fitz threatened to make my life real hard if I didn't call off Schaeffer."

"Imagine that," I said.

"That's when I decided I needed to take action. I'm my own man. Nobody tells Dick Richardson what to do. I knew

PetroPlex was scared of Schaeffer and Gilbert, and I figured I had a good 'in' with Schaeffer on account of the fact that he was already working for me. I thought maybe if I played my cards right, I could use Schaeffer to get some leverage against PetroPlex and beat them at their own game. Get 'em off my back. I knew PetroPlex was looking to find Gilbert on account of some computer virus he was threatening them with, so I convinced 'em that by keeping Schaeffer around and by keeping my eye on him, they'd be able to find Gilbert a lot easier. Then I called up Schaeffer and told him I was on his side. I was a double agent."

"You think he really believed you?" I asked.

"He believed me after I played him my tapes."

"When did you start recording?" Nash asked.

"A couple weeks ago, when I started hearing more about this virus. Fitz and Lewis weren't talking about it directly at the poker table, but it's amazing what people will say when they think nobody's listenin'. I had taken to planting tape recorders in my bar on nights I hosted games because the PetroPlex executives were really starting to lean on me. Also carried one in my pocket and turned it on whenever I could. I was looking for leverage. Fitz and Lewis would go refill their drinks and have whispered conversations. When they went home for the night, I'd play the tapes back. I started hearing things about a plot to raise prices on the energy market. That was about the same time I starting thinking it might be a good idea to convince Schaeffer I was on his side.

"I contacted him, and we talked on the phone briefly. He didn't trust me right away—paranoid, you know—but after a while he started to settle down and open up. He told me about his contact with Cameron and their plan to do a large scale media release, and he asked me if he could use the tapes as evidence. This was the day before your summary judgment hearing. I told him I'd bring 'em to court in the morning and slip 'em into his briefcase while PetroPlex was making arguments.

"I don't know exactly what happened next, but somebody at PetroPlex got nervous and offed him. While I was trying to figure out what to do next, your house got torched and you disappeared. I've been looking for you and Gilbert ever since."

Wow. That was quite the story. If only I'd known earlier. I don't know that I'd have been able to do anything to prevent Schaeffer's death, but I sure as heck could have stayed out of Cameron's old car garage and saved myself some run-ins with thugs. Plus, Nash wouldn't have been shot. I was still mad at him, but I felt bad about his foot, nevertheless.

"We have to get the tapes back to Cameron," I said.

"Where you guys holed up?" Dick asked.

"Gracie's root cellar," I said. "What are we gonna do about the body?"

"Leave him in the creek for now," Dick said. "I'll holler at Old Man Jonas up the road and ask him to call it in. I think I saw him looking out the window when you drove through his barn earlier, anyway."

I looked at Nash. "You okay with that?"

Nash nodded. "As long as it gets called in right now."

Dick made the call while we listened in. Then we helped Nash up, and the two of them limped up the hill to Dick's new car. Nash settled into the front seat, and I curled into the back.

It was almost 8:00 A.M. I wondered if the crime scene techs had found Dorian yet.

We drove the distance back to Gracie's root cellar and went underground.

***

When Lucy saw Dick, she growled. "Good dog," I said, patting her on the head.

When Miles saw Dick, he hopped out of his cot angrily. "Bloody hell!" he said. "What is *he* doing here?"

"Nice to see you too," Dick said.

"He's the inside guy," I told Miles.

Cameron let go of the mouse and looked up from his computer. "Who is he?"

"My boss," I said. "Dick Richardson."

"Don'tcha recognize me from my TV commercials?" Dick asked. He struck a pose and said, "I'm Dick Richardson, and I'll fight for *you*."

"Get outta town," Cameron said. "I *never* would have found you. You're not on the network!"

Dick pulled the tapes out of his pocket again and handed them to Cameron.

"Unbelievable," Cameron said. "Thanks."

We filled Cameron and Miles in on the latest developments. I apologized to Cameron for trashing his car in a creek bed, but he seemed unperturbed, as usual. He was more low key than any guy I'd met in my life.

While we told the story, Cameron converted the tapes to digital format. He attached them to an email packet that also contained copies of internal PetroPlex records and emails between executives, along with a cover letter that explained what everything was. Then he imported all his press contacts into his email from a database file and hovered his mouse cursor over the "send" button.

"Ready, guys?" he asked. "This is it!"

I stared at the computer screen, mesmerized. Did I dare feel any kind of relief? Would this call off the PetroPlex dogs or just whip them up into an angrier frenzy? Would we be free to leave the root cellar in a few hours, or would we be trapped here indefinitely?

"I can't believe this is it," I said. It had been an unbelievable three days. "We finally did it! How can it all be over with just the press of a button?"

"Modern technology is a wondrous thing," Cameron said.

He pressed the button. I held my breath as I watched the progress bar showing the file upload. When the empty bar filled all the way up with blue, I let out a sigh.

CHAPTER 30

Delmont was in the middle of presiding over a slip and fall case when his clerk, a rosy-cheeked youth of twenty-two years, nervously sidled up to the bench and whispered into Delmont's ear.

"Chief Scott's on the phone for you," she said.

"Well tell him I'm in the middle of a hearing, for crying out loud. He can wait."

"He says it's urgent—a matter of life and death. He's refusing to leave me alone until I put you through to him."

"Oh, all right," Delmont grumbled. "I'll take it in my chambers."

Delmont banged the gavel and called a twenty minute recess.

Once in his chambers, he slammed the door behind him and picked up the phone.

"You know I got better things to do than talk to you right now, don'tcha?" he said.

Chief Scott was breathing hard on the other end of the line. He sounded like he'd been running. "You know where I am right now? Do ya?"

"I don't, and I don't care." Delmont pulled a cigar out of his jacket and eyed it, debating whether or not he had enough time for a quick puff before heading back to the bench.

"I'm out in Chandler's creek on the Jonas property. Old man Jonas called the station this morning and said a couple of crazy drivers came careening through his fields and took out half a barn and a length of barbed wire fence. One of 'em lost control and wound up in the creek. You are not gonna believe who was in the back seat."

Delmont decided that a cigar just might hit the spot. This sounded like it could be a long conversation. He bit the end off and spit the tip on the rug. The janitor would clean it up this evening.

"So how come I care?" Delmont said.

"Because it was Frederick Lewis, and he's deader than a doornail! Shot right through the forehead, just like that Schaeffer guy."

Delmont swore.

"And besides that, have you seen the news? First the explosion, and now they're accusing PetroPlex of some kind of conspiracy, and there's a whole lot of evidence to back it up!"

Delmont frowned and flipped on the television. Sure enough, on every channel, some news reporter was playing audio with voices that sounded like Lewis and Fitz.

"It's bad," Scott said. "Real bad. I got a call with intel that Nash and Taylor went to Lewis's house this morning. And now he's dead and the press is all over PetroPlex. Those two are out for blood! It's just a matter of time before they're on to me and you. We're gonna get caught!"

Delmont's heart rate started to rise a little. He lit his cigar and took a long puff. The nicotine calmed him down some.

"Listen here," he said. "You gotta keep calm. You gotta get out there and find Nash and Taylor and shut them down."

"How am I supposed to do that? They could be anywhere! And they apparently ain't afraid to put a bullet through somebody's head!"

"You're a *cop*," Delmont said. "You have a gun, too. If you see them, just shoot first."

"I been behind a desk too long," Scott moaned. "I'm out of practice. I'm not cut out for stuff like this."

"Hey!" Delmont barked. "Pull it together!"

"What are we gonna do? *What* are we gonna *do?*"

"It ain't over 'til it's over," Delmont said. "Get out there and do your job. Whatever happens next is up to you. If you can find 'em and shut 'em down before they do any more damage, then we win. Got it?"

"Okay," Scott said. "I'll try."

"Don't try. *Do.*"

Delmont hung up the phone and took a long drag on his cigar. He felt nervous. Could he really trust the darn fool to find Taylor and Nash before they did any more damage? How much had they uncovered already? Would the trail lead back to Scott and him eventually, or would PetroPlex be the only one taking the hit?

He was unsure of what to do. He glanced at the clock. There were still eighteen minutes before he was due back in the courtroom. He thought he'd take a walk to clear his head.

CHAPTER 31

Cameron pulled up multiple browsers on his web site as we waited for breaking news.

It only took thirty minutes. CNN, MSNBC, FOX News—all of them were all over the story. The Twitter memes all started showing hits on PetroPlex and oil. Google news exploded with stories.

Cameron pulled up some live video feeds. We listened in awed silence for a while as various reporters read the contents of Lewis's and Fitz's emails and played the whispered audio conversations with subtitles, so they'd be easy to understand.

After awhile, Cameron opened his hacking terminal and connected to the PetroPlex network. He started running some searches on words like "media, press," and "news."

The search results were ominous. Now in emergency mode, Fitz didn't bother trying to cover his tracks. He was giving orders, even in writing, clearly and explicitly. Emails between his subordinates told the whole story.

Fitz had launched a county-wide search for Lewis. He had called Chief Scott and told him that Lewis was missing after having met with us early this morning, and that it wouldn't surprise him if Lewis were dead. He had advised Chief Scott that Miles, Nash, and I were most likely armed and dangerous, and Scott had issued orders to shoot us on sight.

Then Fitz had gone into cover up super-drive, sending out emails to every government regulator he had a special relationship with. He argued that the emails the press had were taken out of context and that the voice files were fabricated. He also claimed that the sources of the information, namely, us, were wanted murderers and that local law enforcement was hunting us that very moment. He argued that the word of murderers couldn't be believed.

"That's jumping the gun, don't you think?" I said.

"Well," Cameron said, "it's a convenient assumption for him, isn't it? We already know he had trust issues with Lewis. If we hadn't shot him, Fitz might have done it himself. It would be convenient for him to have someone to blame in advance."

We turned back to Cameron's computer screen, which was hopping with activity. It appeared that Fitz had put his media team into overdrive issuing press releases with statistics about how any criminal investigation into PetroPlex would cost billions of dollars in stock losses, eliminate tens of thousands of jobs, and throw the national economy into a dive.

The spin machine had fully spun to life. If he could successfully convince people they should be afraid of losing their jobs, he could swing public opinion in his favor in a heartbeat. That was always the go-to scare tactic Big Oil used.

"What now?" I asked. "If we stay here and Scott starts going door to door, we're bound to be found."

"I think it's time to get out of town," Nash said.

Cameron started to pack up his equipment.

"You're driving," Nash told Dick. "We're fresh out of cars."

"What?" Dick said. "I can't drive. I'm not leaving."

"Just because you're not being directly threatened now doesn't mean you're safe," I said. "Once Fitz gets out of panic mode and takes a minute to think about things, he's bound to realize you were the source of the tapes."

"Well, that'll give me enough time to get to the bank, pull out some money and. . . call in some favors."

Dick, seeing that Nash was about to physically restrain him, darted up the root cellar stairs. "Don't worry!" he said. "I'll be right back!"

Nash, on his bad foot, wasn't fast enough to catch him. I tried myself, but I wasn't strong enough. Miles and Cameron, deep inside the root cellar, were just too far away. Dick left us stranded there without him.

CHAPTER 32

Cameron, unperturbed as usual and confident that Dick would be back shortly, unplugged everything and packed it up, except for one computer and its wireless connection equipment. Lucy bucked up and down happily, thinking that all the packing meant she might get to go for another ride in the car.

"How long do you think we have?" I asked Nash.

"Well, it's a small police force, so manpower is limited. Probably what will happen is that Chief Scott will go knocking on doors, the telephone grapevine will get going, and before you know it, the whole town will be up in arms and out looking for us."

"Great," I said. "So that gives us what. . . like thirty minutes?"

Cameron planted himself back down in front of his computer screen.

"What's happening?" Miles asked.

"Hold on," Cameron said. "There's so much happening so fast, it's hard to keep up."

He scanned the screen. Miles and I joined him and hunched over his shoulder, reading. Words sped across the screen faster than I could follow.

"Uh oh," Cameron said, bringing the scrolling screen to a stop. "Look at this. They're on to Dick."

Sure enough, Fitz had texted Chief Scott to be on the lookout for Dick. "Quick," I told Cameron. "Gimme your cell phone. We have to warn him." Cameron was the only one of the four of us who had a phone left.

Cameron tossed me the phone, and I dialed.

Dick didn't pick up.

"He probably isn't picking up because he doesn't recognize the number," Miles said. "He hates it when he doesn't recognize the number."

"Who doesn't?" Cameron said.

"If he gets picked up, do you trust him not to give away our position?" Nash asked.

"I don't," Miles said.

"But he's the inside guy," I countered.

"Yeah, but he loves money. If the price were right, he might say anything." Miles folded his arms and stared at me. "And you *know* PetroPlex can hit the right price. Who's to say he wouldn't go triple agent on us?"

Nash blew out a sigh. "We have to go after him."

"What are you gonna do?" I asked. "Hijack his car?"

"If I have to," Nash said.

Wow. His "by the book" attitude sure had done a one-eighty over the last couple of days.

"What about transportation?" I asked.

"I think I saw Derrick's old motorcycle upstairs," Nash said. "I can hotwire it."

"You *can?*" I asked, astonished.

"Can't catch the bad guys if you don't know their tricks," Nash said.

"Wait! Cameron said. "Take my cell phone. I'll risk calling you from Gracie's landline if I learn anything new."

"No," Nash said. "You keep it. I might need to contact you. And if I get in a tight spot, I'd rather not risk a cell phone ringer giving away my position."

He disappeared upstairs. After a few minutes, I heard the roar of a motorcycle engine growl to life and then fade away into the distance.

We waited, all but biting our nails and watching the computer screen for any kind of news. I felt naked and exposed with the line of contact between us and Nash severed. What if he got into trouble? What if something happened to him?

I told myself I didn't care. I told myself I was still mad at him. But the fact is, I cared. In fact, I was only mad at him *because* I cared about him. I wouldn't have been half as angry if I felt nothing for him and he'd kissed and run.

And what about Dick? If something happened to Dick, I might not shed a lot of tears on his behalf. I still didn't like him, inside guy or not. But if anything happened to him, I was out of a job. I couldn't afford to bankroll my cases myself—that would take hundreds of thousands of dollars I just didn't have. And it's not like other jobs abounded, especially for lawyers who'd been on a losing streak like me. My career would be over. Nobody would believe me if I told them all my recent losses weren't my fault.

Ten minutes went by. Then twenty. Then thirty.

"This town is not that big," I said. "Something must have happened."

"I don't see anything on the network," Cameron said.

I stared at Cameron's cell phone. It refused to ring.

"Wait," Cameron said. He had pulled up the PetroPlex security camera feed.

"OMG," Miles said. "There's Dick, walking in, plain as day."

"Did you just say 'OMG?'" I said. "Tell me you didn't just say OMG. What are you—*twelve?*"

Miles ignored me. "Check Fitz's phone records," Miles told Cameron. "See if there were any calls between Dick and Fitz."

Cameron did so. "Yep," he said. "Right there. Ten minutes ago. The call lasted eight and a half minutes."

"What on earth?" I said. "You think they got to him, or do you think he's trying to pull off some crazy hero stunt?"

"Like what?" Miles asked. "You think he believes he could really go in there and talk Fitz off a ledge?"

Cameron's phone rang, and I jumped.

Cameron connected the call and put it on speaker.

"I can't find him," Nash said. "He's not at the bank."

"He's at PetroPlex!" I said. "We just caught him on the security camera walking through the doors."

"With an escort?" Nash asked.

"Nope. All alone," I said. "Where are you calling from?"

"Gas station pay phone," Nash said. "Dick's gotta be headed straight for Fitz's office. I'm going in after him."

"Nash, no!" I said. "It's too dangerous!"

The line disconnected.

"Arrrrgghhh!" I slammed the phone down. "He is going to get himself killed!"

"I thought you were mad at him," Miles said. "I thought he was giving you the slient treatment."

"I am, and he was, but--"

"Now you're a thing and you care," Miles finished.

"We are *not* a thing, but I still care," I said. "That's the problem."

Miles nodded knowingly.

Cameron clicked through the security feed images one by one, trying to keep a trace on Dick. Sure enough, he walked deep into the heart of corporate headquarters, and no one stopped him.

It's amazing what you can get away with if you walk into a building looking like you know where you're going, and Dick could pull off that trick like nobody else. If you project the right attitude, no one questions you. And Dick was projecting the right attitude. He strolled right into Fitz's office unchallenged.

"You got sound on this?" I asked.

"Nope," Cameron said. "Image only."

We watched as the two men talked. The conversation started out pretty tame, but got heated quickly. Dick was gesturing wildly and waving his finger around in Fitz's face.

Fitz stayed calm for awhile, but even on the poor resolution of the security feed, I could see that his face was getting flushed. His gestures became more rapid, more frequent, a staccato complement to Dick's histrionic overtones.

We watched as Fitz opened his desk drawer, pulled out a gun, and pointed it at Dick.

Dick raised his hands and froze.

At that moment, Nash limped into the frame, gun drawn, aimed at Fitz.

"And he thinks *I'm* out of *my* mind," I said. "This cannot end well."

Fitz said something to his desk phone, and in seconds, PetroPlex security, all clothed in black, swarmed Nash and took him down easily, thanks to his bad foot. But they couldn't get to Dick in time.

Dick rushed Fitz.

Fitz pulled his trigger, and Dick crumpled to the ground.

The pit of my stomach sank. Bodies were piling up around me left and right, and I was helpless to do anything about it! I could not stand the thought of one more person dying today—especially if that person were Nash.

PetroPlex security seemed oblivious to the obvious murder. I peered more closely at the camera footage. I thought I saw a familiar face in the sea of all that black.

Sure enough, I recognized black-suit man from Cameron's car garage. Well, that explained a lot.

"Are you recording this?" I asked Cameron.

"Yep. I've got every frame."

That was good. If we got out of this mess alive, the footage might come in handy later.

Fitz put the gun away and sat back down at his desk, calmly picking up his phone.

CHAPTER 33

The fresh outside air calmed Delmont down some. He threw his cigar on the ground and stamped it out, then pulled out his cell phone and took a look at the display. The old battle-ax had been ringing his phone all morning. There were fifteen missed calls, all from her. She probably wanted the inside scoop on what was going on with PetroPlex. She just hated it when she couldn't be the fount of all the town gossip.

When the phone rang again and interrupted his mini-outdoor getaway, he felt a surge of anger. Sixteen calls in the space of an hour was too much. He'd pick up the phone and let her have it, and then when he got home tonight, he'd reconsider making that accident happen after all. A man just couldn't live under constant badgering like this. It was unnatural.

Delmont jammed his finger down on his cell phone receiver without bothering to look at the caller ID and started yelling. "Listen here, woman! I ain't got time to talk to you right now!"

"Can it, Delmont, this is Fitz."

Delmont cleared his throat. "Oh," Delmont said. "You again. What is it this time?"

"Dick Richardson just walked into my office and went ape, wanting to make some kind of a deal."

"Get outta here."

"No, I'm serious. The guy had the nerve to try to call in his poker favor. Now! In the middle of all this!"

Delmont raised his eyebrows. "What'd he want?"

"He wanted me to call the dogs off Chloe and Cameron. Can you believe that?"

"You're kidding me."

"I wish I were."

"What did you do?"

"Well, I would have laughed him right out of my office, but then he started talking about how he had a whole lot more tapes than the ones he gave to Gilbert. He said if I didn't lay off Nash and Taylor and start taking responsibility for all this garbage that he'd release the additional tapes and make things a whole lot worse for me than they already are. The he rushed me. What was I supposed to do? I shot him."

"Right there in your office?"

"Well, where else was I supposed to do it? He attacked me!"

Delmont swore. "I thought I told you, no more bodies!"

"I know, I know. I'm sorry. If it makes you feel better, that fool Nash came in after him, but I didn't shoot him. Somebody else had already shot him in the foot, so he was easy to take down. If he doesn't lead me to Cameron Gilbert, though, I can't say that I won't shoot him in a more fatal location."

"Do it in another town, okay?"

"We'll see. In the meantime, I'm going to get rid of the body. Your friend Chief Scott is flipping out about this. I need you to try to calm him down."

Delmont pulled a cigar out of his pocket and lit up. "I already talked him off a ledge once this morning. I ain't gonna promise I can do it again. And anyway, what about me? You keep things up like this, and I'm gonna need somebody to calm *me* down real quick."

"Look, don't worry about it. You take care of things on your end, and I'll take care of them on mine."

"You better," Delmont said, and hung up. He turned around and headed back for the office.

CHAPTER 34

As I sat stranded in Gracie's root cellar and stared at the PetroPlex security footage, I felt more helpless and more powerless than I had in my entire life. And now I wished I hadn't yelled at Nash last night. What if I never got the chance to make amends? What if Nash and I really could have had something, and I had ruined it forever?

Goodness knows it was hard enough for me to find men. Most of them ran away when they found out I was an attorney. But Nash hadn't. He hadn't been intimidated at all. That was pretty rare for a non-attorney male. As for attorney males, the good ones were few and far between.

As PetroPlex security hauled Nash out of the frame, Cameron paged through various other screens, trying to keep up.

They dragged Nash down the hall and threw him in some kind of a holding room, locking him in and leaving him there.

"What are we going to do?" I asked.

Cameron was pulling up schematics of the building.

"What *can* we do?" Miles asked. He looked miserable.

I couldn't stand the thought of just sitting idly by and letting the scenario at PetroPlex play out. Fitz hadn't hesitated to pull the trigger on Dick. I didn't feel very optimistic about Nash's future under those circumstances, even though he was a cop. I wondered if his cop status was the reason he was still alive at the moment. If he had been an ordinary civilian, would Fitz have just killed him then and there instead of throwing him into a locked room? Or was it that he was going to use Nash to get to us?

A glimmer of an idea started to form in my mind.

I rummaged through the rest of Nash's stuff and found another gun. Carefully keeping it aimed at the ground, I turned to Miles.

"Miles," I said. "Give me your car keys."

"Why?" he asked. "My car is in my driveway halfway across town."

"If I run, I can make it in forty-five minutes."

"Oh, okay," Miles said. "Only forty-five minutes? Well here you go." He tossed me his keys and then let loose on me. "*Forty-five minutes is like, an* ETERNITY *in Nash time.* You think Nash has forty-five minutes *left?* Because *I* don't. And besides that, what if someone sees you running across town? What if Chief Scott finds you? What if the neighborhood brigade calls you in?"

I raced up the cellar stairs and into Gracie's house, Cameron and Miles right behind me.

"Chloe, you *can't!*" Miles called after me. "What are you doing?"

I tore through Gracie's house and into her bedroom, rummaging around in her closet. I felt like I was doing a lot more rummaging in other people's bedrooms these days than I thought I'd ever do in my whole life, but oh well. It's the way it was.

I found a pair of dark aviator sunglasses and a Stetson hat that had most likely belonged to Derrick. Piling my hair on top of my head, I jammed the hat down as far over my ears as it would go. The hat hid a lot of my face as well as my distinctively red hair. With the large aviator glasses, I would be almost unrecognizable.

I shut the closet door for privacy and exchanged Gracie's frumpy pants for a pair of cutoff jean shorts, cinching them around my waist with a belt so they wouldn't fall off. It was hot outside, after all. I didn't want to be running in long pants.

The biggest problem was the shoes. Gracie's shoes didn't fit me, so all I had were the high heels Miles had bought to go with my suit a couple days ago. I'd have to make do with them the best I could.

I hoped that once I got to the refinery, I wouldn't be so funny looking that I couldn't get anywhere inside of it. Maybe I could find some protective gear once I got in and improvise.

I opened the closet door and was ready to go.

"Cameron," I said, "I know it's risky, but set up your network in the house and give me your cell phone. That way you can get on Gracie's land line and walk me through what's happening. If I can get in the building, and if you can keep an eye on the security cameras and get me where I need to go, maybe I can unlock the door and get Nash out."

"With what key?" Miles asked.

"Good point," I said. "Miles, give me your credit cards."

"No way," Miles said. "This is never going to work. You'll just get yourself caught or killed, or both."

At this point, I wasn't sure I really cared. "My boss is dead. I have no job. I have no house. I have no car. I have no money. If anything happens to Nash. . ."

Miles looked at me for a moment, then crossed his arms defiantly.

I raised my gun and pointed it at him.

"Are you *serious?*" Miles said. "*What* is your *problem?*"

"Give me your credit cards," I said softly.

"You wouldn't," Miles said.

Yeah, of course he was right. I wouldn't. I lowered the gun. "Please, Miles. It's important."

"Oh, all right." Miles yanked his wallet out of his pants, flipped it open, and flung his credit cards at me. "But this is never going to work."

"It's our only shot," I said.

"Are you sure you're up for this, Chloe?" Cameron asked.

"What other way is there?"

Cameron hesitated, thinking. "Options are limited," he said carefully.

"Limited!" I said. "That's the understatement of the year. Now, if you're operating inside the house, you'll have to be extremely careful," I told Cameron.

I thought I saw a hint of amusement flit across his face, but surely I was imagining it?

"The cops will be going door to door," I said. "Try to stay low and keep out of sight. If any of the neighbors see you. . ."

"Yeah, yeah, I know," Cameron said. "Trust me. This isn't my first rodeo."

"Ain't," Miles said. "The expression doesn't sound right if you don't say 'ain't my first rodeo.'"

Cameron shrugged.

"Miles, while Cameron's on the computer, you and Lucy sit by the window and look for police or snoopers," I said. "If you see anyone, get out the back door and back into the root cellar. Got it?"

"Never gonna work," Miles said.

"We can try," Cameron said, ignoring the daggers Miles looked at him.

"We have to get it done," I said. "If we don't, Nash is dead."

"And so are you," Miles said. "I don't like it. I don't like it one bit."

"Unless you are prepared to physically restrain me, you don't have a choice." I gave Cameron and Miles quick hugs and raced out the door. "Call me from the landline when you get set up!" I called back to them.

Forty-five minutes was an ambitious estimation of time, since I was pretty out of shape. I raced down Gracie's sidewalk and into the open road, praying my hat and sunglasses would do the trick and hide my identity. If it didn't, I was toast for sure.

CHAPTER 35

Anna Delmont had been calling Joe Bob all morning, but as usual lately, he didn't return her calls. She'd have absolutely no idea what was going on at all if it weren't for that nice Chief Scott, who did actually call her without her even having to call him first.

He sounded like a real wreck, which of course, was understandable. The whole town was in turmoil looking for Detective Nash, Chloe Taylor, and her paralegal, and he wanted her to get out there and help.

This, of course, she was happy to do. The problem was, all the neighbor ladies were calling her up and asking for more information than Chief Scott had been willing to give, and since Joe Bob wouldn't return her calls, she still didn't really understand what was going on. It was downright inconsiderate of him not to have informed her there was a situation brewing. He knew she hated to appear out of the loop.

She kept calling him, but he refused to pick up the phone. There was nothing for it but to go down to his office and tell him what for. The current situation was intolerable. She just knew that catty Mrs. Dagney was wagging her tongue all over. She could just hear her now. "Judge Delmont don't trust his wife. He never tells her anything." The nerve of that woman!

As she drove to the office, she watched the neighborhood waking up. People were out grabbing their papers, watering their lawns, or going for a morning jog, just like that girl in a Stetson hat and jean shorts over there. She couldn't imagine why anyone would want to go jogging in a Stetson hat. After all, those were mighty fine hats, and it seemed like sweat would ruin the brim. Well, there was no accounting for taste.

When Anna got to the courthouse, it was all but deserted. In fact, the whole square, police station and everything, seemed deserted. Everyone must be out on the hunt.

Anna walked into the courthouse and took the familiar route to Joe Bob's chambers. She knocked on the door. There was no response, so she went right on in.

"Joe Bob?" she called.

He didn't answer.

Maybe she could figure out what was going on if she rooted around on his desk. His desk was a fine mess, covered with stacks of paper that were three or four inches high in some spots.

She moved some papers around gingerly, wanting to find information, but also not wanting to destroy the natural order of things. She'd hate for him to find out she'd been all through his stuff.

She picked up a particularly large stack of paper and noticed something brightly colored underneath. A photograph.

No, a *set* of photographs.

She'd recognize Joe Bob's naked behind just about anywhere. And who was that in bed with him? All that blonde hair and the size of those breasts were unnatural. Ain't nobody in the world should have breasts that big, except for maybe Dolly Parton. They looked like way more than a handful for Joe Bob.

Anna began to shake. How *could* he? After *all these years!* After everything she'd done for him! What would Mrs. Dagney say when she found out?

Anna felt nauseated and faint. She swayed and gripped the edge of the desk for support. There was a letter opener lying on the edge of the desk. A fit of rage tore through her, and with renewed energy, she grabbed the letter opener and brandished it above her head. Then, in swoops of pure, unadulterated grief and anger, she brought it down over and over again, driving the point into the offending images beneath her.

The paper ripped and tore satisfactorily as her steel point drove through it four, five, ten times. She would gouge out the very image of this woman's breasts and her husband's naked behind. No longer would this unholy amalgamation of flesh on flesh remain joined in frozen union on coated glossy card stock, a moment captured on film and available for the whole world to see. She would obliterate the image. She would obliterate the event.

Judge Delmont appeared in the doorway.

"Anna! What in tarnation are you doing to my desk?"

Anna, blinded with rage and hardly aware of what she was doing, screamed in tortured fury and rushed toward Joe Bob, steel tip upraised.

Joe Bob seemed like a thin, cardboard excuse for a man. Not the passionate man of flesh and blood she had admired, loved, and married. The man who stood before her was merely a shell of the man she'd been living with all these years. She didn't know who this man was.

She knew he had his faults, but she never in a million years dreamed that he would have betrayed her trust like this. The sanctity of their marriage, the highest holy sacrament of the church, was destroyed! She had taken a lot from Joe Bob lying down, but not this. *This* was too serious. This was not to be tolerated.

Her adrenaline surged. She plunged the letter opener into his heart. It pierced easily. She pulled it out and plunged again. She felt strong and furious. The steel seemed to simply melt into his body with no resistance—it was just like stabbing air. Just like going through paper. It meant nothing.

It was so easy, she stabbed again. And again. And again.

Joe Bob sank to the floor, his eyes wide with astonishment and pain.

Anna lifted her letter opener for one last plunge. She knew exactly where to aim. Her hands, armed with steel, swooped down and plunged into Joe Bob's crotch. It was a clean stab, straight down, and the letter opener lodged in the floor and stuck, skewering him in death through the part he had enjoyed most in life.

And then, Anna's fury subsided.

She looked at Joe Bob's limp and bloody body on the ground and felt nothing. Perhaps the feelings would come later.

It struck her that she was going to need a good lawyer.

That nice Dick Richardson was a good lawyer.

And now she was single, just like he was. It occurred to her that it wouldn't be in her best interests to arrange dinner for him with Widow Schumacher after all.

CHAPTER 36

As I ran, I kept my eyes peeled for faces in windows and cars on the street. At first, I jogged steadily. Then I started to worry that a woman running around in a Stetson hat and high heels might look suspicious. After that, every time I saw a car or a face in the window, I lowered my head and slowed to a walk.

Even though it was still early, it felt like the temperature was already in the upper nineties, and as always in this area, the humidity was high, making it feel even hotter.

It didn't take long for my heels to start rubbing blisters in my ankles. Not to mention the terrible pinch in the toes. I took them off and clutched them hard as my bare feet pounded pavement. The sidewalk was heating up with the day and began to burn me. I switched to the grass, running through people's front lawns.

Unfortunately, a lot of lawns were covered with sticker burr plants, and I kept having to stop and pick stickers out of my feet. Tiny little blood pricks dotted my soles and the sides of my feet. I sighed. This wasn't going to work.

I cursed my shoes and put them back on. I would just have to endure the pain as I limped hurriedly along. I knew I looked ridiculous.

The neighborhood seemed a little more populated this morning than usual. The residents of Kettle were starting to appear in their front yards, watering plants, pruning bushes, and knocking on neighbor's doors for a morning chat. The grapevine must already be active.

I slowed to a walk, nodding good morning to anyone who looked my way. I was starting to freak out a little. At this rate, I'd *never* make it to Miles's house in time to save Nash.

As I rounded the corner onto Fifth Street, only one-third of my way to my destination, I saw rusty gold lying in the driveway of an old wooden house. A *bicycle!* A big, pink girl's bicycle with an 80s-style flowered white basket on the handlebars! If I took it, it's not like I would be stealing it, I told myself. I would bring it back.

Then the lawyer in me remembered a bunch of larceny law, and I felt a pang of guilt. Okay, yes, it would be stealing, even if I brought it back, but it was for such a good cause! And it was necessary. I'd have to use the necessity defense if I got caught.

Willing myself not to overthink it, I glanced furtively around, hoping no one was watching. Seeing no one, I grabbed the bike, tossed my shoes in the basket, and pedaled as fast as I could.

I was almost to Miles' house when Cameron's cell phone rang.

I picked it up. "Are you set up?" I huffed.

"Ten-four," Cameron said. "Where are you?"

"I found a bike. I'm almost there. What's happening?"

"Nash is still stuck in that room," Cameron said. "Fitz is focusing on media spin for now. He's fielding phone calls left and right. I've tried to look up some of the numbers, and a lot of them are to Mineral Management Services and other agencies in

Washington D.C. I have a feeling he's trying to call in some favors."

"What did they do with Dick's body?" I asked.

"I don't know. I can only look at so many cameras at once. I've got one on Nash and one on Fitz."

"How about the building schematic? Do you have that pulled up?"

"Yes," Cameron said. "If you take the Meadow Road entrance to the back of the refinery, there are a bunch of old, rusty barrels stacked out by the creek. There's a door back there that leads through a giant concrete retaining wall in an open-air warehouse area where they fill and load barrels of gasoline and chemicals. Let me know when you're there, and I'll loop the camera feed so it looks like you're not there."

"Okay," I said. "I'll call you back."

I rode the rest of the way to Miles' house. When I got there, I popped inside for a glass of water and a fresh shirt. My body was soaked with sweat, and I felt like I'd lost ten pounds in water weight on the trip over here. I selected one of his designer tees, which was made to fit him tight and show off his pecs. It fit perfectly on me. And it actually kind of looked cute in a redneck punk kind of way with my heels.

I hopped in his car and raced to the refinery, taking the Meadow Road entrance. The trip took me three minutes in the car. When I got close, I pulled out the cell phone and dialed Gracie's land line.

"I'm here," I said.

Miles walked me through parking the car outside of the security video feed.

"All right," I said. "I'm parked. Run the loop. Tell me when."

There was a pause. I used the time to mutter a quick prayer, begging for this plan to work.

"Okay, the loop is running," Cameron said. "When you go in, I'll jump the loop from camera to camera and follow you. If you can try to stay out of sight of actual people, I'll do my best to keep you off the security feed. First thing I'm going to do is take you to a supply closet. That's where they keep the spare protective jumpsuits everyone wears. If you can find one of those and get into it, you'll blend in a lot better. That sound okay to you?"

"Sounds good to me," I said. "Okay, I'm going in."

I ran toward a rusty chain metal fence that abutted the barrels and planted myself behind them. They smelled to high heaven and appeared to be leeching chemicals into the nearby creek. That didn't bode well for the safety of the groundwater in the area.

Edging my way past the barrels, I made a run for a large concrete wall with a door in it. My heels snagged on a piece of scrap metal and I fell, putting a gash in my knee.

Wiping away the blood, I got back on my feet and proceeded more carefully.

High above me, on the other side of the wall, smoke stacks belched smoke and fire. PetroPlex was burning off chemical leaks with flares, filling the air with toxic clouds. The roar of the flames serenaded me on my journey inward.

I crept forward and used the credit card on the lock. It worked. I cracked the door open. Before me was a large storage yard. Big, open—a large concrete-encased room with no ceiling. It was full of barrels and opened out onto a busy loading dock on the other end.

"Try to stay behind the barrel inventory," Cameron said. "If you can do that, you can get to the other side of the dock and get through the door. From there, if you go left, that will take you deeper into the refinery. Right will get you to the corporate offices. You want to go right."

"Okay," I whispered.

I waited until the workers had their attention glued to several of the large barrels that were being crane-lifted out of the warehouse area and into the loading dock. Then I slipped through the door, shutting it softly behind me.

I ran towards the giant drums and wedged myself in between the wall of barrels and the back wall of the warehouse. There was just enough space for a very thin woman to edge through.

I lowered the phone, flattened myself against the wall, and went in. The air was hot and putrid. The chemical smell in such close quarters was almost overpowering. I fought to breathe. Fought the nausea welling up inside my stomach. Even though the barrels were sealed, there had been small leaks during the filling process, and the evaporation from the gasoline leaks burned my nostrils.

I passed one barrel, two, three. Then five and ten. Eleven. Fifteen. Some of the barrels were tighter squeezes than others, and my phone scraped against them as I pressed myself through.

After what seemed like an eternity, I reached the end. There was at least a fifteen yard run out in the open to the door.

I lifted my phone to my ear and whispered, "Cameron?"

"I'm here," he said.

"There must be a hundred people out on the dock. I'll never make it."

"Hold on," he said. "Let me create a distraction."

As I watched, one of the conveyor belts malfunctioned. Dock workers swarmed over it, trying to figure out what was wrong.

"Go! Go!" Cameron said. "Hallway's clear!"

I ran for it, barely breathing in the fifteen yards it took to reach the door.

I slipped through it and found myself in an empty hallway, Cameron's phone glued to my ear.

"Watch out!" Cameron said. "Incoming! There's an empty office a hundred yards down the hall on your right. Run!"

I ran. "Which office?" I whispered.

"Almost there," Cameron said. "Keep running!"

I ran. "Tell me when."

"Now! Now! On the right!"

I grabbed the office doorknob and skidded to a stop, then ducked inside.

"Tell me when I'm clear," I said.

"Okay, wait for it."

I had one ear jammed to the doorway and the phone pressed to my other ear. I heard two guys having a conversation as they walked down the hall.

"It's a bad business," said one guy with a gruff voice. "Bet half of us lose our jobs before it's all over with."

"I dunno," said a guy with a higher pitched, smoother voice. "Fitz is no dummy. Word is, some lunatics killed Lewis this morning, and Fitz already has one of the guys locked up somewhere in the building. He shot the other one in his office."

"What was that guy doing in Fitz's office?"

"After the dude killed Lewis, he came to kill Fitz, too. Fitz had no choice."

So that was going to be the party line. Self defense.

I listened as the voices and footsteps faded.

"Okay," Cameron said. "You're clear. Step out the door and keep going right."

I did. "How far away is Nash?"

Cameron cleared his throat. "Um, far."

"How far is far?"

"Up on the sixth floor at the other end of corporate. It's not too late to turn around and get out of there."

"Nothing doing," I said. "I'm already here. So far, so good. Just keep helping me, okay?"

"Okay," Cameron said resignedly. "Just so you know, Miles is in the other room crying and promising Lucy he'll take care of her when you're gone. He thinks you're never going to make it out of there."

"We'll just have to prove him wrong."

I fast-walked down the hall. "Where to next?" I asked.

"When this hallway dead-ends, take a left."

I stopped at the corner and peeked around it. Seeing no one, and reassured that Cameron was doing his job properly, I rounded the corner and hurried down the corridor.

Several office doors were open. I took off my shoes and stopped at each one, peeking around the corner to make sure no one was looking before I crept past. Luckily, most of the employees inside had their desks turned towards the outside windows and not towards the hallway doors. I couldn't say I blamed them. I'd rather face the sunshine than an empty, beige hallway any day.

Suddenly, three successive chimes rang out. It sounded like some kind of alarm.

"What's that?" I whispered into the phone.

Cameron cleared his throat again. "Well," he said. "I may have engineered a small pressure drop in the catalytic converter. That's the alarm sounding for non-essential personnel to clear out. Most everyone is already down in the control room, though. Why do you think the hallways are so empty right now?"

Oh, geez. I had been so focused on getting inside that it didn't even occur to me that the halls might be uncharacteristically clear. A pressure decrease sounded better to me than a pressure *increase*, anyway, but what did I know?

"Is that dangerous?" I asked.

"Yeah, kind of," Cameron said. "But I think I've got the pressure under control. I won't let it get too low."

"What happens if it gets too low?" I asked.

"The flow reverses and the whole refinery gets enveloped in a big, yellow, oily, toxic cloud. If you haven't got protective gear on, you're kind of screwed."

"Okay," I said. "I hope you know what you're doing."

"Me too." Cameron sighed. "Okay, fifty yards down the hall to your right is the supply closet. Duck in there and see if you can find a jumpsuit that fits."

I continued down the hall, stopping at open doors doing the "peek and go" routine until I got to the supply closet.

When I opened the door, the light came on automatically. I slipped in and shut the door softly behind me.

"Okay, I'm in the closet," I said.

"I know, I see you. The loop is running. Take your time. Nash is still on ice. Find a jumpsuit that fits."

I saw a bunch of boxes on the shelves labeled "DuPont Tyvek QC Coveralls."

I put down the phone, went to one that was labeled "small," opened the box, and pulled one out. It was bright school bus yellow and made out of a coated fabric. The suit included built-in rubber-soled boots, long sleeves with elastic wrist closures, a hood, and a zip-up front. I unzipped the suit, scrapped my high heels, and stepped in.

After zipping it up and tightening the hood around my face, I also grabbed a pair of gloves for good measure and put them on. I topped off the whole outfit with a paper mask, similar to what you'd see doctors wearing in an operating room, and then covered my eyes with safety glasses. They weren't dark glasses, but I felt like they added an extra measure of protection. Besides, all the workers in the dock had them on. I wouldn't want to stand out by not having glasses on, too.

I picked the phone back up. "Cameron?" I whispered.

"I'm here," he said. "I'll have to keep a close eye on the cameras. It'll be easy for you to get lost in the crowd now."

"Great," I said. "That doesn't inspire a lot of confidence." Especially since the catalytic converter alarm continued to chime.

"Did you have a lot going in?" Cameron said.

I chose not to answer. "Where to now?"

"Go out the door and continue right. Take the second left and continue down to the dead end. Go left from there and look for the stairway at the end of the hall."

"What about the elevator?" I asked.

"Better not risk it. You look good, but you never know."

I walked quickly down the hall and found the staircase, the ding, ding, ding of the alarm punctuating my every step.

"Good, Cameron said. "Sixth floor."

I groaned, contemplating a six-story stair climb after my long run and bicycle ride. As I climbed the stairs, I felt my calves burn. I was huffing and puffing by the time I got to the sixth floor, sweating up a storm inside my coated fabric suit.

The thought of getting to Nash kept me going, even though I still wasn't sure what I'd do when we got there.

"Okay," Cameron said. "When you go out the door, hang a right. Walk about thirty yards down and take your second left. If anyone sees you, just say hello and keep walking. Pray they don't notice your lack of ID. Nash is in the room at the very end of the hall on the left. There's a guy standing outside the room. When you get there, hand him the phone. Tell him Fitz wants to talk to him. I'll do my best Fitz impression."

I did what Cameron said, hanging a right, walking down and taking the second left into a very long hallway. I could see a guy in a security uniform standing in front of a door at the other end, shifting nervously from one foot to the other as he stared up at the alarm chime speaker box mounted to the ceiling.

I started talking into the phone loudly, to make sure the guard could hear me. I wasn't talking to Cameron, but to an imaginary Fitz. "Yeah, I know about the catalytic converter. I heard the alarm. Well, what do you want me to tell him? What about the guy? If you leave him in there and the thing blows. . . Okay, fine, I'll get him out of there."

As soon as I'd started talking, the security guard's attention snapped onto me. I looked him in the eye as I walked towards him.

When I got to him, I held out the phone. "Fitz wants to talk to you," I said.

I could hear the faint echo of Cameron's voice as he did his Fitz impression.

"Get Nash out of there and bring him down to my office," Cameron said. "Then get outside with everyone else. I'll handle Nash."

"Why didn't you call me on the com frequency?" the guard asked suspiciously.

"That's none of your business!" Cameron snapped. "When I give you an order, I expect you to move! Do you understand me?"

"Yes sir," the guy said, handing me back my phone and unlocking the door.

Cool. I didn't even have to use my credit cards. I snapped the phone temporarily shut. I'd have to call Cameron back once we figured out a way to get rid of the guard.

Nash was sitting at a bare table in a wooden chair, his hands folded in front of him on the table's surface.

His guard uncuffed him. "Up," he told Nash. "The boss wants you."

Nash got up from the table. He didn't recognize me in all my safety gear. He limped toward the door.

The security guard cuffed his hands in front of him and took him by the arm, leading him forward.

Nash limped along without saying a word, his eyes scanning for any opportunity to get loose.

I purposely walked a bit slower and fell a few steps behind them. I was hoping to make a move before we got to the other end of the empty hallway.

I halfway unzipped my chemical suit and reached around to the small of my back, where my gun was safely tucked away. I pulled it out and softly crept forward.

Both hands on the barrel of the gun, I raised it over my head and brought it down on the security guard's skull. It hit with a crack.

Unfortunately, instead of taking him totally down, it just kind of stunned him a little.

That was all the time Nash needed. Nash lassoed the guy's neck with his arms and pulled backwards, using the handcuff chains to place pressure on his windpipe.

The guard lashed out, knocking Nash back up against the wall. I pointed my gun at the guard. His eyes went wide with a deer in the headlights look, and he stopped struggling. Finally, unable to breathe, the guy passed out.

I lowered my gun and pulled the paper mask down around my neck. "It's me," I said.

Nash's jaw dropped. "Wow. You are even crazier than I gave you credit for."

"What?" I asked. "You're not happy to see me?"

"Oh, I'm happy to see you, all right." He pulled the guard's keychain off his belt and unlocked his cuffs before enveloping me in a giant hug.

The effect on me wasn't quite the same as it would have been if I hadn't been encased in a coated chemical suit, but it felt good to hold him, nevertheless.

"How did you get here?" Nash asked, disarming the guard and taking his gun for himself.

I quickly told him about the marathon to Miles' car and Cameron's hacking ingenuity. "Everybody's either in the control room or outside," I said. "They think the catalytic converter is about to blow."

"Is it?"

"I don't know. Cameron says he has it under control," I said.

My cell phone buzzed. I picked it up. I could hear Lucy barking in the background and the sound of Miles panicking.

"Somebody's coming," Cameron said. "We have to get out of here."

My stomach dropped down to somewhere around my ankles. "What do we do? What do we do?"

"I'm taking down the entire video surveillance system so nobody else can track you," Cameron said. "Get Nash back to the supply closet and get a suit on him. Then walk out of there."

"The supply closet is all the way on the other side of the building! I don't remember how to even get back there!"

"Do your best. I'll call you when we're clear."

The line went dead.

I swore. "We lost Cameron. He took down video surveillance, but if we meet anyone in the hallways, we're dead meat for sure. I have to get you into a suit so we can get out of here."

"Don't bother," he said. "The limp will give me away anyway. Put your mask back on and take my arm, like you're escorting me somewhere. It's a good thing you're tall. Nobody will be able to tell you're a woman in there."

"Where do we go?" I asked.

"I don't know," Nash said impatiently. "Out! How'd you get in?"

"With the Cameron Gilbert GPS system," I said.

"Okay, we'll just have to figure it out."

I took Nash's arm, and he began limping along beside me.

"How's your foot?" I asked.

"It hurts," he said simply.

I tried to remember the combination of turns that brought me here. In reverse, that would be. . . what? Left, then right, then left? I couldn't remember. All the hallways looked the same. Nothing on the walls, which were painted solid beige.

"I think maybe we better just follow the exit signs," I said. "The problem is, we have no way of knowing which way is the *right* exit. We need to get back to the supply yard so we can get out under cover with access to a vehicle."

"Okay, it's trial and error then," Nash said. "Let's go."

For the most part, the hallways were deserted. The chiming alarm continued to sound. I wondered what would happen to the catalytic converter now that Cameron wasn't actively monitoring it. Did that mean we were about to have a real catastrophe on our hands?

We occasionally passed people who were fully suited up and wearing respirators. They were so consumed with managing the emergency they barely gave us a second look.

We were making progress. I started to even think we might have a hope of making it out.

I started hoping just a little too soon.

The alarm chimed again, and Dorian burst out of an office door and barreled down the hall toward us.

CHAPTER 37

In spite of his obvious hurry to get out of the building, he stopped short when he saw Nash and me.

I kept walking, as though to pass him, and tried not to meet his gaze.

Dorian almost kept going, but something in my demeanor caused him to do a double-take, and I knew he'd recognized me.

Dorian whipped out his cell phone and started dialing.

Nash and I drew our guns on him.

"Put the phone down," I commanded.

He did. I didn't need to ask him what he was doing here. Of course he'd be on site during a public relations emergency with the client of his career.

"Chloe, are you out of your mind?"

"According to Nash, yes."

"This is assault!" Dorian said. "I'll have your hide for this!"

"Sure," I said. "My boss just got killed, your client is out to get me, and the refinery is about to blow. I'm really scared right now that *you* might sue me."

Dorian folded his arms and regarded me evenly. "What are you going to do? Shoot me?"

"Probably not," I said. "But Nash might."

Dorian glanced at Nash in alarm.

Nash shrugged. "Don't make me," he said.

I held out my hand. "Give me your phone," I told Dorian.

"And do it slowly," Nash added.

Dorian grasped his phone with two fingers and gingerly handed it over. I pocketed it.

"Now," I said, "turn around and walk that way." I jerked my head in the opposite direction from which he had come.

Dorian put his hands in the air, turned around, and started walking down the hall.

"No," Nash said. "Hands down. Make it look natural."

Dorian dropped his hands. "Just so you know, you're going the wrong way."

"How do you know?" I asked. "You don't even know where we're taking you."

Dorian sighed impatiently. "You want out, right? This way is just going to take you back to the other side of corporate."

"And I should believe you, why?" I asked.

"Because I loved you, once," Dorian said.

Once. Once upon a time. *Once* was the key word.

Even though I had known it was over with Dorian long ago, the way Dorian had intoned the word "once" had a ring of finality to it that had been lacking in all my previous communications with him this week. We had *once* shared so much, but no longer. And now I knew for certain that his pretended feelings for me had been nothing more than manipulation and legal games.

I didn't know whether it was the direness of the situation or the knowledge that the Miller case was most likely finished for lack of a client that had prompted him to drop the "I still love you" act, but I didn't really care. Even though it hurt my ego a little to hear it, I also felt a large measure of relief. At least now, I knew exactly what I was dealing with.

"Once has nothing to do with now," I said.

"And you think I'm holding a grudge just because you left me handcuffed to Schaeffer's desk overnight?"

"Noooooo," I said, in a way that clearly meant 'yes.'

Dorian reached the end of the hallway and stopped. "Which way?" he asked. "Right is out. Left is deeper in."

"Left," I said.

The refinery alarm chimed again.

Dorian sighed. "Look. You don't get it. I want out of here just as bad as you two. This place is about to blow, and unlike you, I'm not wearing any protective gear."

I had to admit, his argument made sense. I had no reason not to believe it.

I looked at Nash. He shrugged.

"Okay, fine," I said. "Go right. No. Actually, take me to the storage tank area."

"That's to the right," Dorian said, and began walking that way.

Nash leaned over and whispered in my ear. "Are you sure about this?"

"I don't know. What do you think?"

"It seems reasonable for him to also want to get out. The less time we spend in the hallways, the less likely we are to get caught. But you know him better than I do."

"The question is, what are we going to do with him once we find the exit? We can't just march him through the yard at gunpoint."

I eyed Dorian nervously. He appeared to be nonchalantly strolling down the hall, but I knew he was straining to hear our every word.

"Did you get all that gear in a supply closet?" Nash asked.

I nodded.

"Were there respirators in there?"

I nodded again.

"If we can get him into a supply closet and stick a desk chair under the doorknob on the outside, that might give us enough time to get rid of him and get away. And if he can't get out, he'll have access to protective gear, which means he should be okay. It's only a gas cloud we're worried about, right? No fire or anything?"

"Um, I think so?" I took a deep breath. Surely Dorian would be okay. We were well into the corporate section of the building now. If there were a gas cloud, it wouldn't be like Dorian would be stuck at ground zero. "We don't really have a choice. I say that's the plan."

Dorian came to another fork in the hallway and stopped again. "Which way now?"

"What's the fastest way back to the storage tank area?" I asked.

"Straight," Dorian said.

I felt like I had no choice but to believe him, so I did. "Okay, go." I waved my gun, motioning for him to move forward.

We walked this way for several minutes, with Dorian pointing the way at each turn. We had to be close. Maybe I was imagining things, but I felt like I recognized some familiar landmarks from my journey in. It was time to start looking for a supply room.

We turned one more corner, and I found one.

Nash spotted it, too. "Stop," he said.

Dorian did.

"Open the supply room door and go in," Nash commanded.

"Aww, come on," Dorian said. "You're not on board with this, are you Chloe?"

I ignored him. "You get him in, I'll get the chair," I told Nash, and ducked into an empty office across the hall.

I emerged from the office with a chair just in time to see Dorian disappear behind the supply room door. I rolled the chair past Nash and toward the closet.

Just as I was about to securely place the chair under the doorknob, the heavy door flew open and knocked me backwards.

The chair spiraled down the hall.

I went flying into Nash, who simultaneously caught me and popped the door back so hard that it slammed into Dorian as he was trying to escape, temporarily disorienting him.

I flung my full weight on Dorian and bulldozed him back into the supply room before he could catch his balance.

The two of us careened into a metal supply shelf, and it toppled.

Boxes of masks, suits, and various other supplies slid to the floor.

I fell on Dorian, who fell on the shelving. I heard a crack, and Dorian groaned.

I immediately rolled off Dorian, not wanting to physically touch him for longer than I had to.

It appeared that Dorian had broken some ribs, because he didn't move. He had fallen directly on top of the edge of the shelf, which meant it could be a pretty bad break.

Or, the crack I had heard might not have been his ribs at all. It could have been caused by any number of things hitting the floor. Would it be wrong of me to hope for a bone break?

In the scuffle, I'd lost my gun.

I backed away slowly, scanning the floor for the gun. Nash stood in the doorway, covering me.

I felt guilty for having to leave Dorian like this, but what else could I do?

Dorian continued to lay across the downed shelving unit, wincing with pain.

I finally spotted my gun lying on the floor by Dorian's hand between the shelving.

I consciously refused to look at it, for fear that I would alert Dorian to the fact that it was there.

Pretending concern, and wanting to get closer to the gun so I could pick it up, I stood and stepped back toward Dorian.

"Are you okay?" I asked.

"I think you broke my ribs," he moaned.

"I'm sorry," I said, and I think there was a small part of me that actually meant it—but only because he looked like he was in so much pain.

"Chloe, get away from him!" Nash warned. He clearly couldn't see the gun from his angle. I had to recover it, or we'd be at a huge disadvantage.

I ignored Nash and stepped over the shelving to lean over Dorian.

Involuntarily, and despite my best intentions, I glanced at the gun. Dorian, being an expert people reader, followed my eyes and saw it too.

I lunged for it, but Dorian was closer and quicker. In a flash, he had me by the hair with the gun pointed straight at my temple.

Nash swore. "You *never* listen, do you?" he said.

"Let me guess," I said to Dorian. "Your ribs aren't really broken. Nicely played. You fooled even me."

"About time. I was beginning to think I couldn't win with you." Dorian glanced at Nash. "Drop your gun, or she gets it."

"Remember, you loved me once," I said, feeling somewhat desperate.

"That's before you cuffed me to a desk, threatened me at gunpoint, and tried to lock me up in a refinery that's about to blow."

I eyed Nash. I didn't think Dorian would actually shoot me, but I was still going to try to get free. I wanted Nash to be alert so he could help me out if I got in a pinch, just in case.

Nash met my gaze and seemed to sense that he knew what I was about to do.

I slammed my fist into Dorian's crotch—something I'd wanted to do ever since I'd learned he was a lying cheater. The gesture was thoroughly satisfying.

Dorian loosened his grip, and I spun away.

Nash fired off two shots in rapid succession, and a shelf that had been suspended from the ceiling dumped all its contents on Dorian's head. Boxes of metal nuts and bolts came crashing down around us in a hard metal rain that sliced his skin as it fell.

Dorian thudded to the ground, wincing with what I knew for a fact was *actual* pain this time.

I stared at Nash in amazement. "Are you *serious?* Don't you think you might have wanted to shoot like that when we were being chased across the open field by an unknown car?"

"I could have, if you were a better driver," Nash said. "And anyway, you better be glad I didn't, or Dick never would have caught up with us."

I had been hoping Dorian would drop his gun, but he didn't.

I decided to just leave it and make a run for the door.

I dove through, and Nash slammed the door behind me. I rushed to grab the chair and place it under the knob.

I could hear Dorian cursing bloody murder as we walked away.

I pulled the chemical suit hood over my head and replaced my mask. It was time to resume our charade.

"Give me your gun," I told Nash.

He did, then he held out his arm, like an usher at a wedding. I took it and pointed the gun at him. We resumed our charade of captor and captive as we proceeded back down the hall toward what I hoped was our eventual exit.

I was still breathing hard from the encounter with Dorian when we rounded a corner and bumped into Fitz.

CHAPTER 38

Fitz's gaze hardened when he saw Nash. Then he lasered in on me.

"What are you doing with this man?"

"Uh, bringing him to you," I said.

"I ordered no such thing," Fitz said.

"I asked," Nash covered. "I thought we could make a deal."

A deal? What kind of deal, I wondered. Did Nash even know?

"I haven't got time for deal making right now," Fitz said. "As you well know, I'm kind of busy. And on top of all the trouble you caused, the catalytic converter is about to blow."

Fitz was looking me up and down. "Who are you?" he barked. "Where's your ID?"

I opened my mouth, but no sound came out.

Fitz shot a hand out and pulled the mask down from my face. "You gotta be kidding me," he said.

I pulled my gun on him.

Fitz, in turn, pulled his gun on me.

We were in a standoff.

"Wait a minute," Nash said. "Let's talk about this."

"There's nothing to talk about," Fitz said. "You make one fast move, and she's dead."

"Not if I shoot you first," I said.

Fitz leaned slightly forward. "If you shoot me, it won't go well for you. You're on my territory. I can claim self-defense.

What can you claim? The police are already out looking for you."

He had a point. Hmmm. My life or my freedom? Life or freedom?

I wasn't sure. I glanced at Nash from the corner of my eye. His gaze was trained on Fitz. Nash was clearly gauging whether or not to make a move.

"Let her go," Nash said. "She's not a threat."

Fitz laughed—a harsh, mirthless noise. "I wasn't born yesterday."

"It's Gilbert you want," Nash said. "If you let her go, I'll take you to him. He's the one with all the data. He's the one who's the threat. Chloe hasn't got anything on you. Cameron has the tapes. He has the hack into your network. You already burned all of Schaeffer's files, and her boss is dead. She can't afford to finance any more cases against you herself. Her job in this town is finished."

I watched Fitz ponder this possibility, praying that he would buy it and that Nash had some more tricks up his sleeve that might allow him to engineer another getaway. Fitz didn't look like he was going to take the bait.

"You'll never find him without me," Nash pressed. "I suspect that's why I'm still alive."

Fitz still didn't say anything. He considered his options.

"Let her go," Nash coaxed. "I'll take you to Gilbert. Look at me. I'm not a threat to you. I've got a bad foot. I can barely walk."

"What happened to your foot, anyway?" Fitz asked.

"Lewis shot it," Nash said.

"I guess that means you shot him back. Thanks for saving me the trouble."

"I didn't do it for you," Nash said. "Let Chloe go. I'll take you to Cameron, I swear."

Fitz took a few more moments to consider this offer before he countered.

"I tell you what," Fitz said. "I'll let you *both* go if you go in my office right now and issue a retraction to the press. Tell the press you made up the whole story about the market manipulation in order to gain leverage on your law suits. Tell them you fabricated the tapes and manufactured the written evidence. Then you walk out of here, I leave you alone, and you can both go on with your merry lives."

My hands tensed on the trigger on my gun.

"The alternative," Fitz said, "is that I shoot you both right here and you die with a bad reputation anyway. The public already thinks you're murderers. Mayor Fillion is delivering a press conference right now. He's telling everyone you're a couple of crazed Yankee environmentalists who launched an armed assault on me in my office in an effort to make a statement. And even if you somehow manage to get the better of me and walk out of here, you still can't win. There will be no rest for you without my cooperation. With the dollars I have to throw at the media and the government, you can't possibly hope to compete with my message. For every statement you make, I'll make three and follow it up with goodwill advertising and a massive PR campaign. I'll launch a four million dollar investment fund into clean energy research and tout it to the press. I'll come out looking like the good guy, and you'll be the crooks."

"Four million dollars," I spat. "That's nothing. Your company makes profits higher than that in two and a half hours."

"That's why launching the campaign will be so easy," Fitz said. "Make the statement. It's your only hope of living the rest of your life in peace."

My trigger finger twitched. Not hard enough to fire the gun, but it was definitely feeling itchy.

On the one hand, shooting this loser seemed like the easiest thing to do. But we'd never get away with it. Knowing Nash and his by-the-book personality, all his guns were registered. As soon as they ran the ballistics report, he'd get arrested. I couldn't let that happen.

On the other hand, if Nash and I made the statement, all our work and all the risks we took would be for nothing. And the rest of America would never realize the shadow of corruption they were living under.

Things would just continue on like normal, and PetroPlex would continue to lobby Congress and make hefty campaign contributions hoping to garner favors in return. Nobody would push for regulation, and the Big Oil machine would churn forward, unchecked.

I had absolutely no illusions that it would turn out any other way. It had been about a decade since the Enron fiasco, and after all this time, that little piece of legislation was still good law, and on the books.

To top that off, refineries all over the country would continue to churn out pollution, killing workers and poisoning entire communities. Nobody would care. That didn't seem like a palatable option, either.

"I won't do it," I said.

Nash rolled his eyes. "I will," he said.

My gaze snapped to Nash. "Nash, no! What's *wrong* with you? You can't do that! If you do that, PetroPlex wins!"

Nash glared at me hard. There was something in his eyes that said *trust me*. "Chloe, lower the gun," he said.

My resolve wavered.

"Please," Nash said. "Chloe, trust me. This is the right thing."

I didn't move.

"Tell her that if she lowers the gun, she can walk away," Nash told Fitz.

Fitz sighed. "Fine," he said. "Give me the gun and you walk."

I still didn't move.

"Move slow," Fitz said.

"Go ahead, Chloe," Nash said. "It's the best thing. You heard Fitz. We'll never be free any other way."

Slowly, I lowered the gun, allowing the barrel to drop. With my thumb and forefinger, I pinched the end of the grip and handed it to Fitz.

I shot Nash a look that said *you better know what you're doing*.

Fitz took my gun, but still didn't lower his own. He kept it trained on me and then pointed the other one at Nash.

"Walk away," Nash said.

I looked at Fitz for confirmation.

"Yeah, get out," he said.

I slowly started backing away.

When I was a safe distance down the hall, Fitz turned his gun on Nash. "Walk," he said.

Nash did.

As I watched him walk away, it started to dawn on me that maybe Nash didn't have a plan. I knew that *this* time, he didn't have a weapon hidden away somewhere. He couldn't possibly get the jump on Fitz with his bad foot, and I didn't really think he'd make a retraction statement to the press. So what was he doing?

Was he about to sacrifice himself for my sake?

For the second time in twenty minutes, my stomach settled around my ankles. I couldn't let him do this. I couldn't let this happen.

"Wait!" I yelled.

Nash and Fitz stopped.

"Take me instead," I said. "*I'll* make the statement."

"Chloe, what are you doing?" Nash said.

"It will make much more sense coming from me," I said. "After all, I'm the attorney here. I'm the one who makes a living suing your company in the first place, not Nash. I'm the one who had the evidence. Schaeffer was my expert witness. I'm the one who worked with Cameron to release it. Not Nash. Nash's connection to all of this is too tenuous. He's just a cop who got on the wrong side of the establishment."

"Detective," Nash said through clenched teeth. "Chloe, shut up."

"Take me," I insisted.

I could see Fitz's wheels turning. He knew I had a point. "Walk slowly towards me," he said. He was still double-fisting his guns, one pointed at me, and the other at Nash.

I began the slow motion walk back towards Fitz.

"Chloe, no," Nash said.

I kept walking.

"Chloe," Nash said. "I can't let you do this."

"I have nothing left," I said. "You do. Go back to your life."

"You have me," Nash said.

"Not if Fitz shoots you."

"Whoever makes the statement is not going to get shot," Fitz said.

"Hear that?" I asked Nash. "What about the person who doesn't make the statement? What about that person?" I turned to Fitz. "If you let me go, are you just going to hunt me down later and force me to take you to Gilbert?"

"Don't be ridiculous," Fitz said, in a way that sounded like an obvious lie.

"Take me," I said. "Look, I'm walking toward you."

I raised my hands in the air and closed the distance between us in the corridor slowly. Carefully. Methodically. When I was about three yards away from him, I stopped.

"Lower the gun," I said. "Let Nash go. I'm coming with you willingly."

I slowly lowered my arms and extended my hands toward him, palms up.

The gesture distracted Fitz. It was long enough for Nash to bring his fists down on Fitz's arms. His arms fell, and one of the guns went off. Fitz literally shot himself in the foot right in front of us.

"That's fitting," I said, jumping into action.

I helped Nash wrestle him to the ground and took the guns, his com device, and his cell phone. Pointing our guns at him, we backed away through some heavy metal double doors with small glass windows.

The doors closed on Fitz, who was swearing up a storm in front of us. Even though we weren't out of harm's way, I felt a sense of relief to have the heavy double doors creating a barrier between us and Fitz.

Fitz hobbled to his feet. We watched through the windows as he lowered a thick metal bar in front of the doors.

Nash and I exchanged glances. We were locked in. My previous feeling of relief evaporated.

We spun around to find ourselves in a chamber that was acres long and at least seven stories tall. Pipes twisted away in every direction, into the floor, through the walls, and high overhead. Giant steel drums loomed above us. The bottoms of them started at about the second story and stretched all the way to the roof.

"Is this the catalytic converter?" Nash asked.

"How should I know?" I said. "Theoretically I know how this all works, but I've never actually been inside here before. They don't like to give tours to people who make a living suing them."

My cell phone rang.

I picked it up. "Cameron!"

"You have to get out!" Cameron said. "While I was gone, Fitz started a chain reaction that's going to make the whole place blow!"

"*What?* Are you sure?"

"Yes, I'm sure," Cameron said. "This was nothing I did. I can only think he's trying to destroy evidence. The failsafes aren't working and the pressure is building across all refinery units. There's about to be a massive explosion—one that will take the whole refinery down. They're evacuating the area. Homes and everything."

"Fix it!" I, said, my heart racing.

"I can't!" Cameron said. "There are power outages all over the plant, and the server I hacked into went down right after I got back on!"

"Can't you get another connection?"

"It's not that easy," Cameron said. "I created the security breach on this server before I quit the company. There's not a lot I can do from the outside without that connection."

"We don't even know where we are!" I glanced around in desperation, trying to spot some exits. "Can you see us?"

"No!" Cameron said. "I told you, my connection's down. You're flying blind!"

I peered through the Plexiglass windows on the double doors we'd just backed through. There was a trail of blood leading down the hallway. Fitz was long gone.

I motioned for Nash to stand back and fired at the windows.

"Save your bullets," Nash said. "That's safety glass. You won't be able to shoot it out."

"Cameron," I said. "I don't know how we're going to get out of here. You've got to think of something."

"Okay, I'm thinking!" he said.

I waited a beat. "What have you got?"

"Nothing yet! Let me let you go and see what I can come up with. Try to get out!"

The line went dead.

I was sweating. I felt claustrophobic. I shoved my gun back in my belt and stripped off the yellow plastic suit, which helped to clear my head some.

I stretched my arm around Nash's back, inviting him to lean on my shoulder for support. He did so.

"Forward, ho!" I said, trying to be brave.

We limped slowly but urgently forward, eyeing the pipes all around us. Some were skinny, some were thick. Some had bolts the size of tomatoes.

A nagging question tugged at the edges of my mind. Maybe it was inappropriate under the circumstances, but I wouldn't be able to fully concentrate unless I got it out of my head.

"Did you mean it earlier when you said I had you?" I asked him.

"Yes," he said. "I meant it."

"Okay, but what does that *mean*, exactly. Like I have you as a friend?"

"More than that," he said. "When we get out of here, I'm going to take you out for a fajita dinner and some really big, really strong margaritas."

"With Patron?" I asked.

"With Patron. And a sangria swirl. And this time, it really will be a date."

I smiled. The only thing dampening my mood was the thought that getting out of here was a big, big *If*. With a capital I. And maybe even a capital F.

We had hobbled our way from one end of the chamber to another. We found another set of double doors and leaned against them, expecting them to budge.

They were locked.

"I think they're sealing off the unit to try to control any potential explosion," I said. "We can't get out down here. The only way out is up."

We headed toward a nearby spiral staircase. I prayed that it would be the right one—that it would actually lead us to a path that might go up and out, not to another dead end.

We began the long journey upward, with Nash practically hopping up each stair on one foot, leaning on me for support the whole time.

Above us, a bolt blew off a pipe and hot steam shot out into the space above us. The condensation dripped onto the stair railing.

"If that's gasoline, we're cooked." Nash bent down and trailed his finger through some droplets, then brought it to his nose.

"Is this. . . *water?*" he touched his finger to his tongue gingerly, tasting the fluid. "I think it's water!"

"It could be," I said. "Refineries run on steam."

"You're joking."

"Nope, I'm serious," I said. "Big Oil uses steam to produce the fabulous toxic chemicals that power our world every day."

"That is an unbelievable irony," Nash said.

Above us, more steam jets popped one by one.

And then the flames roared to life with a deafening noise.

Nash jumped.

I peered high above us.

The flames were isolated and appeared to be controlled.

"I think it's only the safety flares," I said loudly so that Nash could hear me. I could barely hear my own voice over the roar in the room.

"What?"

"Flares!" I yelled. "These are miniature versions of the ones on the roof. When the pressure gets high and there's danger of chemical leaks, they turn on the flares to burn the excess chemicals before they can reach the air."

Nash held his nose. "It doesn't smell like they're burning them all!"

"The flares don't get them all," I said.

We were working our way steadily upwards.

Beside us, another pipe blew, sending a bolt the size of a quarter flying straight in my direction. It hit me in the back.

I doubled over in pain.

"Are you all right?"

I took a moment to catch my breath, which wasn't easy, considering the extent to which this room stunk. I smelled gasoline. Tar. Smoke.

We had reached a platform about four stories up. At the end of it was a door.

"Look!" I said.

We limped towards the door. Below us, three more pipes split open, spewing steam upward. I felt the dewy moisture coat my face. Very steam bath-like, except for the smell. The roar of the safety flares was so loud I could barely hear myself think.

Nash leaned on the door and it opened into another chamber just as large as the first one.

Enormous towers connected by a maze of pipes stretched above, below, and ahead. The platform continued on to another staircase. We hobbled toward it as fast as we could.

In this room, large vapor clouds were forming over containment drums. I smelled a sickly sweet odor and felt a burning in my eyes. Benzene. Gasoline.

I hurriedly pulled my paper mask back over my face, realizing that would provide only minimal protection.

"Take off your shirt and tie it over your face!" I told Nash.

He did, and for a moment, I was momentarily distracted by his bare chest. It was so chiseled and perfect that it looked like he had stepped right out of a Renaissance painting. Hoo weee! I hated to think of all that hotness coming to a bad end.

"We can't stay in here!" I squinted through the vapors, still scanning for possible exits.

"We can't go back," he said. "The only way out is forward."

"Okay, but we have to hurry!"

I tried to take short breaths. The fumes were burning my eyes, and tears began streaming down my face.

Nash was making an effort to move faster, although he winced with every step.

I felt dizzy. Disoriented. Nauseated. My head was pounding, and for a moment, I forgot where I was.

Nash had stopped, seized by a coughing fit. I waited a moment for him. When it was over, he looked like he was about to pass out. "My head is killing me."

"It's the benzene," I said. "This is high level exposure. Take short breaths and keep moving."

There was a door at the top of a staircase ahead. It was padlocked.

I pulled out my gun, tempted to shoot it off, but one spark could ignite the vapor clouds around us, and we'd be crispy toast in no time.

"Don't even think about it," Nash said.

"I'm not."

Nash took the gun by the barrel and bashed the handle down on the lock, being very careful to hit it with the rubber gun grip instead of any of the steel parts.

I shut my eyes tight. One spark of metal-on-metal friction could ignite this whole place. I didn't see how we had any other option, though.

Nothing happened.

He tried again, and this time the lock came loose.

He yanked the broken lock off and we hobbled through the door into a smaller room. Closing the door behind us, we took a few moments to breathe some relatively fresher air. This room was full of horizontal tanks and enough pipes to give a plumber nightmares. I estimated that the floor of this room started at about the third story and stretched to the sixth.

We spotted another staircase and headed towards it. Immediately below us, underneath the metal grate of the platform on which we were walking, the seal on a pipe broke and droplets of liquid spewed out.

We hurried forward. This time it wasn't water. The smell gave it away. Gasoline.

"Chloe, you have to get out of here," Nash said. "Leave me. Run."

"No!" I said.

"This isn't right. You have a chance to escape."

Before I could respond, a steam pipe burst and a section of it went crashing down through the mesh of pipes below it. The metal on metal friction threw out a spark, and the gasoline ignited in a small explosion.

The force of it knocked me off my feet and I fell off the edge of the platform.

Nash's reflexes were as quick as ever. His hand shot out and grabbed my arm.

I dangled over a mess of spewing pipes below. The heat from the flames scorched my feet.

"I've got you!" Nash yelled.

I twisted and dangled in the air, like a yo-yo on a dead string. He slowly pulled me upwards, struggling to get leverage with his bad foot. My stomach lurched, and I felt dizzy, but Nash had a strong grip on me.

I grabbed onto the railing when I was high enough to reach it and pulled myself up and back onto the platform.

"You all right?" Nash asked.

I nodded, pressing forward.

The heat was getting intense. The gasoline leak burned with a steady flame, but I didn't know how long it would stay that way.

We were almost to the top of the room. I could see a door labeled 'emergency Exit Only' at the top of the next spiral staircase. I figured this qualified as an emergency. We were almost there. Just a few more yards, and we'd be out!

We hurried toward the staircase.

Another explosion rocked the room. It knocked out the supports for one end of our platform, and we plummeted. Nash grabbed the railing, and I grabbed Nash. I was holding onto him by the waistband of his pants.

The platform swung downwards like a pendulum, taking out pipes and crashing to a stop at a seventy degree angle. The bottom edge of the platform perched precariously on a thin pipe with a large, round valve wheel.

Steam jets buffeted us from both sides, and I cringed against the scalding heat.

The steam on the railing was making it hard for Nash to maintain a grip.

"I can't hold on!" His hands slipped down, and down some more.

I desperately tried to gain some leverage with my feet, but the platform was slick with steam and the angle was too steep.

He slid ever further backwards, until my feet finally slipped off the platform and dangled over the flames below.

A few more inches, and he'd lose his grip on the railing altogether.

I eyed the Exit sign, which had once seemed so close, and now seemed so far away.

Our only hope now was to grab onto the jungle-gym of pipes and monkey our way up and out. But which ones were hot steam, and which ones were cold chemicals?

It would be a process of trial and error.

I felt Nash slip another inch. I had to get my body weight off him immediately.

I kept one hand on his pants and stretched the other one out, reaching for a nearby pipe, only to jerk it back again quickly. Too hot.

There wasn't another one within reach.

Our combined body weight on the end of the platform was too much for the thin pipe holding it up. It gave way, and the platform crashed down. The screech of steel on steel nearly deafened me. I closed my eyes against the sparks, certain that any second they would ignite some unseen vapor cloud and toast us both to bits.

Down and down we went, until finally the platform hit a ninety-degree angle and bashed into the wall. The impact was too much for Nash. His grip slipped off the railing and we fell.

My stomach did the upward flip associated with free-falling. Panicking, I kicked my feet beneath me, hoping they would catch something other than air before it was too late.

Abruptly, the falling motion stopped. Pain seared through my shoulder blades as I held on to Nash through the jolt. Nash had grabbed hold of a pipe on the way down and halted the fall. He was able to maintain a grip, so it must not have been a steam pipe.

I held onto his pants for dear life, praying they would stay on. They slipped some, revealing a peek of nicely toned cheeks underneath. That was all I wanted to see. For now.

"Can you hang on?" Nash called down to me.

"I think so!"

Nash started doing a hand-over-hand, inching us down the horizontal length of the pipe. If he could make it another fifty feet, he could get us to a vertical pipe that wasn't slick with steam.

One hand in front of the other, Nash swung forward. I swayed over the fires beneath us precariously.

Five feet. Ten feet. I swung in small circles beneath him, the motion creating an additional drag on his grip.

Twenty feet.

Thirty.

Nash's arms and back were slick with sweat, his muscles straining with every movement.

Forty feet.

My own strength was giving way. The muscles in my arms burned, and my shoulder sockets seared with pain.

Fifty feet. We made it.

Now began the climb.

"How are you doing?" I wrenched my chin upward, trying to get a look at his face and gauge his progress for myself.

"I'm fine! Can you climb a vertical pipe?"

"I don't think so!" I said truthfully. I had never had a lot of upper body strength.

"It's okay!" he said. "Hang on!"

Hand over hand, he pulled us slowly up.

I was dizzy with the possibility that neither of us might make it. I felt guilty for being nothing but a weight holding him back, dragging him down. If he wasn't strong enough—if he couldn't hold on—what would we do? He was right. I should have run on ahead. Now I was only holding him back, endangering both of us. As of right now, he would have had a better chance without me.

I worried about the amount of blood he'd lost this morning. I knew he was in pain, but if he felt weakened, he didn't show it.

Up and up he went. High above his head—it seemed like miles—was a small platform with a ladder leading up to a hatch. If he could just make it to the ladder. . .

Smoke and fumes filled the chamber. It was as much of an effort to breathe as it was to hang on to the pipes. If anything else exploded—if there were any more fumes or smoke, I wasn't certain we could remain conscious.

I started to cough as a giant smoke plume wafted upwards and enveloped us. Each expellation of breath racked my body, taxing my ability to hang on.

Nash was coughing too. He had to stop climbing every time he coughed just to hold on.

"Only a little farther!" I called.

He was under too much strain to reply.

We continued slowly upward.

I felt sleepy. All I wanted to do was close my eyes. To take a nap. To rest. To let go and feel a blissful nothingness. Waves of drowsiness swept over me, and it seemed like there was nothing. . . *nothing*. . . more important than just taking a little snooze right now. Just a little rest. Only for a second.

My eyes drooped and my fingers loosened their grip.

Feeling the change in me, Nash hollered down, "Chloe, no! Stay with me! Hang on! We're almost there!"

His exhortations ended in a virtual symphony of coughing. The jerking motions of his body shook me back to a fully conscious state.

The platform was just above us. Maybe only four feet higher.

I willed myself to concentrate on the motion of his hands as one by one they released, gripped, and pulled. Release, grip, pull. Release. Grip. Pull. Only a few more times.

I was so sleepy. Just a little nap. That's all I needed. Then I'd be refreshed and ready to resume our journey.

My eyes drooped again.

And the next thing I know, I must have actually fallen asleep, because I knew I was having a dream. It was one of those falling dreams—the kind that jerk you awake right after you've drifted off. There was a noise that accompanied this jerk. A big ka-boom!

I opened my eyes to see the exit sign getting smaller and smaller as Nash and I slid down and down. *No.* I thought. *No, no no!*

The pipe Nash had been climbing was now slicked with an oily substance that spewed from a nearby barrel. It might as well have been made of ice, it was so slippery.

I tightened my grip around Nash's chest, hoping the slide would eventually stop.

To my horror, Nash actually *let go* of the pipe with both hands.

I screamed.

In one quick motion, Nash rubbed his hands on his jeans and then grabbed the pipe again. The oily substance hadn't run down the pipe as fast as we were falling, and when his hands reconnected, he had a better grip.

We still slid downward, but the fall slowed a bit, and continued to slow the lower we fell. I shut my eyes tight, not wanting to see the ground racing up at me.

Slower and slower we slid, until finally we came to a stop.

"Let go of me," Nash said.

Had I heard that right? He was abandoning me to die?

"Let go!" Nash said again, more urgently this time. "I can't hold on much longer, and if we both fall together, I'll hurt you!"

I hesitated.

"Chloe, look down!"

I did. We were a mere six or seven feet from the ground. All that work fighting to get to the top—and all for nothing. Now, we were surely dead. We didn't have the time or energy to make another climb, and minor explosions continued to ignite above us.

Feeling defeated, I let go, hit the ground in a roll, and moved away quickly. Nash dropped down, landed on one foot, and rolled a few times to soften the blow. Even so, his bad foot must have impacted somewhere, because I heard him groan in pain.

The air was a bit more clear down here, since the smoke and vapors wafted upward away from us . . . and since there was a giant hole in the wall where one of the explosions had blown the doors right off their hinges, safety glass and all. I could feel a draft as fresh oxygen swept in through that door, fueling the fires above.

Nash and I saw the door at the same time. I rushed to help him up, and he leaned on me for support as we hobbled out.

We limped around corner after corner, looking for an exit.

Behind us, we heard another loud ka-BOOM and the shrieking of metal on metal as the refinery infrastructure began to buckle in on itself. We didn't stop to look back.

Acrid smoke billowed into the hallway and a cloud enveloped us.

Nash and I held our breath as we turned the corner again and came upon a door blocked by a chair. A very familiar-looking door blocked by a chair.

I could barely see Nash through the smoke, but I knew we needed to get into the supply closet and get some respirators, pronto—never mind that Dorian was probably still in there and armed.

I moved the chair away from the door and tried to open it as Nash covered me. The door wouldn't budge. The explosions and subsequent shaking of the building had warped the door frame and the thing was stuck.

In desperation, Nash handed the gun to me as he tugged on the door.

In one violent motion, the door wrenched free, and as expected, I found myself staring down the wrong end of the barrel of Dorian's gun.

I aimed my own gun straight back at him. I didn't even know how to use a gun before yesterday, and I certainly hadn't become a crack shot overnight. What was I supposed to do? Duck? Shoot first? Run?

Nash and I edged into the supply room as Dorian inched backwards. We circled each other, Dorian making for the door, Nash and I making for the safety equipment.

I watched Dorian's trigger finger tense as the smoky, toxic air around us seemed to grow even thicker. Walls shook and the floor rolled beneath me as another explosion thundered through the building. The PetroPlex flagship oil refinery was fast on its way to becoming nothing but a memory.

The doorframe buckled before my eyes—our only means of escape. Sharp orange tongues of flame lapped at me from above, sending down a rain of fiery particles as acoustic ceiling tiles disintegrated overhead.

That's when I knew that gun or no gun, I was going to die.

I tossed my useless weapon on the floor. Dorian did the same.

Nash grabbed a couple of respirators from the floor, put one on himself, and tossed the other one to me. I put it on, not for one moment believing it could save me.

"Help me," Nash said, motioning toward a freestanding metal shelf.

Dorian and I both understood. We rushed to the shelf and emptied it of its contents so that we could knock it over and use it as a battering ram.

The roar of the burning refinery around us was so loud we barely heard the crash of the shelf when it hit the floor.

All three of us hoisted it and aimed at a section of wall that wasn't yet on fire.

"On the count of three, put all your weight into it, okay?" Nash yelled.

Dorian and I nodded.

Nash counted, and we rushed the wall.

The impact jarred me so hard I thought my joints might never be the same, but the shelf punctured a hole in the wall, and air rushed into the room.

Dorian was through the hole and gone before I could even regain my balance.

Nash and I moved more slowly, limping along at a wounded turtle's pace. Nash never complained about his foot, but I could tell it pained him more after the drop to the ground from the slick pipe.

I could hear rafters falling and the building creaking all around us. Flames easily caught up with us, and even through the respirator, the scent of smoke and chemical waste scorched my nostrils.

Bits of flaming particles rained down on us, the deluge of the devil, and we dodged as best we could.

Another explosion. The building shuddered, and a flaming crossbeam crashed down behind us, missing by mere inches.

"You have to go," Nash said. "If you wait for me, you'll die."

"I'm not leaving here without you."

"Then I'm afraid you're not leaving," Nash said.

"We can make it! Come on. Just a little farther!"

The building shuddered again, and this time an entire section of hallway collapsed. Nash heard the walls coming down and jerked me into an open doorway, hoping to gain what meager protection he could.

In the space of three seconds, debris crashed down, all aflame, blocking the pathway out completely.

"Look!" Nash said, pointing to a window in the office we'd just ducked into.

I nodded. We weren't on the first floor, but there was a fire escape outside.

I picked up a desk chair and hurled it through the glass.

Then we both climbed through and surveyed the long distance down to the ground. We were six stories high. There would be no quick descent for Nash on his wounded foot.

We began the descent together, one painful step at a time.

Another explosion from somewhere inside shook the stairs. Again, I heard the shriek of metal on metal and knew the infrastructure was beginning to collapse.

I panicked, grabbed onto the railing, and stopped.

"Don't stop!" Nash said. "Go! Go!"

I refused to budge without him.

"So help me God, Chloe, if you don't go now, I will pick you up and throw you over the railing! Go! I'll catch up with you!"

Still, I hesitated. I didn't want to leave him to die, even if it meant saving my own life.

Nash hopped onto the stair railing and slid down. Before I knew it, he was beneath me.

"See?" he said. "Hurry up!"

Reassured, I pounded down the stairs as Nash continued to slide.

When my feet hit the ground, I breathed a sigh of relief.

Too soon.

The refinery grumbled and groaned in its death throes. High at the top of the building, the smoke stacks caved in. The structure swallowed itself and belched fire.

The loudest explosion of all shook the dirt beneath my feet, and I thought the very ground would open up and swallow the entire refinery, and us with it.

"Run, Chloe! Run!"

This time, I ran. I hadn't intended to leave Nash, but sheer survival instinct propelled me forward. A thicket of trees lay ahead of me, and I ran deep into it, hoping its thick trunks and green canopy might provide some measure of protection if the refinery blew.

Nash ran behind me more slowly.

"Nash!" I called. "Nash, hurry up!"

"I'm coming!"

Please, Nash. Please. I mentally willed him to overcome the pain and keep up with me. *Please.*

I ran ever farther into the thicket, frantically kicking my way through brush and weeds until I was in so deep I could no longer see the refinery or Nash behind me.

Nash!" My lungs were on fire. I could barely get the word out.

There was no answer.

Nevertheless, I could not stop. I mechanically jerked one foot in front of the other, over and over, churning out as much distance as I could between me and an imminent catastrophic disaster.

When the final explosion came, my eardrums popped with its force, even though I was far into the woods. I felt the heat and the force of the blast propel me into the air, up, up, and forward. Trees flattened behind me. Splinters of wood and bark shot forward. Leaves burst into the air and caught flame, transforming into embers that floated softly to the ground.

My skin burned. My body ached. I flew forward, my body one with the motion of the forest around me. And then I slammed into the ground.

The last thoughts I had as the world went dark were of Nash and how I'd never see him again.

CHAPTER 39

From out of the darkness, I felt a repetitive, wet pressure on my face. A sponge? No. A tongue. In the distance, I heard a voice. It sounded like Miles.

"She found her!" called the voice that sounded like Miles.

I opened my eyes to find Lucy standing on my chest, frantically swiping her tongue over and over my cheek.

"Lucy," I said. "Good dog."

I figured I must be dead. I had to be dead, and this had to be some Heavenly incarnation of my dog, because otherwise, what on earth could she be doing here?

I glanced around. I lay in the midst of flattened trees and stripped bushes. I didn't see Nash anywhere. If I were dead and in Heaven, wouldn't Nash be here, too? And my family members who had gone before me? Angels? Harps? Singing and that sort of thing?

I saw none of that. Instead, I saw only Lucy and the semi-flattened woodlands around us. But I could still hear the voice that sounded like Miles calling my name.

I turned my head in the direction of the voice and saw Miles, Cameron, and Gracie racing toward me. Wait. . . *Gracie?*

I did a double-take. Yes, that was definitely Gracie.

"Oh, thank you, Sweet Jesus!" Gracie said, coming to her knees beside me. "Thank God you're okay!"

"Where's Nash?" Cameron asked.

"I don't know," I said. "I think he might be dead. Am I dead, too?"

"You're not dead," Miles said, "which is an ever-loving *miracle,* I might add! I swear that if you ever try to pull any more crazy stunts like this *ever* again, I will kill you myself!"

So I was not dead, but Nash might be. *Please, God, no,* I prayed. *Please don't let Nash be dead.* I just wanted to spend some time with him. Any time—even just one day. There was so much I still wanted to learn about him. So much I still had to tell him. So much of his lips, body, and soul I wanted to explore.

"Find Nash," I murmured.

"We'll keep looking," Cameron said. He stood up and called to some dark shapes in the distance. "Over here!"

Large, looming men jogged towards us. They were dressed all in black except for the letters 'FBI' in white across their torsos.

The men in black arrived and began checking my pulse and testing my bones for breaks. For the first time since I regained consciousness, my body began to register pain.

One of them looked up at Cameron and nodded.

"It's okay," Cameron told me. "You're okay."

It was then I noticed that Cameron was *also* dressed all in black with the letters FBI across his chest.

I frowned at him. "Wait a minute. Where'd you get that uniform?"

Cameron flashed me a badge.

A tsunami of conflicting feelings washed over me. Relief. Anger. Happiness. Rage.

He bent down to help me to my feet. When I was up, I hugged him. And then I slapped him.

"You are *FBI* and you let me go in there *by myself?* All alone? To most likely die?" I punched him in the ribs. *"FBI? For real?*

So that's why he was able to kill those thugs in the garage so easily. So that's why life on the run didn't seem to bother him. That's why he could be so cheerful in the face of life-threatening stress. He was trained to handle all of it.

Before I could punch him again, Miles grabbed my arms and restrained me.

"Lay off," Miles told me. "It was necessary."

"I'm sorry, Chloe," Cameron said, "but I've been deep undercover for more than five years now, and I was under strict orders not to reveal myself, no matter the cost.

"But why?" I said. "Why the press release and all the sneaking around and stuff? If you're FBI and you knew you had probable cause, why didn't you go in and raid the place?"

"This was never meant to be a public operation," Cameron said. "Can you think why?"

I was so tired and hurt and stunned that I could barely think at all, let alone piece together the secret motives of the FBI.

Cameron saw my blank look. "Certain government officials are aware that our energy policy needs to change. And they're aware of the need for stricter regulation and a move toward green energy. But these officials, who will remain nameless, are also aware that Big Oil is the richest industry in the world and also one of the biggest campaign contributors. There is hardly anyone in office that is not beholden to PetroPlex in some way, shape, or fashion. If these officials came out publicly against PetroPlex without popular opinion behind them, their careers would be over."

It all began to make sense to me now. "So instead, they launched a covert operation to expose the dirt and corruption in the industry and spark a public cry of outrage. Then when the country cried out for effective regulation and clean energy, the PetroPlex lobby couldn't hold them back."

"Right," Cameron said.

Wow. I felt like my world view had been rocked. "But if it was so covert, why risk the operation by revealing yourself to Miles, Gracie, and me?"

Cameron gestured toward his team. "As soon as it became clear there was going to be a massive refinery explosion, I called in my guys. At that point, I knew we wouldn't get out of this without a Congressional hearing, and we would need Gracie, Miles, you, and Nash as witnesses."

"Let me get this straight," I said. "My life became valuable to you *only after* you knew there would be a Congressional hearing? What if Fitz hadn't set the refinery on fire? What if I went in there and he killed me?"

Cameron put his hand on my shoulder. "You can't say I didn't do my best to get you in and out of there, considering the orders I was under."

Even so. While the logical part of my brain understood, my emotional side still felt a little bit betrayed. I swayed on my feet, but Miles caught me.

"And Gracie?" I asked. "Where did you come from?"

Cameron answered for her. "Remember when I had to hang up on you because someone was coming? Well, it turned out to be Gracie. She saw the news and came home."

"I knew y'all wasn't murderers," Gracie said. "I had to tell someone down here, didn't I? But when the refinery exploded, we thought you was goners for sure!"

"But Cameron agreed to search the area anyway," Miles said. "We told Lucy to find you, and she did! We might have missed you in all these trees if it wasn't for her. Your dog's a hero!"

I always knew she was.

"Can you walk?" Cameron asked.

I thought so, and I let him take my elbow.

"We're going to escort you to a secure medical facility and take you into the Federal Witness Protection Program. We have to hurry. We're still trying to do this without alerting local law enforcement."

"We have to find Nash," I said.

Cameron frowned. "I thought you said he was dead."

"Find his body," I said. "I'm not leaving him out here to rot."

Lucy was prancing around my feet joyfully.

"Lucy!" I said. "Go find Nash!"

She stood still and cocked her head up at me. I don't think she knew what that meant.

"Nash!" I said. "Go find him!"

She cocked her head the other way, uncertain.

Suddenly, she heard something. She spun and growled, then took off running through the trees.

I felt unsteady on my feet, but hope surged through me and I chased after her. Miles, Gracie, Cameron, and his FBI entourage followed.

Lucy stopped beside a fallen tree. I could see something pale and white pinned underneath.

As I drew nearer, I could see that it was a body lying face down in the dirt.

Lucy sniffed it.

It was a man, but his hair color was wrong. Not Nash. Not Dorian. Nobody I knew.

Lucy took off again, and I kept following. A couple of FBI guys stayed behind to check for vital signs, but I instinctually knew they wouldn't find any.

We were definitely in the kill zone. I felt sick in the pit of my stomach. How on earth could Nash possibly have survived if this other man hadn't?

As we moved forward, the ratio of flattened to still-standing trees increased. The destruction around me seemed even more evident, and I could see the flames of the refinery still raging only a short distance away.

"Chloe," Cameron said, not unkindly, "it's not safe to go any farther in. We can't be seen."

Before I could answer him, Lucy sniffed the air and took off again.

"Somebody get that dog!" one of the FBI agents barked.

We all took off after Lucy.

She wasn't heading straight for the refinery. Instead, she veered a bit to the east parallel to the heap of ruins that was once PetroPlex.

Lucy stopped when she reached a clump of several fallen trees.

The trees appeared to be moving, and Lucy barked at them frantically.

"There's somebody in there!" I said, daring to hope that by some miracle it might be Nash.

Agent Roberts and his men jogged ahead of us and pulled the trees back to reveal a sinkhole—a natural phenomenon that was common in this area, especially near the refinery.

Then I saw the impossible.

Nash's shirtless silhouette emerged upward out of the hole.

Cameron helped him climb out, and Nash limped and lurched through the foliage toward me. Lucy pranced around him, her tongue lolling out the side of her mouth as she panted happily.

Nash had some minor burns and scratches on his torso, and his pants were torn to shreds, but his perfect face was unscathed. He must have found the sinkhole and dived into it in the nick of time. It was more than I had dared hope for. *Thank you, God*, I breathed.

I ran toward him, and Nash caught me in his arms. My lips found his. My eyes sank shut, and it was as though no other part of my body existed. I felt no more pain. Only the rhythmic, pulsating motion of his lips on mine. Wave after wave of pleasure washed over my soul, erasing the hurt, anger, and loss of the past few days. Kiss by kiss, Nash was making me whole again.

Nash pulled his lips from my mouth and kissed my eyelids, my forehead, my nose. He covered every inch of my face with kisses before moving down to my neck, my shoulder, and then lower.

"Ahem," Miles said.

Nash moved back to my lips for one last, deep, hungry connection. Then he pulled away. "To be continued," he said.

"Yes, please." I grasped his hand and we turned toward the crowd.

"Wait a minute," Nash said. "Am I seeing things? Cameron is *FBI?*"

"You're not seeing things," I said. "I'll explain later. Right now, we have to go."

One of Cameron's agents, who was apparently unwilling to let Lucy get away from him again, had scooped her up and held her in custody in his arms. She didn't protest.

Cameron led us to a van parked in a remote location, and we all piled into the back. I wasn't sorry when an agent put the car in gear and drove away. If I never, ever came back to this place, that would be just fine with me.

However, there was one last order of business to attend to before I disappeared.

I asked Cameron if I could borrow his cell phone.

"It's not safe," he said.

"Please," I begged. "I promise I won't do anything to give away the operation or location."

Cameron still hesitated. "You owe me," I said. "You let me go in that refinery to die, and now you're about to hold me captive as a witness for God knows how long. One measly three minute phone call before I go is the least you could do for me."

Cameron sighed, but forked over the phone.

I dialed Dorian's number.

"Dorian Saks," came his voice on the other end.

"Now would be a good time to thank me for getting you out of that refinery alive."

Instantly, he recognized my voice. "*Thank* you! I am going to *sue* you! False imprisonment, assault with a deadly weapon, intent to kill, emotional distress. . ."

"Feel free," I said, "if you can find me. In the meantime, let's talk about the Miller case."

Dorian sighed. "That again? Are you kidding?"

"My client is back in town, so I'm going to give you one last opportunity to settle this case equitably. If you don't, it's going to court, and let me tell you, thanks to Cameron Gilbert, I have some incredibly damning video of your client committing murder, which I *will* use against him. In light of recent events and all the media scrutiny surrounding your client, I doubt if it will end very well for you. I can promise you that I will do my very best to make sure it gets high profile coverage, and I'll pull out every trick in the book. In addition to nailing Fitz for murder, I'll prove that his history of flagrant safety violations and cost cutting measures also killed Derrick Miller. A jury will have absolutely no doubt believing it after the explosion that just devastated this town. But if you settle it right here, right now, it goes away, and you'll never hear about it again."

"I'm listening," Dorian said grudgingly. I knew the last thing he wanted to do was settle with me right now, but he wasn't a fool.

"My client refuses to settle for less than ten million dollars," I said.

"Heavens to Betsy!" Gracie gasped.

"Petroplex makes that much in profit in only a few hours. It won't be much of a loss compared to what you'll get if you let me add fuel to an already raging PR fire. Take it or leave it," I said. "Last chance."

"Under the circumstances," Dorian said quickly, "I think I can speak for my client in saying we agree to that."

"Good," I said. "I'll draft the agreement. No pushback, or it's a jury. Got it?"

"I understand," Dorian said.

"I want the check in the mail in a week."

"Okay, fine. Whatever."

I thought I could hear him call me the c-word under his breath, but I figured that since I'd just beaten him at his own game, I'd let it go.

"So long, Dorian," I said, and hung up.

Gracie's face welled up with tears. "I don't know what to say," she said. "Thank you! Thank you so much! Lord a'mighty, I don't need that much money. Seeing as how you risked your life for it and all, how about I give you half?"

"No, no, a standard fee would be fine. Actually, a less than standard fee would be fine," I said, since the original fee agreement stated forty percent. "Send the check to Cameron when it comes in?"

Gracie looked at Cameron for confirmation.

"I'll give you my address," he said.

Perfect. My eyes drooped, and my thoughts turned to Judge Delmont. I guessed I wouldn't be needing to hold those blackmail photos over his head anymore. That was too bad, really. But I supposed karma would catch up with him sooner or later.

That reminded me. Where had Miles gotten those photos in the first place? I decided to ask him, even though there were other people around.

"Hey Miles," I said. "You know that piece of evidence we used to get Delmont to grant a continuance? Where did you get it?"

"Dick gave it to me," he said.

"What evidence?" Nash wanted to know.

"Just something pertaining to the case. I won't bore you with the details," I said.

I could only imagine how *Dick* got his hands on the photos. Probably Delmont was stupid enough to set up a rendezvous with his mistress during a poker game and Dick caught it on tape. Then he figured he'd follow Delmont to the motel and snap some photos for leverage on down the line, just in case. He was crafty like that, always making deals and securing insurance.

I wondered for a moment why he would have given them away instead of just using them himself, but then the answer became obvious. He couldn't have used them without destroying his relationship with Delmont and the poker crew, thus staunching the flow of his inside information. He knew I'd been up against the wall on the Miller case and must have been afraid of losing a hundred grand in expenses. Hence the exchange. That was my theory, anyway. It seemed to fit.

Lucy left her spot at the window and crawled into my lap, where she promptly fell asleep.

"Too tired to enjoy riding in the car, huh?" I asked. "Alert the media. I can't believe it."

"I believe it," Nash said.

My head sank onto his shoulder as I contemplated slipping into my own land of dreams.

"What's next?" Nash asked agent Roberts.

"After the hospital, a nice farm somewhere in Montana for a couple months. And then Congressional hearings, most likely," Roberts replied.

In a perfect world, we'd be able to convince Congress to fully close the Enron Loophole, institute campaign finance and lobbyist reform, and add some more teeth to the *Clean Air Act*. One could only hope.

"After that," Nash whispered into my ear, "We'll go spend some of the fee you just earned in Tahiti."

I couldn't argue with that. "Can we get one of those little huts that stick out over the water and have glass bottoms so you can see all the fish swimming around underneath?"

"Sounds good to me," Nash said.

"And margaritas," I said. "We have to have margaritas."

"And margaritas," Nash agreed. "With Patron and a sangria swirl."

Nash and Patron margaritas and a beach. Heaven. Sheer Heaven. And then afterwards, I could take the money I made on Gracie's case and start my own firm. Be my own boss. No more having to deal with jerks like Dick. No more blackmail. No more subterfuge. Everything on the up and up. Things were looking better for me, finally. I breathed a deep sigh of relief. I was going to be okay. Better than okay.

Look out, world. Chloe Taylor's on the loose. *Here I come.*

Thank You, from the Author

Wow, since you made it this far, I'd like to personally thank you for reading this book. I hope you enjoyed it. If you did, will you please do me a favor and post a review on amazon.com? Please also feel free to drop by my blog at http://www.blackoilredblood.com and leave a comment or send me a message. I'd love to hear from you! While you're online, take a moment to connect with me on Facebook and Twitter, too!

Facebook: https://www.facebook.com/dianecastle10
Twitter: https://twitter.com/#!/Dianecastle10

Finally, I'd like to invite you to join the **Blue Bulb Project**. Show your Congresspeople you support clean air and clean water by replacing your porch light with a blue bulb or by tying a blue ribbon around one of your trees. We live in a world where some politicians think it's a good idea to dismantle the EPA, which would adversely affect the safety of our environment. Every blue bulb your representative sees will be a reminder to them that people want clean air to breathe and clean water to drink. Learn more at http://www.bluebulbproject.com.

About the Author

Diane Castle is the pseudonym of a Texas attorney whose practice experience includes assisting plaintiffs with wrongful death and personal injury cases against Big Oil giants such as ExxonMobil, ChevronTexaco, BP, and ConocoPhillips. Diane has published short fiction under a different name, and she has also written a stage play that was translated into German, produced in a castle near Munich, and sold out three seasons.

Prior to her career as an attorney, Diane was a staff writer for *The Dallas Morning News.* She also feels privileged to have been honored with two awards for humor and satire and one award for literary criticism. Diane lives in Dallas with her husband David and her three dogs: Lucy, Gracie, and Mouse.

Made in the USA
Charleston, SC
10 February 2012